Life
Of
Zanna

Life Of Zanna

Emily Jane Hodgkin

Black&White

Black&White

First published in the UK in 2024 by
Black & White Publishing Ltd
Nautical House, 104 Commercial Street, Edinburgh, EH6 6NF

A division of Bonnier Books UK
4th Floor, Victoria House, Bloomsbury Square, London, WC1B 4DA
Owned by Bonnier Books
Sveavägen 56, Stockholm, Sweden

A CIP catalogue record for this book is available from the British Library.

ISBN: 978 1 78530 545 0

1 3 5 7 9 10 8 6 4 2

Typeset by Data Connection
Printed and bound in Great Britain by Clays Ltd, Elcograf S.p.A.

www.blackandwhitepublishing.com

Grandma Eve, my ever-constant inspiration, this book is for you.

Mum, Dad, Grace and Vijay, you can have the next one.

Life of Zanna Documentary

Transcript

Embargoed until January 00:01

MUSIC UP: [MAROON 5 "MEMORIES"]

VISUALS: Still images scroll down the screen through a mock Instagram interface, displaying pictures of two girls, one around twenty, the other twenty-five, having fun together. They are drinking and laughing. One kisses another on the cheek.

VIDEO RE-ENACTMENT FEATURING ACTRESSES: Two girls sit on the upper deck of a London bus, brown cardboard boxes on their laps and suitcases around them. They are moving house. One holds a box, "Zanna" written on it in marker pen in bold capital letters. She is pretty, with long, dark brown hair and a tan, stylish. She leans her forehead against the other girl's cheek in a sign of friendly intimacy. The other, paler, with mousy brown hair and blue eyes, holds a box that reads "Paige".

Zanna pulls a Polaroid camera from a box and snaps a selfie of the two young women, sticking her tongue out while the other smiles. The flash illuminates their happy faces, full of excitement.

PAIGE WHITE VOICEOVER: I couldn't believe the most beautiful person I'd ever met was my best friend and we were moving in together in London. It was going to be the start of an amazing life together, working on the blog; it took us all over the world.

It was the dream for two girls our age, making it big in social media. When the free makeup started rolling in, I thought, *This can't get any better*. I was already so lucky just to know Zanna. To have met my soul sister. So lucky. Blessed.

Then came the free bags, the free holidays, invitations to hotel openings, exclusive events with celebrities and private cars, all because of our vision, mine and Zanna's. I was so blessed just to know her and to have become a part of her magical world. I had a pass to the most incredible life I could have imagined. But it was never about those materialistic things. It was my friendship with Zanna that brought me here, where I am today.

That's why, sometimes, I still can't get my head around the fact she's gone.

TITLE TEXT ON SCREEN: "*LIFE OF ZANNA*"

The Present

In Paige's flat, overlooking the Albert Bridge

I wake up this morning to sweet, harp-like chords swelling from my sunrise-mimicking alarm clock. Groggy and unsure at first, I'm still half asleep. It's as if someone has rubbed Vaseline in my eyes, like on the lens of an old movie camera. I read somewhere they used it as a trick to hide old actresses' blemishes, like Marilyn Monroe. The fine hairs on my body ripple upright. My heart flutters. Something's unusual. I haven't woken to the sound of my alarm for a long time. From the left of me comes a murmur.

"Paige."

A warm arm brushes across my back, reaching feebly for the noisy device. It's a nudge for me to get it, not an earnest attempt to shut off the jangling sounds, so I reach out towards the clock that cost far more than any clock has a right to. There's a wet sensation on my cheek and glistening drool on the pillow. I slept well, for once. I press snooze, turn onto my side, and there's

Shane's profile, backlit by the morning sun streaming in through our large windows. No Vaseline necessary to make him beautiful. I want to make the most of being here, in this warm, big bed, next to my warm, big boyfriend. I dreamed of spilled wine, hot sweats, shaking hands, bile in my stomach. As always, the bad dreams linger in snippets. Snippets that slip through my fingers like a breeze. I try to grasp them, a disquieting sensation there's more, a nagging idea that I need to retain something — not to forget. I could tie a knot in my pillow to remember, but it would be no good. It fades away too fast.

Most days I'm wide awake in the dark of the early morning, transported from a nightmarish dreamscape, scared, startled, and full of energy. Awake in the way we only are at night. Some ancient part of us knows we're vulnerable in the dark. Weak primates with poor vision and worse hearing, relying on sheer cunning to get to the top of the food chain. Machiavellian in our very DNA. I hate to lie in bed next to Shane as violent nightmares of hushed, frightened voices ebb away. His breaths are steady and sure, trusting in the safety of this home, in me. I love him so much it's like someone inflating a balloon in my bowels. I love him so much, I wince.

Normally when I wake early, tormented by these visions, I take my trusty packet of tablets from the locked drawer in the side table, where I keep those nasty, ominous white envelopes with their various warnings in red:

REMINDER
UNPAID
OVERDUE

hidden where Shane can't see them. I want to throw them away, but I'm afraid someone will find them. Even if I tear them apart, someone might piece them back together. No. Better safe here with me, where I can keep an eye on them.

I've been walking around the house on these late nights or early mornings, shivering at the delicious cold of the smooth wooden floors in the hall, tiny bumps rising on my body. Each spot in the foot relates to a different body part, and the nerves travel through the body from the soles. I learned that when I worked with a celebrity reflexologist who paid £500 for a mention on my Instagram account, a while ago now. I've always hated people touching my feet and grit my teeth through the experience, #dreamy as far as my followers were aware. A big payout, though. God, I needed it. What I suppose I didn't need was my nerves irritated by some pseudoscientist with a foot fetish. They are frayed enough.

I tread around my big top-floor flat, alone, silent. This is not my beautiful house; this is not my beautiful wife. That's from a song I think. Well, it's not true in this case. This is my beautiful house, or flat I guess, and that *is* my beautiful boyfriend. Mine, mine, mine. No one's taking it.

I pour a glass full of cold water and pop a prazosin pill from the silver foil of the packet in my hand, and some diazepam, although I do try not to. They're highly addictive. The little tablets wrap you in a warm cotton-wool cloud of purring kitten fur. I place my forehead against the window to soothe my thoughts. Dilute the apparitions of the last time I saw her face. The Albert Bridge is lit up like Selfridges at Christmas. Some of the Battersea Power Station flats have lights on, even at this early hour.

By the time Shane comes through to the open plan living room and kitchen, rendered in white with cool grey marble (Charcoal Mist the designer called it, who in hindsight, frankly, we should never have paid top dollar for), I've answered the dwindling number of emails from brands looking to collaborate, finalised my captions for that day and gone over the agenda for any meetings. Shane sinks down next to me on the dark velvet sofa I got free from that really expensive but oh-so-millennial furniture company in exchange for a post. His full, soft lips pull at the sides. An imitation of a smile, a grimace. But it doesn't carry to those oil-black eyes, ringed with feathery lashes. He's not surprised I'm awake, and he doesn't ask why.

That's what usually happens. But this morning I am, miraculously, still in bed. It's not gone unnoticed by Shane, who is already running his warm hands over my back and pulling me close to him. He's most like this in the morning. In the sliver between night and day, unconscious and conscious, when the world's troubles haven't fully manifested. What happened last night?

A black dress and Dior kitten heels are lying on the white and black patterned Moroccan Berber rug. I remember now. We were at a beauty launch at the Dorchester. We didn't stay long, of course, just long enough to kiss a few cheeks and get some content and a goodie bag full of pricey products I'll list on eBay later. I don't get drunk at these events, and none of the other bloggers do either — at least not the professionals. If I drank at every event I was ever invited to, my life would be a 365-day-a-year hangover. And I'd probably be fat. Shane, on the other hand, threw the glasses of bubbles back. I don't know how he does it and still looks so good, but I suppose besides enjoying a drink he does treat his body like Angkor Wat itself, working out for hours and hours every day, never breaking his strict personal trainer's diet.

Back from the party though, he persuaded me to open the bottle of Veuve Clicquot in our goodie bag. Shane, so often busy, had no early clients the next day. I saw that animal look in his eyes and felt a carnal desire to get drunk, to quiet my mind. These factors combined overrode any desire to sensibly call it an early night. So, we relished a rare moment of being all one another's, getting tipsy and laughing on the sofa, forgetting our worries, me lying across him and silently marvelling at the firm muscular mounds of his torso, the soft but unyielding pectorals

I rested my temple and cheek against, my head bouncing a little as he laughed. His shirt smelled so fresh.

Too drunk for sex last night, we were both already exhausted. At 1 a.m. Shane lifted me, falling asleep on his chest, in his arms, enjoying the ease of it. What is it with men and women? We are endlessly fascinated by our differences more than our similarities, always comparing our big and small hands. We brushed our teeth in the quiet solidarity of the drunk.

This morning he wants to recapture last night's missed opportunity. He presses himself into my back and moves his hands between my legs. I let it happen, even as the nausea of a hangover gurgles away in the pit of my stomach. Alcohol and I don't mix too well, no matter how many times I've tried to make it work out between us. Some relationships are too toxic.

Today is the day I'm getting together with some of "The Girls". I've big news. Big enough for an impromptu get together. Both Maggie and Sara immediately accepted my texted invitation. It's often tricky to get all three of us together these days, although I know their cocktail nights go on, courtesy of their social media. I'm never invited. But perhaps they sensed something different. Something in the tone of my text, if it's possible to decipher text tone.

There were more of us in Zanna's "inner circle" once, but Gianna moved to some market town in Surrey to have her baby. She still leaves long gushing comments on the memorial Instagram posts, such as, *You burned too bright for the world, the angels needed your light.* Ultimately well meaning, but probably copied from Google. She was grey and sick at the funeral, morning sickness playing a part by then, in hindsight. You can't expect someone to stick around after a mutual friend dies, though it ought to be a time to pull together. Not everyone responds to death in the same way, some choose to run, some forget, some live in denial; and some stay, to remember, to pay tribute, to hold it all together. And then there's some who can't run, even if they wish they could, stuck in the memories.

Maggie and Sara keep a polite veneer of friendship where I'm concerned. They stay close-ish to me, I think because I'm their connection to Zanna now. If they want to take part in her memorials, they have to go through me.

This morning, they arrive at the flat, one after the other. First Maggie in a fuzzy, mostly wool, ensemble. Sara clops in five minutes after in a full model-off-duty look, fashionable flared sweatpants and square-toed boots, and she bumps her sharp cheekbones against our faces as a form of greeting. The artificial odour of menthol vape pens lingers on her breath and in her hair.

Sara's got perfectly polished honey blonde hair. God knows how much it costs to have highlights woven in like that, like fine gold in your hair. She's tall and thin and gorgeous, so no shock when she married a rich guy, a salesman, but a super luxury one, dealing in watches, cars, that kind of thing. He sold Alan Sugar a watch for £250,000. That's why he and Sara often attend dinners with Saudi businessmen and footballers, trying to convince them to spend money on one of the few things they don't have. I suspect he sells other, less legal, things too.

I open some of the breakfast goodies I've ordered fresh from Pain Quotidien as Shane chats with the girls and gives me a kiss on the cheek — the picture of a good boyfriend — before he leaves us to it. He has little patience for "girl time". One of those men's men. Off to the gym, his everyday routine. Out early, back late. He works hard. Maggie's eyes linger on his back and his broad shoulders in his puffer jacket with the faux fur trimmed hood as they vanish behind the front door. I bring out some yoghurt and some fruit to nibble on. I'm more than a little hungover now and morning sex didn't help. In fact, it sort of mixed everything afresh.

Sara has some yoghurt and half a croissant. Maggie helps herself to more than both of us.

"So," I say, after a cough, picking a raspberry from the tray as I wait for their attention. "I have big news."

I'm woozy. My hangover is suppressed by coffee, fructose and willpower alone. The fatty dairy smell wafting from the croissants almost sends me over the edge.

"I've been approached by a streaming platform about a documentary," I say, "about Zanna."

Maggie pauses, pastry flakes stuck to her thumb and forefinger.

Sara echoes. "A documentary about Zanna?"

"Yes, about her, what happened to her — and me."

Maggie's brow furrows, still trying to compute what this means. Sara's eyes flick to the top of her head when I mention myself. Bitter and jealous.

"Is it one of the big streaming companies?" Sara asks.

I nod. "Really big. But I can't tell you much about it yet. I'm asking you if you want to do it."

The documentary marks the five-year anniversary since Zanna's death. When I'd been approached by the streaming platform, my agent Tom had been beside himself. He bargained at a very reasonable rate for me, even though a huge streaming platform like this was the real prize, for us both.

"Think of how many people are going to see it. Who gets offered something like this?" Tom ranted down the phone, high as a kite from excitement alone, "And it's in memory of Zanna, you can't *not* be in it."

Life of Zanna, named after the Instagram account we crafted together, would look at her life and the events of her death, and who better than me, her very closest friend, to play a key role? In reality, I simply can't turn down the fee.

"Who else would be involved?" I'd cautiously asked in those preliminary meetings.

"Family, friends, the police—" If they have noticed a flash of concern in my eyes, they never let on. "—but it's a positive piece,

11

focused on preventing this sort of tragedy in the future. From the perspective of her ghostwriter. You want that, don't you?"

Funny, how they call me the ghostwriter. Zanna's the ghost now.

"We would be concerned that my client is treated fairly, with appreciation for the fact she's happy to give her time and access to her life for this documentary," Tom said.

I'd squirmed in my seat.

The filmmakers looked at one another.

"Of course," they said. "Of course."

I fill the girls, wide-eyed over breakfast, in on the details. It would take three months to make with the release date scheduled for New Year's Eve.

"Three months, is that it?" Sara asks.

"I know, I was surprised too." Three months, it made my stomach do flips and my toes curl. Excitement and fear, what a cocktail.

"I'm nervous," Maggie says. "What if it doesn't come out right?"

"I don't think I'll do it." Sara leans back in the low seat, a fashionable grey modular one I'd treated myself to. It went perfectly with our burnt-orange rug. It would look so good in pictures, I rationalised, as I put it on the plastic.

"I've seen enough true crime documentaries to know it's never that simple. They always try to dig something up, uncover something."

"Well, neither of us have anything to confess," Maggie says with a little laugh.

I raise my hands in a pantomime pose, as though an officer has a gun pointed at me. "No confessions here."

Sara smiles, closed-lipped.

"I'm sure it will be fine. Great. There are experts, charities involved; it's going to be heartfelt, you know, not sensational at all, Mags." I soothe my anxious friend, though her fears mirror mine. In fact, I can't ensure this, as it was made clear to Tom and me during negotiations. There'll be no reviewing the footage.

"This documentary is a journalistic endeavour, we do not offer footage approval," a producer said as they smiled at us.

Another period of quiet falls over us. Maggie fiddles with the plate resting on her knees. Sara takes out her phone and checks it.

"Five years," Maggie says, in the silence hanging over us like a cheap wedding marquee — stuffy and hot.

Five years since I lost her. Five years since I stepped into her shoes, coming out from under her wing, out from her shadow, running the Instagram account and blog where I'd leaned my skills as a writer to her seven years ago, when it began. She'd selected me to help with the blog. She'd called me "whip smart".

"You have a way with words," she'd told me, a sparkle in her eyes. She finally saw me.

The girls harbour some jealousy, especially given what it's become. They resent me for it, and the benefits that come with it. Sara bristles with every glance at my Louis Vuitton bag, my Cartier watch, my House of Hackney cushions. Judgemental, since her husband foots her bills, but it's the inheritance of the business she resents, I suppose. The idea I got something I didn't deserve. If only she knew the reality of my financial situation now. So far in the red it's a Mourvèdre. If only she knew how hard I really worked to get here.

Spending time with these two women is a hangover — only slightly more bearable than the one I'm suffering now — from a headier, happier time when we were closer. A montage of highly filtered images, a group of girls together, shiny hair, white teeth, the coolest clothes in the room. Fake filters on fake friendships. Without Zanna, our keystone, our glue, our reason to be, we fell apart.

"I have to get this back in time to catch my train," Sara speaks to Maggie and nods her head towards a Harvey Nichols bag by her feet. On cue, Maggie looks around for somewhere to put her plate and I extend my hand to take it.

"We should be off," she says, in an apologetic tone. "I'll get back to you about the documentary."

"What have you got planned?" I ask in a nonchalant way, I hope.

"I'm just going with Sara into town to return something, nothing exciting."

I'm not invited. Maggie makes every attempt to lessen the slight, making things worse, while Sara, uncaring, looks at her phone as she gets to her feet and shuffles mindlessly towards the door, attention on the screen.

Maggie stops at the door on the way out, pausing for a moment and looking directly at me. I'm aware of my hand on the door frame, my arm held out ninety degrees from my body at short little Maggie's eye-line. How long has it been since I saw her? Since before she bought her home somewhere in the suburbs. I've never visited, despite a few invitations, which have trailed off now. I suppose it takes two to drift apart.

"Shame Gianna didn't come," Maggie says. "I extended the invite."

Of course she did, Maggie the peacemaker. I purse my lips. We lock eyes. I say nothing. Gianna had not liked me while Zanna was alive. She'd cut me off immediately after her death. She had much to say, things that meant I would hardly welcome her here, in my home.

"You don't have to run yourself ragged over this Zanna thing you know." Maggie changes tack. "We're all worried about you, how much you take on."

"I'm fine. I can handle it."

Locked in the grip of her steady eyes, I shrug. I try to be nonchalant. I seriously doubt their worry is any more than a momentary thought. I seriously doubt any of them have ever cared about me.

"Every year you do so much for the anniversary. Taking control, doing everything. Now, taking part in this documentary. It can't be easy. We want you to know we're here to help with whatever you need if you want to share the load."

Sara is in the hallway after a curt "Bye" and another bony, cold, half-hug. She stares at an old Art Deco light fitting on the mansion block's communal interior wall, avoids my glance. "Thanks, Mags. But I really don't think that will be necessary. I like doing it. It makes me happy. Like she's still here."

"I get that," she says with a sigh, "but you can move on, we all need to."

Easy to say for you, Maggie, but you didn't know her like I did. My best friend forever, but forever was cut short. Zanna never leaves me. I speak to her in my head, I hear her words as though she is peeking over my shoulder at every moment. I struggle to know which are my thoughts and which are hers.

Never alone, even as the girls leave me — the only living soul in the flat — ghosts are here. I wander over to the remainder of my breakfast spread, mostly untouched, shiny mounds of pastry oozing chocolate spread and marmalade, like grisly organs and bodily fluids. I shove half of a pain au chocolat in my mouth. It's a moment of heaven as chocolate spread, butter and a little hint of salt hit my palate. I chew and open Instagram with a flick of the thumb. No exciting updates, just my influencer colleagues showing off their coffee dates or morning workouts. I flick to the business email account. It's the one on my website hyperlinked under the entreaty "collaborate with me". It's here I check for paying jobs, the kind that aren't so forthcoming at the moment. There is a new email, though, from an unrecognised email address with nothing but a collection of numbers where a name ought to be. The subject:

I know what you did, Pooh Bear.

As I read the words lit up on my phone screen, my stomach rebels. There's a familiar lurch before it expels what has been slopping around in there since last night. I make it to the sink just in time, hot palms pressed against cool marble worktops. My guts empty, sweet orange juice and bitter stomach acid, onto stainless steel. I don't fight it.

I twist the long, modernist tap as clumps of things that were recently inside me circle and fall down the plug into the creaking abyss of an ancient London mansion block pipe system. My heart pumps. It hurts. I feel fire in my chest and ice in my feet. I retch as the sick, guttural, wet growling turns my stomach. That gurgling has something wretchedly, awfully familiar about it.

The Past

I've always suffered with anxiety, so much it became a corner-stone of my personality, my existence. My first memories, the crunching bowel before a panic attack. I figured everyone else must feel this way, feel as much as I do. It never occurred to me that some people's insides don't seize up that way. They don't fear entering a busy room. They don't go over every conversation every night, in search of the wrong thing they said. And while I've always felt out of place, it wasn't half as bad as how I felt at university halls, forgotten like a remote left under the sofa, or an elderly relative in a care home, withering away, existing a little bit less every day.

I'd started at university a month or so before I met Zanna. While "A" grades in the first assignments had not been hard to come by, friends had. My new flatmates in halls had mostly stopped talking to me. I'd walked in on one, Sammy, a lanky Northerner who had a nose ring and wore a knock-off Burberry shirt, saying: "She's weird, though, isn't she?" I knew from the way he stopped speaking when he saw me, I was the "she". I wasn't a stranger to this sort of thing. This kind of bullying. I knew it early. I remembered the snickering down the hallway at school. Girls turning their backs to me, cupping their mouths, laughing.

Still, that night, a girl from my halls allowed me to follow her out and let me stand by her — for lack of a better option, certainly. That was when I first saw her in the flesh.

Zanna oozed the effortlessness of a person gifted with looks, and latterly with everything else, and who never gave this fortunate happenstance any second thought. Her parents were rich. I could tell by looking at her. You learn to do that when you grow up poor.

Passing a bottle of Blossom Hill between us, the girl from my halls scoffed at Zanna.

"So embarrassing," she said to me from the side of her mouth, sneering at the brunette on the sofa, dressed like a budget Lady Gaga. Disdain can bond you with unlikely people. "You know, Zanna isn't even her name — she made it up."

I did know. I had heard about her before I first saw her. Naturally, everyone talked about the gorgeous Zanna and her posse of girlfriends, all nearly as attractive. People always talk about those girls.

Zanna Zagalo. Some names are so fun to say, you can't keep them out of your mouth. Like gum, you want to spend time masticating on it. Of course, Zanna's name wasn't really Zanna, her parents were too sensible for that. A solicitor and a house-wife, they settled on Hannah Zagalo for their little girl, but they really should have known it would never be good enough for someone with the otherworldly glow of Zanna. So, naturally, she gave herself a new name, easy as a haircut. She breathed it into life with sheer will and charisma, and it stuck. If I gave myself a new name, people would laugh.

She wore skintight, wet-look leather trousers and a totally sheer mesh body with a red bra. Zanna wrapped herself in a huge leopard-print jacket from Topshop, a jacket way too warm for the room but she wore it anyway. Holding a bottle of Prosecco, she drank straight from it. When she wasn't drink-ing from it, she held it with a limp wrist, waggling it while she talked. She held a cigarette in the other hand in exactly the same way, like the pictures saved to my Pinterest board of Kate Moss in the nineties.

My fellow party guest said: "She looks like Patsy from *Ab Fab*." Zanna studied fashion. I, journalism. I was destined to watch her.

Sprawling out over three men, five foot seven and not a pound over nine stone, she talked to a girl sitting on the floor. Legs all over the place, feet sticking off the end of the sofa, she wriggled around, obviously uncomfortable. It didn't look comfortable for the men she lay upon either, who winced but allowed her to stay there anyway. She lay there because lying there looked powerful, sexy, and most importantly, people were watching.

"Yeah," I said, agreeing with my party companion, "so tragic."

But I was utterly drawn in by Zanna. Every moment a pose, every drag on her cigarette a moment. Her lips red, like the bra. I'd seen her type before. I'd sat on the edge of the playground, wistfully, as gaggles of teenagers I feared to approach socialised, the girl in the middle orchestrating the show. I never kept friends for long. School had been like halls over those first few weeks, and I had a terrifying feeling it might really be my fate to be alone.

As my companion had got talking to a guy lacquered with dark tattoos, I slipped away, through the crowd, unnoticed, drifting between bodies like a draught. They moved their bodies just enough to accommodate my progress without so much as a glance in my direction. I manoeuvred next to her, in the smoking area, stomach churning. Hand almost shaking, I lifted ten Marlboro Lights from my pocket, the hot girl's cigarette of choice. I took a deep breath, steeled myself.

"Do you have a lighter?"

Walking home on my own from the party a few hours later — my halls mate had gone home with the tattooed man — the phantasm of a hopeful smile tugged at the corners of my mouth. I felt dizzy. I hadn't even drunk that much. But Zanna had asked if I wanted to go shopping.

"I'll find you on Facebook," she said.

I refreshed my Facebook messages when I arrived home early that morning, and again when I woke, a mass of excitement, at around 7 a.m. In the evening she finally messaged me. A date was set for Saturday. She sent me her phone number. I did a little dance around my room in halls.

"You should never use the testers," Zanna said that weekend, in the nearest shopping town to our university, as I reached to try some serum on my skin. She'd slapped my hand. "You don't know who else has touched it. You can get herpes."

I nodded and put the tester back on the shelf like it was an activated grenade. Zanna smiled encouragingly, eyes twinkling. We moved down the shelves and she dropped products in my basket.

"Now, you could really do with some vitamin C, to brighten you up, and salicylic acid, for your oiliness."

Later she whispered to me, "That's not a real Louis Vuitton," nodding at the bag of a woman sitting near us in a café, keen eyes narrowed. She pronounced it properly, "loo·ee vwee·ton".

"The bag looks older but the trim is light. Louis Vuitton trim tans with age. It's the Vachetta leather."

I followed and listened. Tried to remember the names of the products. I studied the ingredients on the bottles later, when I smoothed the products, bought with my overdraft and used as sparingly as liquid gold, onto my face.

No more than a month into our friendship, and we were what my grandmother called bosom buddies. We drank wine and smoked cigarettes out of the tall windows in her bedroom. I seemed to make Zanna laugh, and we lay in her bed until the early hours, giggling too much to sleep through eyelids weighed down by exhaustion. I told her my childhood nickname, Pooh Bear. My mother, mostly, used it for me after she'd bought me a little Winnie the Pooh. Zanna found it hysterical, and used it liberally, when it was just the two of us. Like a little sign that she knew something classified about me. Knew me like family.

In that bedroom, she showed me some crystals and she loaned me a book, *The Secret*. She told me, "Our thoughts create our reality." She said to imagine already being what you want to be. So, of course, I imagined being her.

In Zanna's room, in that cosy bed with its soft as butter sheets, I spoke about the things I'd never discussed with anyone before, spanning from fairytale wedding planning to conversations that at first seemed so dirty I blushed.

Zanna said: "Paige, you should tell me what you want for an engagement ring now, so when your future husband asks me for help to choose one, I'll know exactly what to suggest."

I've never forgotten her dream ring.

"A brilliant cut solitaire on a micro pave white gold band."

She made me repeat it back to her. I could say it in my sleep.

We talked about sex more than weddings, though. We talked about virginity, how we didn't have it now, how that came to be. We totted up the number of boys we slept with. Zanna, mainly, because she'd slept with many more people than me. I'd slept with my secondary school boyfriend, Michael, and had a one-night stand during Freshers' Week. A rite of passage and an effort to claim my womanhood backfired spectacularly when I discovered the man I chose, another first year in my halls and a graphic design student, had told everyone about it in detail the next morning.

"Fucking boys," she erupted in anger when I told her. "Why do we have to like them so much? It would be so much easier to be a lesbian. I'd just date you."

My heart could have glowed like ET's, lighting up our under-the-covers tête-à-tête. Curled up under the sheets, top lips daubed with bleaching cream, a treatment Zanna both prescribed and performed, Zanna turned our conversation to her boyfriend.

"He's amazing," Zanna said. "So kind to me. So wonderful to women in general. Treats me like a princess. Doesn't drink though. His body is a temple, and I worship at it. He's so soft. I think he'd only ever want to do missionary and stare into my eyes if I didn't get him to experiment a bit more. He loves me so much, he's happy with the basics, I guess. But I like it rough, like when they spit in your mouth."

I visibly cringed at the revolting thought and she laughed.

Usual patter for Zanna, her foul mouth part of her modern, millennial, feminist charm. She would spout blue language and graphic sex anecdotes as easily as she would tell you the time, although the former she did unsolicited. But she also had a sort of girly dreaminess, the classic heterosexual dreams of rich middle-class girls. I loved it, lapping it all up like glittery honey. She made me laugh out loud. She explained away my awkward shyness with imposter syndrome, she told me my feelings were "valid" until they were spilling out of me. She opened me like a string purse, said what I'd thought were novelty gems were diamonds.

She described her father, Santiago, to me, as I had broken through to the soft and intimate part of her.

"So, like, what do you want to do when you graduate?" she'd asked.

The question always caused a tug of anxiety in my guts. What do you want to do? *I can't believe I've got this far*, I'd think. And, *I get to choose?*

"I want to be a journalist, I guess." My rehearsed reply with a self-conscious caveat did not get past Zanna.

"You guess?"

"No, no. I know, I do," I said.

"You don't seem sure," she teased.

"Who's ever that sure about what they want to do? If I've not done anything yet, how can I really know I want to do it?"

"Mm. I guess." Then she laughed. "Now I sound like you! You can definitely do it. You're clever and insightful. I bet you're a great writer."

I tingled with a warmth that started in my stomach. I couldn't remember the last time someone since primary school had been so encouraging of my writing.

"You should show me some, I'd love to read it," she said.

I nodded, already the heat of embarrassment creeping into my cheeks at the idea of showing her my meagre blog with its pointless musings and zero readers.

"What do you want to do?" I asked.

"Well, I wanted to be an actress."

"You can still be." I trailed off weakly as she shook her head violently.

"Nah," she said, a broader sound than she usually made, brash, forceful, pushing the idea away aggressively with a syllable. "I never got cast in anything, besides a few small bits, and anyway, it's not really me. Being an actress is all about being told what to do. And I don't want to be told what to do. Plus, my dad hated it."

She left it dangling there, a tasty morsel to pluck from a low hanging branch. The gate leading to knowing her more intimately left purposefully off the latch.

"Your dad?"

"He's super Catholic." Zanna shrugged, an attempt at noncha-lance, with an edge to her voice put there by hurt. "He doesn't

27

think acting is appropriate for his daughters. That's why he's so thrilled with Sophie and Clare, and always so pissed off with me. I break the rules, he hates it."

"Catholics are really so strict?"

"He is," she spat. "A woman without discretion is like a gold ring in a pig's snout. That's what my dad says, it's from the Bible. Doesn't mind a bit of corporal punishment either, does Daddy Dear. Doesn't spare the rod, as it were. He's a self-made man. Really clever, like, unbelievably clever. He runs his own companies, like I want to do one day. Be a boss. Like him. But I don't think he sees that in me."

Her voice swelled with pride, as well as pain. Her eyes glittered with the beginning of tears. Her jaw hardened. That moment I knew we'd fallen in love. Not love, love, but the love of two best friends.

I wanted to tell her about my parents. My dad and his rolled newspaper smacking my cheek when I dared show my face downstairs amid another argument with my beleaguered mother. But I didn't want to put her off. I didn't want her to see me that way, to know the full sad story of me. I wanted a new start, without all my squalid history. I deserved that, and now I had my Zanna, I could do it.

"That sucks," I said. I waited a little. Then, "You're studying fashion, right?"

28

"Yeah. That will annoy my dad as well," she said with a chuckle, "but not so much as acting. I like fashion, but I don't want to design. And I've done the internships at *Vogue* and *Stella*, they shove you in a closet putting clothes in bags and writing out addresses, but like, fuck that. I want to make money. And I want to be the boss. I want to be the boss as quickly as possible.

"I've always felt I belong in the public eye," she said, her eyes searching my face for a response.

I'd never heard someone say it like that, so brazenly. Again, she shocked me into a moment of silence. In front of me, bleached moustachioed, lay a woman who'd lead me, one hand in hers, into a future where we said our ambitions out loud.

And what did I want? Whatever Zanna wanted.

The Present

In a studio

Did you know three inches of fast running water is enough to take you toppling down? Is enough to drown in?

That's what I think of when my agent Tom tells me this documentary is my "stepping stone". I focus on those words. Repeat them in my head. Stepping stone. Stepping stone. Stepping stones take you over cold, rushing water, and — if the water is too high — you'll fall in.

We're doing my makeup in a studio the production company has rented, somewhere in Hoxton, on a third floor. An enormous space with high ceilings, white walls, and a wooden floor. A big, white, plush sofa is set against a white backdrop with bright lights directed at it. That's where I'll sit.

On the makeup table in front of me sits a stack of magazines. *Grazia, Vogue, Cosmopolitan, Love, Glamour, Stylist.* In my sweaty palms, the *Sunday Times Style* magazine, the familiar sheen and inky aroma of its pages gleaming under my gel-manicured hands.

I read the Editor's Letter, as always, trying to imagine being the woman in the picture above the words. Arms clad in a quirky print silk shirt, folded across a jaunty, could-be flirty, angled torso below a face with a red-lipped smirk. Not friendly enough to be conspiratorial, but not cold. It's special to me, this magazine. A kind English teacher, Ms Quinn, who noticed a talent for writing and love of clothes in a quiet girl, brought me the supplement one Monday morning. My parents didn't read *The Times* and wouldn't buy it for me weekly. Their meagre budget didn't stretch to Sunday papers for precocious children.

I remember when news of Zanna's murder covered front pages and column inches in magazines such as these. She wanted to be in the public eye, and eventually she really, truly was. Sadly, she didn't live to see it. I collected each clipping and webpage I saw, as if I could show her later. She'd have laughed, sparkly eyed with gleaming teeth, to see herself the main topic of the news.

Thanks to this documentary, I'm closer than ever to being the woman above the Editor's Letter, her image printed onto semi-glossy pages. I'd been reluctant of course, as had Shane. Living the life of an influencer, it feels like your whole career can be at stake when posting a selfie, let alone taking part in something like this. But Tom had worked his agent magic.

"If this comes off," he told me, "The *Sunday Times* are offering you a column."

Something I'd dreamed of. My words finally in print, in a magazine, not on a blog or in an Instagram caption.

"This could make you legit. More mainstream in the eyes of the public. From influencer to media personality. We could pitch you to TV."

The column was something I'd dreamed of, yes, but TV money? Now, that's something else. Something I need. I almost salivate thinking about it, dangled in front of me, a carrot leading me into this documentary like a starving donkey out of one of those Christmas charity ads.

I ought to be enjoying this moment, having my makeup done, taking the spotlight. Truth is, I'm too anxious to enjoy anything since *it* arrived. That email, lingering in my inbox, another dirty secret correspondence like those white-enveloped overdue credit card payment notices. But this has far worse ramifications than bankruptcy. I'd been so sure I'd made the right decision, being talked into this documentary by Tom, lured by money, tormented by the minus sign in front of my bank account, certain the past would stay the past, some of its aspects well-hidden and secret.

I accepted a risk. A huge one. But I'd been too confident, cocksure. One email turned this whole documentary into a living nightmare. The eyes of producers and interns alike are on me. Murmuring. Consulting clipboards. I wonder how many of them believe the rumours, rather than the truth.

I shudder as I think of it. *Pooh Bear*. Reflexively, I reach for my phone, the rectangular device still a little warm from the last time I held it. It comforts me to do these everyday things, these compulsive robotic movements. Sheryl, an employee of the streaming company, flinches a little, her brow cross-stitched before she relaxes and says in a tone tinged by tension, "No pictures!"

I nod. Of course, I know. I signed the NDA like everyone else, after a brief flick-through. All content I post about the documentary must be cleared with the streaming service first. I can't even really tell anyone about it, in any capacity. I'd needed express permission to tell Sara and Maggie, to invite them to take part.

Now the neurotic Sheryl has been assured I'm not uploading details of the process for my followers, I check the stats on my last post. It's a series of pictures of me smiling in the kitchen, surrounded by veg with a tool in hand. It's an ad for said tool, which is used to pulverise hard vegetables like swede. *I love to use it as the base for healthy sauces,* I promise my followers in the caption. I've never done that. It sounds thoroughly disgusting.

This is not the content I usually go for, but offers to collaborate or promote brands — the lifeblood of an influencer's income — have been coming in less frequently in the past year, as have the likes and follows. They are linked together, of course. My growth has stalled, interest in me evidently waning with my followers. I was set to take home a third less than I normally make in a year, before I signed up to this documentary. And, if I'm honest, I didn't make what I'd make in a normal year last year, or the year before that. Shane has no idea that many of our expenses have been spread across a few credit cards, but I've had to keep up appearances. I can pay those mounting bills back once business gets better. That's why I agreed to this. Between a rock and a hard place, you could say. This accursed email, however, transformed that hard place into a pointier, sharper place, moving slowly towards me, Indiana Jones booby-trap style.

God, I really need this kitchen tool post to do well. I get a bonus if anyone buys the product through my link or if I bring a certain number of followers for the brand's own page.

I share the picture to my stories, adding:

"You guys, the algorithm is hating on my posts. Please give this a like and a share to boost my content to your feed."

I hate to beg, but you have to do what you have to do.

You have to do what you have to do.

I glance over at that couch. Today, I'm going to tell the story of me and Zanna from the beginning and my stomach is already churning. The story is etched onto my heart, but the email has knocked all my confidence.

One of the producers, the aforementioned Sheryl, is a small, pointy young woman, sharp elbows, sharp nose, even sharp ears poking out from the side of her face with a perfectly shiny head of blonde hair pulled back, skull-cap tight, into a bun. I bet she has "Look like a lady, think like a man and work like a boss" framed in her bedroom. Her name doesn't suit her. She is about my age, thirty, and my job is a little bit of a joke to her, while she works long days for far less money. She talks slowly to me, like the intricacies of television are far above my intellect. I've looked at her Instagram; her page is full of snaps of cocktails, homemade bread and marathon training updates.

"It's a chance to tell your side of the story. Explain what happened. Address anything unfair, any misconceptions you feel the public might still have about you and Zanna," Sheryl said, during those early meetings about the documentary.

I had questions.

"What is the point, though? What is the documentary looking at?"

"A very good question." Sheryl smiled at me, patronisingly. "We are looking simply to shine a light on Zanna's life, her influence, her achievements. And yours. We want to prevent tragedy in the future while honouring her memory."

"And it's not going to be cheesy with horrible re-enactments and stuff? Not going to focus too much on . . . what happened to her? The horrible stuff."

"We feel," Sheryl answered, seamless and controlled, "re-enactments are a great tool to help an audience understand

a story, to feel an emotional connection to those involved —
Zanna, and yourself."

I pressed on. "But it's going to be positive, about her life,
right? Not like a true crime thing about, you know—" A word
hard to say out loud. "—the murder."

Sheryl smiled reassuringly. "Absolutely. This is going to be
positive, uplifting, inspiring. All things Zanna."

So, I agreed.

But that was all before that email. That nasty little email. I
have no idea where it came from. No idea how to trace it. It
hangs there, making me sweat each time I check my inbox. Of
course, anyone else would think, go to the police. But I can't.
There's too much to lose. The blog. Shane. I've run myself ragged
thinking about it, bringing on dark circles under my eyes. I've
had abusive emails before, of course; it's par for the course.
I've had many over the years. But this one is very different.

Who would call me *Pooh Bear*, besides Zanna and my
mother, both of whom were quickly struck from the list of
potential suspects for obvious reasons? Zanna, dead. And my
mother, who — living miles away and being a practical stranger
by the time of Zanna's death — would have no idea about anything. No one, in any of the emails before, has used that most
secret of nicknames. Zanna must have told someone. The hair
on my neck prickles with shame as I think of her laughing with
someone about it. My stomach drops. My best friend.

A wave of nausea washing over me, I check my emails again. The email is still sitting there. My tongue dry and stuck to the roof of my mouth, I open it again and regret it instantaneously.

I know what you did, Pooh Bear.

My hands tremor violently, so I put the phone down on the table, too loudly, slamming it. The makeup artist jumps. Tom and Sheryl look.

"Sorry," I murmur, afraid to open my lips too wide in case my quivering heart jumps out of it, flopping onto the floor. That would be something for the documentary.

"Don't be nervous, babes, you're going to be amazing," Tom says, giving me the thumbs up.

Sheryl squints at me, raises an eyebrow and makes a note on her clipboard.

I stare at myself in the mirror, my armpits moistening. The white couch beckons. I try to forget the email and unstick my tongue, so I fixate on my nose and breathe in for five and out for ten. I told Zanna I'd like it straightened once, my nose, explaining how it broke after I tripped over my dad's boots in the hallway. He smacked me on the leg for it. Never treated at hospital, no one took me, I soothed it with ice myself and it remained always a little skew-whiff.

"Don't you want anything done to the bulbous bit at the end too?" she'd asked, squeezing her own nose, crafted with help of a surgical hammer and a few stitches.

"Yeah, maybe," I'd said, turning back to my bedroom mirror, unsure.

"Don't worry, you're gorge either way. Look, you can contour it."

She'd sat cross-legged in front of me and dusted on a new nose with dark powder. "Beautiful," she'd pronounced, touching the makeup brush to the end of my nose like a tickly little kiss. I miss that Zanna so much my heart convulses.

The closer my face comes to complete under the hands of the makeup artists — cheekbones, eye sockets, a jaw filled in with darker powder — the sooner I'll have to start talking. As much as I want to at this moment, I can't stop her fingers from finishing their work and, once she's done, I settle down on the well-lit sofa.

Sheryl sits down in front of me, a list of questions on a clipboard, questions that are going to call on me to speak the truth about my relationship with Zanna.

Hello, Paige. Welcome to the set.

Life of Zanna Documentary

Paige White Interview

PRODUCER: Hello, Paige. Welcome to the set. First time, how exciting.

PW: [Smiling, lips together.] Thank you.

PRODUCER: How are you feeling?

PW: Alright. [Wrings her hands together.]

PRODUCER: Are you sure you're okay? You look white as a sheet. Do you need a moment?

PW: No, no. It's okay. Let's get on with it. I mean, let's do it.

PRODUCER: Well then, why don't we start from the beginning? Nice and easy. How did you become friends with Zanna Zagalo?

PW: Um. [Pause.] How does anyone make friends? I guess I don't really remember. I think we got talking at a party. [Chokes a little on her words, frog in her throat.]

PRODUCER: Do you want some water?

PW: [Nods.] I'm sorry. I don't really know what to say. I'm nervous. I'm not used to cameras and lights and . . . stuff.

PRODUCER: Really? Not even as an influencer? I would have thought it's all lights and cameras and stuff.

PW: Well, not quite like this. This is . . . different.

PRODUCER: It's okay, take your time. We can take as long as you need. You don't need to feel anxious.

PW: Yeah, it's just, there's a lot to say. It's hard to know where to start. There's a lot to keep track of, you know. Remember. Like, there's a lot of history, so it can be hard.

PRODUCER: Let's forget all that and just focus on you and Zanna. What's the first thing you said to each other?

PW: Oh, I don't know. [Laughs.] Let me think.

[Long pause.]

PRODUCER: Where did you meet?

PW: I honestly don't really remember. It's all a bit of a haze those first months or so of university. Making so many new friends in halls, getting invited to all the parties. Having a little more fun than doing your uni work — if you know what I mean. [Laughs.] But yes, we became very close. Thick as thieves. It was a happy accident that we met. I honestly couldn't imagine my life now if fate hadn't brought us together.

PRODUCER: How close were you exactly?

PW: Well, Zanna used to say she and I were soulmates. I'm a Gemini, she was a Sagittarius. Those signs form a very deep bond. Opposing signs. Opposites. Or two halves of a whole. That's what she told me. Zanna was very into star signs. So, yes. She said we were soul sisters. I never had a sister. I don't have any siblings. They are opposing signs and opposites attract, don't they? That's why we were a good team, Zanna said. God, sorry, I'm rambling, aren't I? Star signs, how painfully millennial.

So, yeah. We met and then we got on really well so, as we got closer, it made so much sense to work together, to live together, to do everything together. We never really fought. It was so easy — just us against the world. Two girls supporting one another, accepting one another, going after our dreams together. Girl bosses. That's what we wanted to be. I was so lucky to have a friend like her, I know that for sure. I feel sorry for anyone who doesn't have a Zanna in their life.

PRODUCER: What was Zanna like to someone who knew her as well as you did?

PW: What was Zanna like? That's such a hard question. How to describe someone like Zanna ... It's like asking you to describe a rainbow to someone who's never seen one. She was such a force to be reckoned with, you had to see it to believe it.

She made you feel important. She made you feel you could do anything. She lifted me up. She wanted to reach all these starry highs, wanted the most amazing life, and wanted to take you with her. She was fierce and she lit a fire underneath everyone else. She never accepted "no", she never let anyone tell her she couldn't get what she wanted, and she made life the best, most amazing, most glittery, most fabulous thing it could be.

Before I met Zanna, so many possibilities in life never occurred to me. She talked about living in multiple homes, she took me on my first holiday abroad and talked the people at the front desk into giving us the suite. We'd be having drinks and the next minute we were off to an exclusive club with some rich guys from the next table over. These things didn't happen for people like me, with my background. Zanna, she just made things happen, and things happened when you were with her. She was magnetic.

PRODUCER: So tell me, how did you begin working together?

PW: Zanna had read my old blog I wrote when I first started uni. It was full of silly stuff, really. Writing about moving to university, being a journalism student. Urgh, honestly, it makes me cringe to think of it now. [Laughs and rubs cheek with hand.] She said she loved it. Read it over and over. But I was still shocked when she asked me to start writing for her. She said my writing was the best she'd ever seen. Plus, no one knew her better than me. She didn't want to be bogged down with the writing side of things. "I need to focus on steering the blog in the right direction, and the visuals," she said.

At first, she offered to pay me £50 per post for three a week. I was like, *hell yes!* I was struggling to live on my money from working at a local pub, fitting shifts in between my uni lectures, so an extra £150 was like winning the lottery. [Chuckles.]

For an aspiring writer, just out of university, struggling even to offer their services for free at unpaid internships at newspapers and magazines, this was an amazing opportunity.

She said, "You can put it on your CV. You can say you're my editorial assistant." [Shakes her head.] Honestly, the money was unreal, but I would have done it for less. I loved working with Zanna, spending time with her on the blog.

PRODUCER: How did it work? Did you imagine you were Zanna when you wrote?

PW: Erm . . . that's a good question. Kind of, but then I always let my voice come through. I couldn't help it, really. And Zanna liked it. She wanted it to feel real, authentic. Anyway, it was easy to write like her, it was like we shared a mind sometimes. She told me: "No one knows me better than you."

PRODUCER: What did you write for her?

PW: Lots of beauty reviews, mainly. That's what was really popular at the time, beauty blogging. She asked me to write stuff about her haircare, mentioning a brand she had a deal with. It was exciting, the closest I was getting to any real journalism. When comments came in on the site and Instagram praising the content, I knew those were my words. People were reading what I was saying, caring about it. It felt amazing, honestly.

PRODUCER: What was the experience like? Having your best friend as your boss?

PW: It was so fun! She was the best boss ever, and the good thing about working for your friend is they let you open the prosecco from 4 p.m. on Fridays! [Laughs.] No, seriously, it was the best. The best time of my life.

PRODUCER: And there were never any issues? Any disagreements? I know I'd struggle to work with my friend.

PW: No, there were no disagreements. It was a perfect partnership. That's how close we were. Working together like a well-oiled machine. How many friends could say they are that close?

PRODUCER: Not many, I'm guessing.

PW: Exactly. You know. Zanna, she, like . . . [Pause.] She believed in me, in my writing. She saw something in me no one else did. Talent, ability. Before Zanna, I was no one. No one cared about me. No one saw me. She was my best friend. I loved her so much. I miss her every day.

PRODUCER: And that is why you have agreed to take part in this documentary?

PW: Yes. Yes, absolutely. It's a tribute to her. To keep her memory alive.

PRODUCER: And how do you feel about taking part given the speculation around your involvement in Zanna's murder?

PW: Oh, gosh. [Puts hand to chest.] I feel afraid. I do. Those were some of the worst times of my life. A lot of terrifying things happened around that time, including my own safety being put in danger by people who thought they knew better than the police. Thankfully, I have a great relationship with the police now. They have been brilliant. I'm very thankful for that. For the sake of mine and Shane's safety.

Life of Zanna Documentary

Maggie Jenks Interview

PRODUCER: Thanks for agreeing to speak with us, Maggie. It took some convincing.

MJ: [Chuckles nervously.] It's a little out of my comfort zone. But yeah, I want to do what's best for Zanna in the end, so you and Paige convinced me.

PRODUCER: We're so excited to pay homage to Zanna. She was clearly an amazing woman, and an important person in your life.

MJ: [Nods and begins to tear up.]

PRODUCER: [Holds out a tissue pulled from a box.] Oh hun, tissue?

MJ: Thank you. [Takes it and dabs her red eyes.]

PRODUCER: Can you talk me through how you met Zanna?

[Pause as MJ steadies her breathing.]

MJ: Zanna and I met at uni in our first year, during Freshers' Week. In halls. Her room was two down from mine, and we shared a kitchen.

I was super nervous that first day, when I got dropped off, and I'd been crying, and I'd come out of my room to get a drink of water or something. My mum and dad, we're a close family, so I just balled. Zanna came in too, and she must have seen my blotchy face because she left straight away. I thought she was giving me privacy, but then she came back a few minutes later with this huge sparkly pink bottle of prosecco, it must have been a magnum or something, and said: "You need something stronger than that, hun!"

It always makes me laugh thinking about it.

We got drunk, listened to music, screaming at the top of our lungs until a boy down the hall came and politely told us to shut the fuck up. [Laughs.] I ended up sleeping in her room and we were friends ever since.

I felt like I already knew her straight away. Zanna was like that — people gravitated to her. But she was kind, that's what brought us all together. I had an on-and-off boyfriend who was basically a dick and Zanna was always really good at making me feel better, always there for me. For all of us. She went above and beyond for her friends, no denying that.

PRODUCER: How did the other girls come into your lives?

MJ: Zanna, she sort of collected people. First Sara, she was in our class on the first day. She was sitting in the front row, by herself, looking through her phone, and she looked so cool. Zanna sort of manoeuvred us down behind her and said, "Oh my gosh, I love your handbag, do you want to come for lunch with us?" She made friends easily, like that. Then Gianna, we met her at the student union, drinking Jägerbombs. Classic uni. [Laughs.] That was our first year, and the four of us were thick as thieves for a while, happy and loving life.

PRODUCER: And Paige, how did you meet Paige? Was she one of these people Zanna collected?

MJ: I'm not sure how Paige came along, but it was a few years later, when Zanna and I were finishing uni. One day she wasn't there and the next she was, always with Zanna, stuck to her side, like a limpet.

The Past

I was absorbed into Zanna's "girls", ones I'd watched shimmering and shining and parting crowds of men at the uni bar like a biblical sea. The induction was made about six weeks after we met.

"The girls and I were thinking you should come to dinner with us."

My stomach fluttered.

"Come round to mine to get ready first," Zanna said, giving me the time of five o'clock.

When I got there, Zanna had Lana Del Rey's debut album on, sounds of glamour and sex. She wore a slinky dressing gown and the top section of her hair sat in three large rollers.

"Yay! I'm so glad you're here, come in!" She threw her arms around me. She pressed her whole body against mine, the soft silk of the dressing gown wafting against my hand and her powdery perfumed sweetness enveloping me, engulfed into her world, where finally someone was genuinely happy to have me — not just happy, thrilled.

She drew me into the small kitchen at the end of the long hallway, giving me prosecco in a pink flute. I followed her back into her bedroom at the front of the house with a large bay window, shielded partially from the quiet road outside by foliage, drink in hand. The scent of shea body butter, biscuity fake tan and the more acidic and brittle-sweet notes of perfume filled the room. And human smells, the musk of sleep on her pillows, the slight tang of a laundry basket, lacy thongs hanging over the top.

If Zanna was an eau de parfum (and she absolutely would insist on being at least an eau de parfum and certainly not an eau de toilette), a beauty editor would describe it like this: head notes of peppy orange, uber-feminine peony, the sparkling mint of really clean teeth and nose-wrinkling curiosity of expensive hairspray give way to a heart of Moroccan-souk-purchased incense and proper leather handbags. Finally, indulge in a base of rich girl body lotion, deep comparison of the self to others, and tonka bean.

I had my overnight bag, which I'd been instructed to bring. It had a thong for the next day and a T-shirt. I had my outfit for dinner on.

"Is that what you're wearing?" my hostess asked.

"No," she said before I could answer. "Paige, we're going to Sushi Samba, not Slug and Lettuce."

54

"I didn't bring anything else."

"Never you fear, my dear," she smiled. She dug in a bag by the end of the bed, one of those posh, wide paper bags with ribbon handles you get from designer shops. Pulling out a long, hot pink, silky dress, she tore the tag off with aggressive enthusiasm. The tag hit the bag and flopped to the floor. I read the name, Alexander Wang. "Put it on," she said, thrusting it at me.

"Is it going to fit?"

"Yeah! We're the same size, silly."

We were the same size, but here the physical similarities ended. While the skin on Zanna's stomach pulled tight like skin on a drum, mine had the squishy give of an old leather sofa. I hoisted the dress above my head and let it fall over me, cool on my skin like a breeze.

The doorbell went, and a flock of women filled the flat. There were kisses on cheeks. Zanna poured more prosecco into more pink flutes.

"Wait. Is that the dress you bought when we were shopping the other day?" Sara, an icy blonde in all possible manifestations, asked, addressing Zanna.

"Yeah," Zanna said, shrugging, "looks better on Paige, I think."

"It's so nice! Where is it from?" shortish, squattish Maggie asked, stroking the soft, shimmering fabric. She'd met me with the warmest smile.

"Alexander Wang." The words were strangled coming out of my mouth and I cast a glance at Gianna, her gaze cold. Jealousy.

That night the sushi wasn't the kind I'd had before, the kind you buy in ready-meal boxes from M&S or Tesco. Brought out on trays, rhubarb pink strips of fish entwined with creamy avocado the colour of a perfect, ripe Granny Smith apple, wrapped in rice. On some of the rolls sat blobs of a yellow sauce with slivers of chive, each one identical in size and shape. On another balanced a dollop of seventies bathroom-suite pink with tiny perfect pink balls. Fish eggs, like those Nemo hatched from, before he had to be found. I ate strange and beautiful food, served on a communal dish in the middle of the table, an edible kaleidoscopic mosaic. The restaurant crowned the top of a tower so tall that riding the lift, shooting heavenward and sending the lights of the City of London far, far below me, left me dizzy.

"I love it here," Zanna sighed as we checked our coats in the cloakroom, my New Look faux leather jacket among a row of thicker, more expensive versions.

The girls ordered off the menu like they were speaking a foreign language. I said as much. "It's Japanese, you idiot!" Zanna said.

Sara added, "It's Japanese, Brazilian *and* Peruvian."

"Where actually is Peruvia? Is it Europe?" Gianna asked, after making her wish for a dry white wine known.

We ordered some starters, including some green pods I didn't know how to eat, spelled out phonetically to me by Zanna as "ed-ah-mah-may" and a bottle of "san-saire".

"She is actually such a stupid hoe," Zanna said after Gianna excused herself for the toilet.

"A moron. She's lucky she's so hot," Sara agreed. They looked at me, the message clear. Join in, or set yourself apart.

"A shocking indictment of the British education system," I said.

Zanna lolled. As in, she actually shouted, "Looooooool," in a drawn-out screech.

"Oh my God." Sara put a hand over her mouth and leaned forwards, stifling a laugh. Even Maggie smiled. A glow, a warmth emanating from within me. Zanna's friends liked me. Her eyes twinkled at me over the arm of a waiter pouring white wine into her glass, her maternal smile telling me I did well. Of course, I wanted the other girls to like me, but only to be close to Zanna. Until then, Zanna was the only person I cared about.

I wanted whatever Zanna wanted, I was more than happy to quickly make her dreams my own, as she manifested some of mine. A group of glamorous friends, dinners in towers. So, when she suggested I ghostwrite for her new blogging venture, about six months into my university course, I was flattered, my heart fluttering at the idea that above all the other people she could have asked, Zanna asked me.

In only a few months we had amassed more followers than I could have imagined, and paid opportunities were coming down like April rain. We were ready to take it to the next level, we agreed. But my boomer-generation parents did not understand.

"You're writing someone's website for them?" my mum asked. "And they pay you for that?"

"And you're writing about lipsticks?" my dad said, frowning.

"It's a fashion, beauty and lifestyle blog," I told them. "And we're up to over fifty thousand followers on Instagram. That's really good."

Eating pizza at a Bella Italia on Shaftsbury Avenue, close to Euston so they could easily catch their train, I tried to explain it to them, my nonplussed parents who thought I'd be interning at a newspaper by now. I couldn't bear to travel home, out to that abysmal suburb, and my parents were not natives to London and viewed the city with hostility. Mum, who had a bad knee, refused to get the Tube, worried about bombings. Dad categorically would not pay the extortionate taxi fares, worried about being ripped off, making a fifteen-minute walking radius from Euston the limit. Nix Wagamama and Wahaca — Mum didn't like "funny" food — and your options were limited.

"Honestly, it's a new media thing. These blogs are the new magazines. A lot of real-life magazine websites don't have anywhere near fifty thousand readers."

"Sorry, Pooh Bear, when your aunties ask what you do, I don't know what to say." My mum looked older, I observed. "You know, Sheila's daughter Talia is doing really well at the estate agency. It's lovely after everything she went through. She's on a really positive path, now."

I rolled my eyes at the mention of Talia, an old school cohort. She'd been my friend at primary school, until come secondary she turned into one of the many who bullied me in those drab, never-ending comprehensive hallways of grey walls and blue locker doors. I still refused to make the trip back to Birmingham to see my parents; the memories were like ghosts.

Dad sighed and said, "Just make sure you're getting paid properly and it doesn't get in the way of your real work — your degree. And call your mum more often, she worries about you."

Sweating in my seat, I struggled with a pepperoni pizza, in anticipation of a coming storm. Even in my early twenties, being in my father's company transported me back to those late nights in a small house where the front door slams closed at night and drunken steps make their way unevenly up the stairs. Hitched breath. When does the shouting start?

"Mum, Dad, there is something else." Fiddling with a crust, I couldn't bring myself to look them in the eye. "I'm leaving university."

"Oh no, Pooh Bear," Mum whispered, collapsing into her hands, eyes already beginning to leak.

Dad froze, fork in hand. "You better be joking."

My silence said it all, and he banged his fist on the table, mild shock rippling round the restaurant.

"Look what you're doing to your mother," he said, gesturing at my mum with a huge, rough hand. Her greying blonde hair, blow dried in a style not altered since the eighties, bounced with her sobs.

"Please don't cry, Mum."

"Well, that's rich. What are you thinking of? You're daft!"

"Dad, it's the future."

"You were the first person in either of our families to go to university, Paige. Your mother was so proud."

What about you?

I stayed mute.

"Alright, you bloody idiot. And don't think you're welcome back at home. We've put enough of our time and hard-earned money, the little of it there is, into you," he said, before asking for the bill.

Later, Zanna dried my tears with a glass of prosecco and a reiteration of the original sales pitch she came to me with when she had the idea for me to leave my course and work with her full-time.

"Paige, no offence but your parents, they don't know anything about the media and publishing." She tucked her manicured feet under the sofa and gesticulated with her iPhone in her hand. "This is where everything is going, social media. Magazines are dying. If you say you built a huge social media platform, they'll hire you in an instant because at the moment we are stealing all their advertising."

She soothed my fear. After all, if uni was so essential to success, why were my work experience applications overlooked while my peers with parents who "knew someone" walked right in the door? On the occasion I was bestowed with the honour of doing a week's free labour, they shoved me to the back of the newsroom with transcriptions while my middle-class male cohort got taken out for drinks by the news editor.

With Zanna, I wrote words that were engaged with on a daily basis by a collection of fans. And it wasn't just that. We arrived at events and had our names on a clipboard for the man on the door to check. We walked into events where paparazzi were waiting at the door. We left events with goodie bags. We were so important, someone else paid for our taxis. We were part of something big, even though when I explained it to my parents, and a host of other people including the unimpressed head of journalism when I told her I'd chosen to leave the course, they exhibited blank faces.

More importantly than that, as Zanna sat with me and soothed me the evening after the argument with my parents, I got to sit in her arms with her soft, expensive jumper around me. Not only making the best career move of my life, Zanna assured me, but working with her, my very best friend. Detaching myself from an old life and starting a new one, with Zanna. With her. We were together. A team. My first and only real friend and now my colleague.

Leaving university meant leaving halls. So when Zanna asked me to move in with her in a flat near London Fields, I said yes immediately. Of course, it wouldn't be the two of us. She had a boyfriend. Jealousy panged in me whenever she mentioned him; whether of her or him, I remained unsure. We'd yet to meet. This was the perfect opportunity, she said.

As she got ready for a date one night in early summer she told me how they met. "He was the best-looking boy in town, it was him or no one." Naturally, she would be with the best-looking boy, there was simply no other way. The world accepted things just so.

She told me how her boyfriend had the most wonderful penis possible for a man to have. Then she described his body, perfect, "toned but not too big". She told me how now he had lived with his dad, her lip curling slightly.

"It's only so we can save for our dream home," she told me. "And his dad can do loads of the work for us for free. He's a carpenter. His dad doesn't speak English, really, so he feels like he has to stay to be there for him, you know? His mum left when he was little. It's sad. Dads leave their kids all the time. Mums? Not so much. I was worried it was going to make him kind of hostile to women and a total psychopath or something when I found out. But he's amazing to women, you know. Has so much respect for them. If anything he's too good to women, if you know what I mean."

I lay on the bed as she talked and talked, tittering, as she dug through drawers stuffed with makeup for the perfect colour of nail polish. She'd been looking forward to this dinner for weeks, at a French steak place she raved about to me, and which I'd read a review for in the *Sunday Times Magazine*.

"You have two courses of steak, it's amazing," Zanna said.

She painted her toenails khaki, her body divided by the slabs of bright sun streaming through the tall windows of her soon-to-be former flat like a magician's Zig Zag Girl — lacerated with shadow. She painted the nails, neatly clipped and squared off, on top of a fashion magazine spread, where models posed wearing a similar shade. Scattered around her on the floor were scraps of cotton wool soaked with nail polish remover and stained coral — last week's shade. The acrid, but not unpleasant, bite of the remover stung my nose and eyes a few metres away from where Zanna sat, carried further by the suffocating, dense and warm summer air beating in through glass pulled shut specifically to keep it out. A cheap fan sputtered in the corner, pointless.

"Won't the remover damage the wooden floors?" I asked. Zanna shrugged, paying little attention, focusing on preparing for her date. Her eyes set on her work, her face beautiful but as inflexible as the hardware on a Chanel bag, hair glistening so bright I thought the room would fill with smoke if you pressed your fingertip to it.

Behind her, a cool blue satin dress hung off the top of a mirror, expelling the light that beat through the windows with a vengeance, cascading it in all directions in a rainbow-white light. On the hanger, around its tapering neck, fell a multitude of sparkling strings, her chosen jewellery. Tucked underneath where the glitzy dress hung were gold sandals with a bedazzlement of straps that wound around the ankle like spun gold when laced.

Zanna had said, "You should hang out until he comes to pick me up, help me get ready. I could do with your expertise. You have great natural taste. And then you'll finally meet him, and you can check each other out before we all move in together. Future roomies!"

I lolled on her large bed with its curling, old-fashioned headboard, wordlessly watching as she got dressed and talked to me all about her boyfriend for the millionth time.

"When I first met him," she'd started saying, returning from the shower with a white towel wrapped around her wet body, water like oil giving her the glossy sheen of Charlize Theron in a Dior perfume ad. "When I first met him, he was ugh." She sat down on the floor in front of the tall mirror and put her hands up like a mafia boss reluctantly surrendering.

"Urgh," she repeated, pushing her hands out again for further emphasis, "a mess. For our second date I spent all day cooking the most incredible Greek meal you could ever imagine. I did my hair and makeup perfectly. Dressed up. I was like an amazing domestic goddess. Guess what he did?"

"Was he late?" I asked.

"No, he was on time but he was wearing shorts and a vest, and flip-flops. Flip-flops! He'd come from the park. I was so fucking pissed off."

As she went on, it struck me Zanna had a lot of complaints to make about a man who was, at the same time, allegedly perfect. He wasn't ambitious, he didn't appreciate good food, he wasn't cultured, and he didn't understand art. He did everything for her. Drove her here, there and everywhere, bought her a vintage pouffe she had loved at the market, took her to Paris on his own dime, although she complained he'd got them a hotel in the wrong "arrondissement". I dreamed of setting foot in an arrondissement, never mind being taken there by someone who loved me.

By the time the doorbell rang and lazier sun loitered around chimneys across the street, turning Zanna's hair, thick yet weightless, tourmaline brown, I had such a conflicting report of her boyfriend I had no idea what to expect of the man I was about to meet. Zanna checked her makeup in the mirror and fluffed her hair, before leaving the bedroom to answer the door, hips swinging with excitement and anticipation.

"Hello," she answered the phone in the hall, both syllables soaking with sensual promise. "Come up."

The buzzer hummed and the door outside opened and swung closed. Heavy feet sped up the stairs and the upstairs door swung open too.

"Hello," Zanna cooed again, the sound of rustling plastic and then arms being wrapped around bodies. "My friend's here," she said, the sound muffled and yet coming closer and she stomped towards the bedroom in the dazzlingly sexy sandals she probably would not take off later when she came back to this very bed.

The realisation struck as the "best-looking boy in town" walked towards me, and here I sat on a bed with a swollen, red face like one large popped spot from the hay fever, wearing a sweaty white T-shirt with no bra and basketball shorts. Zanna, on the other hand, shone like an invitee to the Vanity Fair Oscars After Party. With seconds to spare, I sat on the bed and crossed my legs. But my stomach had rolled up, poking out under my top. I uncrossed my legs, and at this moment — as I sat prone on the bed — Zanna walked back into the room, followed by the world's most perfect man.

Zanna carried a bouquet of yellow roses, which she later told me were the best roses "because red and pink are too girly and cliché". Now it's sadly prophetic, they're also funeral flowers.

He stepped into the room behind her. Not wearing shorts and a vest now, he had on a pair of black desert boots, black faded jeans and a light tan shirt in a corduroy sort of fabric. This was how I took him in, feet to face, fascinated to know what sort of footwear Zanna's boyfriend wore post flip-flop ban. Upon coming to his face, it didn't matter one bit to me what this man wore.

His face was a roadmap to the original man if God's blueprint was perfect. His skin tawny, his eyes umber. If being around Zanna was like riding a rollercoaster on a hot day, all stomach flips and slightly scorching, being in his presence for the first time was like falling into an icy plunge pool.

"This is Paige," Zanna said, sweeping her arm out in my direction, presenting me. "Paige, this is Shane."

They were dressed for a night on the tiles, and I was sitting among the bedsheets with my hair tied like a pineapple, like an ape in an exhibit. Shane cast a glance at me, smiled a smile that enhanced the strong, blunt shape of his jaw and said simply "Hey" before turning his eyes back to Zanna, ready to take the next cue. His eyes focused on her so intently, with so much adoring love. He drank her in, I — and the rest of the world — barely there.

On the way out, Zanna shut the flat door behind the three of us and turned to me.

"You know how to get home from here, right?"

"Yeah, I'm going to get the bus."

"Cool, see you later."

She waved. Shane smiled and waved. As they walked away, the vague outlines of her body shimmering perfection in the blue dress, he raised a hand, slipping it behind her hair where it wrapped around the back of her neck. That hold said, "You're all mine." It made something in me twitch. To be touched like that, to be wanted like that. A new type of cold emptiness settled down in my stomach to rest. I'd been thrown out of a club I was never in. I'd never wanted a hand on my neck so badly.

Zanna and Shane walked away, two people who simply lived in a different place and time to where I spent existence. While it seemed as though we inhabited the same world, we never would, due to barely understandable laws of class, beauty and luck. Amber sun still lingered on the pavement, like me, cold now. It was warmer wherever Zanna went with him.

The Present

In Paige's Flat

When my phone rings at 6:05 a.m. it doesn't matter, because I'm already up. In the dream before I woke, an hour or so ago, I cut long flower stems. Then the stems were my fingers, pinging off under the scissor blades. I look down at the large, pink flowers in the sink. They are covered in blood. But I look down at my hands and they are intact again, dry, pristine. It's not my blood.

The device on my bedside table peals and I take some medication to soothe me. I've been spending the past fifty minutes picking at spots on my skin as I stare at the emails in my inbox. There's been no follow up, no second email yet. I read the simple words over and over again, as if they will reveal a clue. Rearrange themselves, conveniently spelling out who this sender is, jeering at me behind a screen. Eating at my beauty sleep.

I stare at the combination of numbers before the @ sign. Are they code? A message? Zanna's birthday? No. The birthday of anyone else I remember? No. But I don't have any other friends whose birthdays I'd know off by heart.

I convulse so violently when my phone buzzes in my hand that I wake Shane, who grumbles as he stirs and pulls a pillow over his head. He doesn't rise graciously, Shane. He's often nursing a hangover.

Fucking hell. Tom is calling, and I answer, breath knocked out of me with fear, heart flopping like a fish in a bucket, desperate. My agent sounds matter of fact.

"Morning, darling. It's a leak."

I don't understand initially. I picture water dripping through a ceiling in my bleary sleep funk. In the short time I take to respond, Tom has already grown tired of waiting for the penny to drop.

"In the press. They know about the documentary."

I sit up, covers dropping from me. Ears ringing as my stomach drops away from my ribcage.

"Oh."

Shane grumbles, making me aware of his annoyance. Tom goes on.

"Yep. Sheryl is fuming but ultimately they're used to it. Apparently it came out on Prattle."

"I see."

"Well, darling, it's not really a problem. I wanted to let you know before Sheryl gets hold of you. I'm sure you had nothing to do with it."

"No! Of course not."

"Exactly. Just a reminder, no posting and if any press contact you tell them you aren't in a position to talk about the doc yet, or direct them to me, babes."

He rings off. I google Zanna's name and it's true. The *MailOnline* reports: *Infamous influencer murder case to be re-examined in true crime doc.* The *Guardian* writes: *Zanna Zagalo documentary to shine light on women's safety in the influencer age.*

I reach for my laptop and navigate to Prattle. As I wake the machine up with the touch of a button, there is the evidence I spent last night googling bikini pictures of celebrities for personal comparison. We all have our toxic habits.

Prattle is there, ready to select as soon as I type a "P" into the search bar. My internet history knows me too well and puts me to shame. Prattle is a forum site where users discuss influencers — mainly what they don't like about them. They debate the surgery they've had, how they really made their money. They ask why mirrors aren't clean, fume when clothes aren't properly ironed. They pick apart shallow, soulless, utterly watchable lives. It's a gossip forum of fans-cum-detectives, eagle-eyed sleuths, many of whom are motivated by holding influencers to account where the law is failing to catch up. Highlighting undeclared ads or diet drink promotions.

Zanna both feared and hated the discussion board and so, of course, she checked it regularly. "Saddos", "fucking losers", "jealous bitches, get a life" she'd say, reading her own feedback. Then she'd read what had been written about her rival influencers aloud to me with glee. Now Prattlers discuss both of us. Zanna never lived long enough to see them come to write about me.

Today, the most popular thread on the whole site is about the documentary. It started late last night, last updated ten seconds ago. It must be abuzz, and the thought awakes dormant, queasy butterflies in me.

The comments are varied.

So happy we are coming back to this case. Zanna was my favourite influencer.

Good people are keen to see the documentary, I suppose.

I really like Paige. I think she's really down to earth and sweet to keep up the blog in her best friend's name.

My eyes lap up positive comments about me like a camel at a puddle in the desert. I can't help it, I'm desperate, parched for praise. Sadly, they're not all positive. I suppose you can't win them all, can't make everyone like you. God knows that's something you learn fast as an influencer.

It never sat right with me how Paige still runs her Instagram with her name. That's weird, right? Talk about riding coat-tails.

There are a lot of theories that Paige was more involved.

Definitely freaky to steal her dead friend's job. I know someone who works for the documentary company and they think there is definitely something dodgy about Paige. Said they've had some interesting calls from people claiming to have information no one knows about her.

Sheryl? Had she told someone about my nervous behaviour? Surely, that's not enough to imply I killed my best friend. And calls? My head spins. My email correspondent, or someone else? My ribcage is constricting, pushing down on my bowels. Of course, there's no way to know if any of this is true. Any of these anonymous posters could be liars. But any of them could be someone I know. Someone I should worry about. I click the comments under this one, and more than twenty people agree.

Snakey.

Shady.

I unfollowed a while ago. The girl has been dead five years — time to stop using her name to make money.

People like this, they are the reason the money's drying up. Now Zanna's dead, they think, why am I following an account with her name? Who is this try-hard? She's not Zanna. They don't know. They don't know I built Zanna. They don't know what I went through working with Zanna. I created Zanna's voice. I was half of Zanna. Maybe more than half.

I slam the laptop lid down, woozy. I breathe deeply. I check my emails and already a number of brands have reached out, interested in me thanks to the doc. I'm lightheaded with relief — no more emails from my new mystery pen pal.

*

Sheryl moans about the leak during filming the next day. She humphs her way around the studio and eyes me narrowly, as if it'll prompt a spontaneous confession from me, or someone. No dice, Sheryl. But she keeps it up, so much so that I'm entirely depleted later, after answering question after question about Zanna.

Exhausted, finally home, I'm lying on the sofa with the TV on, solely for the noise, while I numbly scroll Instagram, check *MailOnline*, my WhatsApps, and back again, almost unthinking, on autopilot. When Shane comes back, he's wearing his black motorcycle leathers and I drink in his rugged face as he pulls his helmet off with one hand and puts it on the shining kitchen island, alongside some supermarket gin and tonics (slimline for the personal trainer, of course) he pulls from a bag with a crumpled bunch of pink flowers. He cracks one tin open and takes a sip, before he turns to me, sighs and smiles a small smile.

When he kisses my lips, falling down on the sofa beside me with his boots and motorcycling suit, his mouth is cold and the scratch of his facial hair on my chin is rough. He tastes like the refreshing, tannic-bitter drink. The plastic wrapping around the spray of roses and baby's breath crackles beneath my hand as I take it from him and smell them with a performative flourish, hoping my eyelashes are as abundant and soft as the petals while he looks at me from under dark eyebrows. The fact he pays attention to my favourites always swells my heart. Not that he can identify them on sight. Shane's idea of differentiating between flowers is "big pink ones" and "small white ones". He knows not to buy me peonies. Peonies are bad flowers for a number of reasons.

1. They attract ants.
2. They look like eyeballs, then cabbage, then tissue paper.
3. They were Zanna's favourites.
4. They make me think of dead bodies and bloody eyes.

I reach a hand up and run a finger over one of those thick dark eyebrows, down his cheek, along the chiselled jaw. I know love warps the mind but I've never seen anyone so handsome. It's never gone away, that utter admiration, total besottedness, from the moment I met him. There are people who don't believe a love like this exists, which makes my heart ache because they should look at me and Shane. The perfect love story.

Of course, I'm guilty, as my eyes swivel to check the price of the flowers. He doesn't know about the issue with the finances. Shane always figures it's all going to work out, he always has. He's impulsive, hardly a forward thinker. He's all passion, no forethought. He never even asks about how the rent is paid. He doesn't know about the email either. It's awful lying to Shane. It's not like us. We have a very unique kind of bond, based on total trust of one another. Nothing can break that trust. And yet I undermine it, when I know all too well how badly Shane responds when his trust is broken. It's risky. All lies are risky, especially those told to the ones who love you.

He pulls away from me, grabbing the remote and turning on the TV, before crossing his arms.

Shane is emotional, sometimes cagey. Since I told him about the documentary, though, it's been more pronounced.

"You know I think it's a terrible idea," he said. I did. But, of course, Shane doesn't know about the money. How much we need it. He huffed and puffed and worried and sulked, but ultimately it was my decision to make. But still, he's holding a grudge. He'll come back around to me. He has to. He always does.

"These flowers need water."

I heave myself off the sofa. I can't stand the flowers in my hands like that, suffocating in the air. Slowly, silently dying. Unable to scream.

*

I feel much like those flowers, the next day, as strangers ambush me outside of my flat. I had figured it would come, sooner or later, and the leak had done it. Taken me right back to the time after the murder when public interest was firmly latched onto me, Zanna, and the case, like a leech. Now one little leak has burst the dam and released the deluge of obsessed loons, only slightly more insane than the most prolific Prattle posters, the true crime fanatics. How they have the nerve to call themselves *true* crime, I don't know. I studied journalism myself, I know a little about objectivity and facts. These podcasters, YouTubers and bloggers, they have their reasons for following murders like others follow *The Great British Bake Off*, drawn to the daker side of life, sceptical and suspicious. I can't understand why they do it, but it's hurt Shane and me over the years. They crawled from the woodwork when Zanna died; like the bacteria that feasts on rotting flesh, they covered every inch of her. Her history, her life, our blog. Hunting ludicrously for "clues" in captions posted before she died. They're consumed with the idea that I murdered Zanna in cold blood. They have no evidence, of course. But that doesn't matter. That's not what these people do.

They were using Zanna's tragedy to spin a yarn, wrapping me up in it, carelessly and callously. You'd think libel laws would scupper their speculation, but alas. They did it for likes, for views, for subscribers. True crime nuts are carving out a living like any other content creator. No one clicks on a YouTube video entitled "Easily Explained Murder".

I knew these three lingering outside the flat were trouble. Their anorak vibes. One younger woman with reddish purple hair wears too-tight, too-light skinny jeans, plimsolls, and a faux leather jacket. An older woman with greying hair wears a khaki jacket and a paisley scarf wrapped around her neck. A skinny, short man with wispy facial hair leans against the wall. The way they look around, they don't belong here. There is a distinct sense of Megabus about them. They see me coming, murmur, and shuffle into action. I brace myself. True crime nutters, for sure. Not well dressed enough to be any followers of mine.

I put a hand between my face and the phone camera, its steady light in my eyes, while the other scrabbles for something in my bag. The three have been waiting here God knows how long.

"Can you not film me, please?" I ask, although it's feeble.

"Why," the shorter, younger girl crows. "I thought you love filming your life?"

The older woman steps between me and my taxi, which is there to take me to the studio.

"Excuse me," I say. I want it to sound dignified, but it's strangled.

"We just want to ask some questions," she says. She has lines on her face, the skin dull, grey. She has wet eyes behind wire-rimmed glasses. I feel bitter hatred towards her.

"I don't have to talk to you," I say, trying to move past her. Incredibly she steps in my way, small and pigeon-like though she is. The man steps towards me and the short, stocky woman pushes the camera closer into my face.

"You can't escape the truth," the younger woman says, in a high, hysterical voice. "You did it for the blog, you did it for the money. You killed Zanna, and the police failed in their duty."

I barrel through the small, greying woman, who shrieks and grabs the strap of my Stella McCartney handbag. "Fuck off," the words come from my chest, barking and gruff. I wrench the strap from her hand and use it to swing the hard leather body of the bag into her face. She makes a strange noise, shock on an inbreath, guttural, like an animal. I grab the handle of the taxi like an outstretched hand in the dark, pull and tumble inside.

As I slam the door shut, the woman screams, "You've got a lot to answer for, with the wrong man rotting in jail."

"You alright, love?" the studio driver asks.

"Yeah, yeah. It's okay," I murmur.

"Looks like bad stuff," he opines.

I close my eyes and breathe. It was inevitable, as soon as the documentary leaked. With shaking hands, I check my inbox, as if I know what will be there. I blink away tears so I can read it, another email:

You were jealous of her, Pooh Bear. She was beautiful, young, and popular. You wanted to be her. And when you couldn't be . . . you killed her. I know it was you.

I shut my eyes and tears wet my cheeks. I imagine Zanna is here to wrap me up in her arms, like she did at the start, and whisper that it will all be okay.

Life of Zanna Documentary

Shane Seacole Interview

PRODUCER: I'm so sorry to hear about the trouble you've had outside your flat recently due to the documentary leak. I hope it's not been too disturbing?

SS: Yeah, it's not been nice. I mean, me and Paige knew it would happen if news of the documentary got out, but I guess we didn't realise how soon that would be. Good news travels fast. You know, or at least, not good news but, news. You know what I mean. It's been quite distressing, we had to call the police the other day.

PRODUCER: Oh God, how horrible. But is it in hand now?

SS: It's better. The police put a pretty stern warning out. It's unbelievable what these people get away with. Paige was pretty upset about it all, but it's okay. She's very strong. Very. Like, crazy strong, man.

PRODUCER: How sweet. Well then, let's get down to brass tacks. Count us into the filming and three, two, one.

PRODUCER: So, Shane, how did you meet Zanna?

ss: I met Zanna kind of just around. I know it seems mad now to not remember the very first time I met her, but there were always a lot of girls around. When I was a young guy, I had a lot of girls' numbers on my phone. She was, you know, she was fit — obviously.

[He shrugs, pauses and looks down.]

PRODUCER: Take your time, I know it feels strange.

ss: Yeah.

PRODUCER: You do get used to it.

ss: So, Zanna, yeah she came to a few parties and we got talking, I guess. It happened slowly. She linked me first, I was like, damn this girl's keen. There were some Insta messages, then texts. Next thing I know we're three dates in and I'm agreeing to be exclusive. It was funny though, I liked it, really. A lot of girls don't have much about them. Zanna was so focused, man. And she was beautiful.

She came from a posh family. We were different like that. All my mates were jealous. It was cool, you know. She was cool. Yeah.

Honestly, I'm a pretty laid-back guy, you know? I like things the way I like them. I got up, I went to the gym, I trained my clients, I came home and had a few beers and dinner with Dad. Before Zanna, anyway. My mum wasn't around. She left when I was little. Dad's not native to the country, he found it hard to meet people. I think I inherited some of that shyness. I guess that's why I didn't really date when I was young either. You know, stuff with my mum. Zanna was my first official girlfriend.

PRODUCER: How did you make it official?

ss: For me, I wanted to keep the relationship casual at first, but I didn't have much choice in the matter, if you know what I mean. On our second date I turned up in shorts and a tank top and flip-flops, she told me she was taking me shopping. Once a woman buys you clothes it's a done deal. You're hers now, bro, she's got that tag on you. Stamp on the forehead, innit? "He's mine." [Laughs.]

PRODUCER: What did your friends and family think of Zanna?

ss: [He makes a whipping sound and mimes the action, then laughs.] My mates called me pussy whipped. Sorry, can I say that?

83

PRODUCER: You can say whatever you like.

ss: So they called me pussy whipped, you know what that means, when a girl is, like, the boss? Everyone said that about us to be fair but, yeah, I didn't mind. I didn't mind.

PRODUCER: Is that what your dad said?

ss: Well, my dad's from a very different background. He's a labourer, he's worked with his hands all his life. And he would never say the P-word, he's probably going to slap me on the back of the head when he sees I've said it. [Chuckles.] He never really got Zanna, her family. Don't get me wrong, you know, he liked her, just two different sides of the track. But he always looked out for me first, always. Still does. It was just me and him, always there for each other.

But Zanna, yeah. Look, things weren't perfect, as you know. As the world knows, at this point. But yeah, I did love her.

PRODUCER: We can circle back to that later. I'm curious — what are you hoping to get out of the documentary, Shane?

ss: Oh man. I'm just wanting to move on. To put it all behind me. You know, Paige, she wants to do this, so I did. I just want to put this all to bed and never wake it up, if you know what I mean.

PRODUCER: I do. So, let's start at the beginning. When did you find out about the blog?

ss: [Shrugs.] A few months into our relationship was when she started it. Then I guess it took about six months to get to the point where she hired Paige. I didn't pay much attention to it, to be honest, except that she'd started asking me to take pictures of her outfits. It was funny, really. She'd stand on the step of some hotel we were just walking past and then look away from the camera and look back and ask me if I'd taken it. I'd say, "No, I'm waiting for you to smile."

She'd say, "I'm not supposed to be smiling." [Laughs.] My days, looking back it was funny, really. I thought she'd gone mad. But I went along with it. Happy wifey, happy life-y.

She wouldn't be happy before she got a picture. And there would be this, like, stressful vibe over the whole evening before she got a picture she wanted to post. Obviously, I loved being with her, but that did annoy me. I got the hang of it eventually. Being the "Insta Boyfriend". [Makes air quotes with his hands.]

Then she started getting sent free stuff. The first time I remember, I was over at her flat and she got this package, it was all blue and wrapped with a big bow. I thought, *It's not her birthday, what's going on here? Maybe she's got a secret admirer.* I'm not a jealous guy, but gifts start turning up at your girlfriend's house and you've got to wonder, haven't you?

I was shocked when she told me she was leaving her job to do it full-time. And worried. Then she laid out this whole business plan to me and it blew me away.

I had no idea what she could make from all this. She had ten thousand followers, and she was making like £200 off one Instagram post. One post. Made me want to throw the towel in on my personal training altogether at first. Then, she started showing me all these personal trainer accounts, guys who were raking it in showing what they did in the gym and taking selfies.

I could do that, I thought. And she was like: "You could do this." It's thanks to her I have the career I do now.

It was around then I moved in with Zan and Paige, in London, after Zanna graduated and they started working together. It was fun around that time.

PRODUCER: And what did you think when Zanna invited Paige to move in with the two of you? Quite an unusual set-up. Would most boyfriends be happy living with their girlfriend *and* her best friend?

ss: I think it was Paige that suggested it, actually. I mean, that's what Zanna told me. That Paige was having to leave her uni halls and she asked Zanna if she could move in for a bit. She said Paige didn't have much money, she didn't have her parents' help or anything, and that it would make our rent cheaper anyway. So I said yes. I didn't mind.

It was generally a really chill set-up. It wasn't the most masculine environment, if you know what I mean. The whole flat was like one big wardrobe. You couldn't move for clothes and make-up and shit, everywhere. Literally everywhere. [Laughs.] Paige and Zan were constantly signing for packages and the doorbell rang all day. The poor supervisor for the flat block, Mr Mazur, I guess you know about him, he was the favourite, and he loved the girls. He was always taking fancy packages for the flat. Literally constantly, his office was full of them.

Every month or so we loaded the products into the back of a taxi and headed to a car boot sale. We would take like a hundred shampoo and conditioner bottles and make £250 off them. And the girls got sent such expensive stuff, they would walk away with over £1,000 in a day from those sales. I always wondered if it was against the rules, like, do these companies know how much cash the girls are making selling their freebies? There was so much money to be made. Honestly, I think selling the things she got sent second-hand made up half of Zanna's income. You had to admire the entrepreneurial spirit, you know?

PRODUCER: What did you think of the public aspect of the blog, Zanna posting pictures of herself online? She must have had a lot of admirers. Were you jealous at all?

ss: Jealous, me? Nah, no way. I'm comfortable with myself. Never jealous. No. That's not me, man.

PRODUCER: Did the blog take a toll on your relationship in any way?

ss: No . . . No. The relationship was fine. It was good. I mean, I guess, sometimes. Like, there were things that got Zanna down, like, things that were posted about her online. Nasty trolling. Some really, *really* bad rumours got made up. People just posted things that weren't true. Total strangers, making up things about her. That's going to fuck with anyone's head. And, you know, she felt a huge amount of pressure to show that what she was doing was legitimate. A proper career. Her dad, especially, was . . . harsh about it. He never really gave her credit for what she'd created. And then, of course, they fell out.

But I was proud, I still am. Of everything she achieved and continues to achieve even now. The yearly charity event, for example, is part of her legacy. We — me and Paige — we love doing it, every year.

The Present

A charity event in Holborn

It's been five years and four charity galas since we lost Zanna.

I type quickly. I've got used to writing about her in the third person, instead of as her, through her.

This is what Zanna would have wanted, I wrote in an Instagram caption, months after she died and I swore to carry on with the blog, despite her parents' protestations.

> *She was dedicated to this blog, to you, to making content. She had so many plans for this platform, and I know she would want you to see them.*

I found catharsis, using the platform as an outlet after she died, writing weekly posts to our followers, updating them on my wellbeing, and the process of grieving. Soon mental health charities were asking for me to work as an ambassador. Clothing and beauty brands still sent me products to try, which I did. As long as the followers remained, the collaborations and deals remained too. In fact, they inundated me. Creating content for bereavement charities. A posthumous jewellery collection inspired by Zanna with a major online seller, proceeds going to charity. And soon, the opportunity to work with a charity to create this annual event, inviting the world's biggest influencers to honour Zanna and raise awareness.

Now, standing at the side of one of these glittering parties, my fresh gel nails are clacking away on my iPhone's keypad, 'squovals' freshly painted with a peachy skin-tone colour called Sin and Tonic.

The irony is not lost on me. I will certainly not be drinking today. It's too important I get everything right. Look right. Look the way everyone expects. I doubt I'll be eating either, as if I could stomach food with everything else I have on my plate. The same cannot be said for Zanna's slightly insane mother, who is halfway through her second glass of champagne, munching on little bits of salmon on blinis.

You wouldn't believe half the things that happen at charity galas. Put the grief-stricken in a room with free booze and remind them of their loss? It's not going to be pretty. Which is also ironic, because this room, this whole event, has been carefully curated to be visually stunning, the way Zanna would have wanted it. Peonies everywhere. But really, this is Angela Zagalo's night. She laps up the high status afforded to her by being in close proximity to the dead, and boy does she enjoy it. You could argue she deserves it. I often wonder how Zanna's sisters deal with it, knowing each year Zanna's fundraising event will be carried out. A reminder of their mother's favourite daughter, stolen from this world, with canapés.

Last night we honoured Zanna's memory with friends, special guests and some of you, who won tickets to attend and be with us in the special moment. For those of you who couldn't be th—

I'm cut off from writing tomorrow morning's caption by Shane walking towards me in my peripheral vision.

"Come on, get off the Insta," he says, wrapping an arm with a warm bulging bicep around my shoulder.

"Sorry, sorry, sorry," I say, deftly shutting my phone off and guiltily flipping it over in my hand. Looking up at his sombre face between my eyelash extensions I say: "I'm just reading all the lovely comments about her."

I couldn't tell him I had typed the caption for tomorrow night's post about the gala, he'd chastise me for working at an event like this, where I should be the epitome of hope in the face of death. Most would think it cold and a little calculated to be writing those gushing posts in advance, copying and pasting the most heartfelt of sentiments. Not Shane, though, after what we've been through together. He understands. Influencer life has never been authentic, but saving meaningful words about death in your drafts takes the piss.

"It's hard, I know," he says, putting his hand over mine clutching the phone. "Keep it together," he whispers in my ear, before lifting his chin up and resting it on my head, wrapping me up in a boa constrictor grip. He's a typical bloke. He's always so much more affectionate in public. I love it, relish it.

"Oh Shane," I giggle, "you'll crease your suit."

And my face powder will get all over it. I wiggle from his grip, and stroke his lapel with my hand, perfect pinky nails glinting, trying to calm myself.

While my nails are nude, everything else is black. Shane's suit is black, and the room is a sea of black, albeit glamorous and glittering black, an ocean of Tahitian pearls. Perfectly made-up faces surrounded by glossy hair bobs above the pool of shifting darkness, to give kisses on cheeks that never touch down.

Black makes me look drawn. It accentuates the dark circles under my eyes, wrought by sleepless nights. The dreams are getting worse. Blood, gurgles and panic as my email inbox filled up with multiple clone emails. I read those digital words, lit up on my screen. *I know what you did. I know what you did.* I read them, and then I heard them. A scream, a whisper. The emails crouched in the world wide web, a deadly poisonous spider.

"Let's get it over with." I put a hand through Shane's arm, as smooth as threading a needle. It's so natural and comforting, my body close to him. My nervous shakes are calmed as we move into the centre of the room, filled with a bustling crowd.

It's a large, airy room with light streaming in through sash windows. Boom mics hover above the crowd and impressive cameras are being operated at points around the room.

Sheryl approaches with Sissy — from the charity — in tow. Sissy is Sheryl's opposite. Taller, about fifty, but not a glamorous fifty. She's dowdy, doughy in body, her brassy blonde hair is greying and she wears glasses, awkward in an ill-fitting suit. She smiles at me. You might make assumptions. In a room like this, Sissy instantly draws pity, but Sissy is a happy, confident woman. I've known her since Zanna's murder and the subsequent media frenzy. Sissy is an expert, her life has been touched by this kind of tragedy, and she does a job she's passionate about; she makes a difference. I like her. She gives me motherly vibes. And I think she likes me. Sissy held my hand before my first TV appearance after Zanna died (on *This Morning*, arranged by Tom, from which I got ten thousand more followers), there on the famous sofa to give advice I couldn't to the hosts and the audience.

"Hi!" I wrap my arms around her.

"I've just been filling Sherry in on how the night will go." Sissy smiles.

"Sheryl," the TV type corrects.

93

The night'll go like this. I'll walk onto the long, high platform at one end of the room and ask everyone to be seated. The models, writers, TV presenters and YouTubers will find their seats at the round tables dotted around the room, before all turning to face me. I'll give my hasty speech, holding back the urge to vomit (I hate speaking in front of the public about Zanna like this), then Sissy will relieve me of my duty and give a speech, before dinner and a performance. This year it's a singer, a young woman with long red hair that is done all in plaits and who wears huge platforms on stage.

"I'm just going to the loo, then shall we get the show on the road?" Sissy asks.

I nod, sweat pooling in the creases of my palms.

As Sissy goes, Sheryl turns to me. "It's quite the event."

"Well," I say, pressing my squelching palms together, "it's such an honour to have you here. I'm so happy to bring awareness to the cause."

Sheryl purses her lips slightly and then says, in a vaguely bored tone: "It's such an important issue that takes so many women's lives."

Her tone then changes, back to business. That's how she's most relaxed, I imagine. She asks, "How are you finding filming the interviews?"

"It's okay. I've only done two so far. It makes me miss her." I study Sheryl. *Has she watched my interview? What does she think of me? How am I coming across? How is Zanna coming across? What about Shane?*

"Was my interview okay?" I hate how little and squeezed my voice sounds, like King Kong's fist is compressing me.

"Oh yeah," Sheryl says. "I've heard you are one of the favourites to interview. Very loquacious." She quickly shoots me a look and adds: "Talkative."

This bitch thinks I'm a moron. She's one of the stuck-up jealous types, assuming it's easy to write engaging captions on a daily basis, to be interesting on a twenty-four-hour rolling schedule. To have the number in your bank account depend on it. I've learned to let people like Sheryl believe I'm stupid. They end up telling you more than they realise.

"What about the girls?" I ask.

"Oh yes, we've spoken to Maggie. Excellent. Really good to get some more voices to give us a view of Zanna, when she was alive."

An electric tingle zips up my spine. I desperately want to know what was being said about Zanna and me. I go to rub my sweaty hands on my dress, then remember how much it cost and stop myself, leaving them to dangle, exposed. All the blood in my body has rushed to my temples, pulsating like beating hearts.

"It's sweet. Worships the ground Zanna walked on, she does," Sheryl goes on, in relation to Maggie.

I smile, and it aches.

"I'm so glad Gianna agreed to take part," she says, taking a sip from her drink, soda water and lime.

I start. "Gianna?"

"Oh yes, we managed to get hold of her."

I look around in the crowd, feeling hot, mouth filling with saliva.

"She's not here," Sheryl says. "She's unwell."

My skin prickles. Gianna hates me, and she's still holding a grudge. The hate only intensified after Zanna's death. The way she looked at me the first night we met, Sushi Samba with the girls, was unfriendly and hostile, and it got worse after Zanna and I were working together and she started creeping around Zanna — after the freebies and the exclusive invites Zanna could get her. And at the funeral, it was clear. I'd tried to keep her away from the documentary, consistently "forgetting" to pass on Gianna's contact details to Sheryl. Pieces of supporting evidence start to align and I nearly drop my glass. It's her. Gianna must have leaked the documentary to the press and sent that email. Zanna and Gianna always had their little friendship on the side.

I can imagine it now: Gi, ever the sycophant, snorting as Zanna said, "They call her *Pooh Bear*."

A familiar voice cuts through the buzzing in my head. I'm relieved by the soap-clean shining face of Chief Inspector Jessica

Baines. She is here, out of uniform for a change, but still conservative, still representing her post. I clasp her in a hug. Indispensable to me during the aftermath of Zanna's murder, during the investigations, and for dealing with the likes of those true crime lunatics. I'm thankful for her.

"Thank you so much for your help the other day," I say, after we exchange happy remarks over seeing one another again.

Jessica rolls her eyes, and I do as well, before blowing out my cheeks in exaggerated exasperation.

I have Jessica's number, after everything with Zanna's death and the case and the trial. She was just a phone call away and had come to my aid yet again, sending out her PCs to remove the anoraks who called themselves journalists from my porch.

"Any time." She smiles, her peaches-and-cream cheeks dimpling.

"It's just a lot, you know," I go on.

Jessica frowns at me. "Have you had more of the hate mail?"

My insides go cold and my underarms hot. *How does she know?* "The prank messages?"

Of course, she means the emails from the past. The stupid ones from idiots, just trolling and busying their sad little lives with hoax emails. They were common in the aftermath of Zanna's death. I nod, quickly.

"Oh yes, just the usual sort of thing." I feel breathless. "Nothing out of the usual."

Jessica purses her lips and squints. But before she speaks, Sissy taps me on the shoulder. "Time to get the show on the road," she says.

Jessica mouths, "I'll catch you later," and I'm pulled away from her.

"Thank you for coming tonight," My hands shake as I read aloud from my cards. It never gets easier. Here on a raised little makeshift stage, all their eyes are on me, and not many belong to friends.

"I can't believe tonight we are marking the fifth anniversary of the tragic event of Zanna's untimely murder at the hands of a dangerous stalker. This devastating crime affects so many women whose stories are sadly ignored or hidden thanks to shame."

I resist the urge to flap my arms and allow the tepid air in the room to cool my comparatively roasting armpits, peppery sweat pooling in the waxed folds of flesh.

"All of us have been touched by this real-life horror and its terrible consequences. Thank you again for coming, for joining us in raising awareness and preventing other women from going through the terrifying and ultimately fatal experience Zanna did. I'm now going to hand over to Sissy Thomas, a renowned expert in the field of stalking and homicide. Please put your hands together."

Dinner is over. I struggled my way through black sesame tiger prawns, then leg of lamb, leaving most of it. Also at my table are Zanna's mother and sisters. Angela, who is so little like her cherished daughter in every way, is making small talk with Shane while downing the white wine, pouring more into the glass of Sophie — who drinks it up — while Claire sticks to just one. She's the fitness fanatic of the family, although all of them have been blessed with tall, slim bodies. The girls look pretty. Not as beautiful as Zanna was, but still, they have the healthy glow, white teeth, glossy hair and sparkling eyes that come with wealth. Sophie's engagement ring is sparkling, a square diamond flanked by two baguette cut stones. Claire rankles each time she sees it, each time the wedding is mentioned. She thought she'd be married by now. The best laid plans of women . . .

"We are planning a wedding in Italy, renting a villa, it'll be small," Sophie says in her *Made in Chelsea* Fulham drawl.

"But expensive!" Angela jokes, chuckles reverberating around the table. Zanna's father is noticeably absent. "Tell the engagement story!" Angela coos.

At the words "Eiffel Tower" I zone out completely.

Finally, blessedly, the night is wrapping up. Grief gives me an excuse to feign tiredness and Angela allows me to blend into the background as much as possible, not because she is understanding and compassionate, but I'm still grateful for her accidental mercy. A hired photographer takes pictures of journalists, advocates, charity workers, Instagram models and one or two reality TV stars with arms around one another's waists. All here with the greater good of "the cause" in mind, or so they'll write in their captions tomorrow, posted at the opportune time of day to harvest likes.

"Oh Paige." Angela's face is now sodden and her skin, dropping ever downwards throughout the years, is red and blotchy from being firmly scrubbed with Kleenex, then a napkin, and now, toilet roll presumably taken from the loos. I hope she cancels any exfoliating facials over the next few weeks. She won't need them. Now, with a portion of her makeup sloughed off, she's nothing like Zanna. The ghost of her beauty haunts her absent father's face.

"I just can't believe she's gone. But this documentary, I hope this helps girls like my Hannah. You know, you never forget. Every morning I wake up with fresh pain." Large globs of tears splash earthwards, some caught in the deep grooves of skin on her décolletage.

"Oh," she cries dramatically, throwing her arms out wide, giving me no real choice, with the eyes of her family and the lens of a documentary crew to boot, but to give in to her and allow myself to be folded into her bronzed arms. She has a huge shelf of cleavage, which must be supported by a hell of a lot of brassière technology, the crêpe-like skin wobbling like a waterbed beneath it. She pulls me right in, my chin dangling over her shoulder with no way to turn it without looking odd. I can't look at the cameras in my periphery, so I close my eyes and try to hug her, meekly placing my hands on her cushiony back.

She breaks away from me, and as she does, Shane approaches.

"You know, Paige," she goes on, "none of us were sure about you, what you did with Hannah's Instagram after it all. Or 'Zanna', as you all call her. Kept it for yourself, carried on going with it even though she was dead. Making your money."

Claire whispers, "Mum, don't."

"I thought you were a sneaky bitch." She throws her head back and laughs a crazed, drunken laugh, moving to flick a strand of hair from her face, forgetting she is holding a glass of prosecco and throwing it on and over her own shoulder. "You even took her boyfriend!"

People are turning in our direction as Angela's remaining daughters reach for her, aghast. Her face changes, her alcohol-soaked brain zipping from thought to thought, emotion to emotion; and then, fully engulfed in it, forgetting what she said only moments ago.

"I wasn't sure of you from the start. From the first Christmas. So standoffish when all we ever were was nice. You didn't even act grateful when Zanna wanted you to have a proper family Christmas, after your upbringing."

Angela nods her head at me, blinking unnervingly slowly. In a state of shock, I'm cold and frozen on the spot, keenly aware of journalists and camera operators around us. The smirk on Sheryl's face if she caught wind of this scene flashes before my eyes.

"Sometimes I even wondered . . ." Angela is going on quietly, her eyes hazy, booze-soaked, bringing an accusatory finger to my face. My breath catches. " . . . if you had something to do with it all. You were so jealous, after all, you wanted to be her. Well, now you practically are."

She laughs hysterically. My stomach drops, the familiarity of those words. The email. My head swims.

"You know, she told me about you," Angela goes on slurring. "Badgering her to be revealed on the blog. She wanted you gone."

I sway, exposed under the mortified stares of attendees close enough to us to hear. Shane is the one who comes to my rescue. He puts a heavy hand on Angela's shoulder, breaking her out of her trance. She looks up into Shane's face now, and instantly her emotions switch. It's like a tap has been turned on behind her face. Fluids, tears, phlegm and spit at the orifices.

After smiling and kissing cheeks all night, Sophie sputters, like her sobs have been held behind a creaking dam. Behind the hand bearing the gleaming engagement ring, her face collapses in on itself with pain, and she takes a rattling breath, her throat leaping raggedly. Claire, who's pale and detached, wraps her arm around her sister. My stomach twists in knots. Shane, white as a ghost, is looking at me, his jaw clenched.

Life of Zanna Documentary

Sissy Thomas Interview

PRODUCER: Hi, Sissy. It's nice to see you again after the success of the event.

ST: Thank you, it means a lot to me to attend every year.

PRODUCER: So, how did you become involved with Zanna's story and the event?

ST: Well, when Zanna was killed I'd very recently had my own brush with this hideous crime in a pretty high-profile case. I'm sure you've heard about it.

PRODUCER: Yes, I have.

ST: Most have. So, when Zanna's case hit the media, I was asked by a number of news outlets and TV programmes to give my insight. Then I was asked to appear with Paige on *This Morning* for her first TV interview, to give another perspective on stalking, and to support Paige. She was very nervous. Bless her. She is such a sweet girl.

PRODUCER: And how did you become a stalking expert? What prompted that?

ST: As you know, it's a very personal story for me. My daughter was, tragically, the victim of a male stalker, someone you would never suspect could commit such a crime. After Phoebe was taken from us, I became a little, well, obsessed with trying to understand why. When I looked into it, I was fascinated. Why do men act in this way and why, why do we allow it to happen? To woman after woman? I knew this was something that had to be understood better to stop it. So, I retrained in criminal psychology. Ever since, I've been working closely with the Met.

PRODUCER: I'm so sorry for your loss.

ST: Thank you. It doesn't get easier for me, but I can try and help someone else.

PRODUCER: Turning our attention to the Zanna case. What elements do you think played a part in causing this tragic murder?

ST: Well, stalking is a crime based around a fantasy, and there are few lives that better exemplify that of fantasy than Hannah Zagalo's.

Social media, like Instagram, gives us the ability to curate our lives. What we see on the feeds of social media users are fantasy lives, highlight reels. And when it comes to big, famous profiles like Zanna's, this is exemplified tenfold. Being gifted designer bags, flying around the world for free and visiting beautiful places, who doesn't want a part of that fantasy?

Celebrities have always had stalkers because their very essence invites the allure of fantasy; it's how movies and magazines are sold. But celebrities have traditionally lived in gated communities, sharing only small slivers of their lives, drip-feeding fans in carefully chosen magazine interviews. Now, celebrities and social media stars are fused together, one and the same thing. This makes the job far easier for stalkers. When you share almost every aspect of your life it makes it easy for dangerous people to know where you are, and to feel like you are engaging personally with them.

PRODUCER: So, social media intensifies all that, and intensifies the experience the stalker is having?

ST: Exactly. Social media makes followers feel close to that individual, like they are living their lives with them — even if they have never met them. Every Instagram video from inside their home, every candid caption and holiday vlog showing minute details makes followers feel more and more connected, and more and more entitled, to details about the lives of these social media stars. The feeling of intimacy tricks the brain of a stalker and leaves some convinced they have relationships with these stars, friendships even.

PRODUCER: So stalkers think they are friends with the victim?

ST: Not always, no. Some stalkers believe they are friends with these people, or they will be, once they meet. A stalker feels such connection with someone before ever meeting them, they have the idea that they and the target are known to one another, although in fact they are not. We call these parasocial relationships. Most will have had one of these in some form. A sports fan, for example, is in a parasocial relationship with the members of their favourite team. Oftentimes these relationships help to soothe stress, and strained relationships in our own lives. But when these relationships intensify, they can become deadly.

Others are driven by disdain, or hatred, for someone, for an influencer. Perhaps what they represent. Perhaps they don't approve of the person's use of social media. This is something we see in cases of disgruntled exes or family members, fixating on the victims' use of social media.

When it comes to more generalised stalking behaviour, though, with social media stars and fans, this is where we tend to see the lines get blurrier, and things get riskier. It's all about sharing personal, private, real details. This — what some might call "oversharing" — encourages their star to rise and fosters intimacy between them and their viewer, until the scales tip. Now they find themselves world-famous or at least hugely popular with a devoted demographic, with the increased stalking fears that come with it. A great example of this are the YouTubers who shared the journey of purchasing their million-pound home, posting images of the inside of the house, the garden, and home tour videos on their channels. They invited fans to get involved on their moving day with a vlog.

Yet the stars were then faced with fans turning up to the house, peering over their garden fence. Parents lifted their children over the fence to take pictures inside the house. They were accused of "moaning about the price of fame". The question seemed to revolve around whether individuals who found their fame by inviting strangers into intimate parts of their everyday lives deserved the same privacy as others.

PRODUCER: So stalkers can be motivated by hatred, or jealousy even?

ST: Absolutely. The most common form of stalking, the one we are most familiar with here, is a stalker who believes they

are in love with their victim. But stalkers are not always motivated by romantic love either, that's a common misconception.
Sometimes, as I mentioned, they believe they have a friendship
with the victim. Sometimes, they feel hatred towards that person. They may be envious. They may be acting out a feeling of
being vindicated, or in the right. Perhaps they feel their victim
is a fraud or a phoney. But does that mean stalking behaviour
is justified?

PRODUCER: How do you spot a stalker?

ST: Well, that's the frightening thing. We think stalkers are
deranged people. Dangerous and rare people, people we would
never know. Would certainly never *be*.

But how sure are you about that? How can you be sure
someone you know, and know well, isn't engaged in stalking
behaviours now?

Researching someone online, "friending" someone, checking
their profile, following someone you want to gain more information about, keeping tabs on someone via their social media,
checking for constant updates on someone's profile — these are
all signs of stalking.

How often do you check the profile of an ex to see where
they are? How often do you look up that old school friend
to see how they are doing? How regularly do you use social

media to look into the lives of people who may barely know you? How often do you "hate stalk" that frenemy? Have you set up a fake profile to follow an ex that blocked you? If so, there may be a secret stalker hiding inside you. Can you say for sure there isn't?

The Past

I loved being bathed in the warm glow of Zanna, and Zanna and Shane together, in the flat we shared. The three of us. Nothing had changed since I first saw him. He stole my breath doing nothing. He made me dizzy. It was a quick process, learning to become immune to his presence, like building a tolerance to liquor. He was the kind of man I wanted to be with, I told myself, someone exactly like him. He brought Zanna flowers, kissed her on the head when he held her.

Their relationship was idyllic to me. I saw her in a new light, as a more domestic woman. She was determined to excel at a fantasy version of housewifery, baking, like Blake Lively, protein brownies, one of the few treats the body-conscious Shane would eat. Cooking for Shane, feeding him like a doting mother, washing his clothes. She was softer in his arms. I enjoyed a twinge of something — longing, jealousy, or a sort of refracted love of my own — when they flirted, play-fought, kissed or touched one another around me. As flatmates, I was absorbed into their relationship dynamic and, at first, I revelled in taking part in the theatre of domiciliary bliss. Like the warm, happy family life I never had.

We were a funny little threesome. They let me tag along with them, going to the little independent café down the road, getting croissants and Zanna persuading me to flirt with the barista, going on their shopping trips, sometimes even to dinner with them as a date night novelty. So, when the idea of spending Christmas together was floated to me, it sounded like a fairy tale.

"Christmas is my favourite time of year," Zanna sang the words as she spun around the room.

Lights had been hung on the lamppost next to the alleyway opposite the new flat. Someone was stabbed in that alleyway. The young man's bereft mother handed out leaflets in the street reading "Make our streets safe — install CCTV now". And we, as much as anyone else, were glued to the news when a young woman was stalked, abducted and killed by her ex-boyfriend, also a Met police officer. Zanna had me write a heartfelt Instagram post about it. About women's safety and fear. Now, she looked out the frosted pane at the lights wrapped around the lamppost with the glowy, childlike Yuletide wonder people with affluent childhoods tend to have. I was researching ideas for Christmas beauty blog posts, like Zanna had asked me to.

"Aren't you excited?" she asked, leaping onto her bed gymnastically and landing on her side, brown eyes glowing at me, shining from exertion. There was a little freckle under her left eye.

"I don't really like Christmas," I said, reminded of our terraced house at home, always a bit grey and drab in my memory, carpets worn out by the door frame so you'd accidentally tread on a painful stud crossing through. One Christmas my dad smacked me for picking at the bobbles of the stucco walls out of boredom. I cried, my mum cried, Dad went to the pub.

Zanna sat more upright, staring at me in disbelief. "Who doesn't like Christmas? It's magical. At my house we all get together and have this amaaazing feast." She was always drawing out "ay" sounds. On this occasion she tilted her head back all the way exposing the little metal strip glued across the back of her teeth to keep them in place after expensive orthodontia. "I think it's the best Christmas ever. I bet you'll like my Christmas."

So, I ended up in the back of Shane's VW Golf as the three of us drove through an indiscrete electric gate in an otherwise discrete country hedgerow.

In actual fact, Shane drove Zanna through the gate after she turned to me in the back seat and said, "Can you get out and press the buzzer?"

The road this gate guarded was narrow, too modest for the over-the-top gate, and it ducked down a little hill so what lay before us was concealed. The silver car ground to a halt on the unpaved road topped with a sprinkle of gravel, sending little chips cascading. The horizon was flat with brown-grey winter fields, and the road was only faintly distinct from a stone December sky. Stark but still bright, white billows of cloud backlit by the sun left retina-frying streaks across the sky. At three o'clock, darkness would soon fall. I braced myself against cold gusts of wind as the car drove past me. Shane shook his head as Zanna madly gesticulated.

Tiny rocks crunched beneath my feet as I reached for the door handle. Zanna shouted "Do it!" as I pulled the car door open and slid into the warmth of the small car.

"Aw," Zanna cried, raising her hands up to the sky like she was praying for rain. She turned to me in the back. "I wanted Shane to drive away, you know, like when someone keeps trying to get in and then you drive."

She laughed to herself. I laughed too, self-consciously. I silently thanked Shane for sparing me the humiliation.

"You are a loser," Shane shot at her, but with a grin. "No one finds that funny anymore." He winked at me. "I've got your back."

I smiled back at him, the moment our eyes met stretching out like bubble gum.

"Let's go," Zanna commanded, bashing the dashboard with an open hand and then pointing forwards, as though she led a cavalry. I jumped and Shane swivelled back to the road, revving the engine and making her squeal in excitement.

Over the hump in the road, the house came into view between a number of trees, shivering naked in the wind. It was an old, big, detached house. It was strange to me that such a house stood alone, isolated. My childhood room was full of the sounds of the kids next door playing, running up and down the stairs with thunderous feet as their mum shouted in exasperation.

The house was square and made of sandy-coloured stones, with a shining red front door, newer than the rest of the house, framed by ivy. To the left, the lower floor jutted out in a bay window, the kind I'd dreamed of reading in in a romantic tableau. Red tiles on the sloping roof decorated with three real chimneys and two little white windows sat like doves. There was a roundabout with a rose-planted plinth in the middle of the drive occupied by a BMW and a Mercedes E-Class. Shane parked up on the side of the house. A terrier rushed towards us, scrabbling on the gravel and grunting.

"Dottie!" Zanna grabbed the little dog's head and ruffled its ears, and it spluttered in ecstasy. A black lab with grey hairs on its muzzle and a low-hanging, barrel-like belly ambled over, like it took all the effort in the world. "Blackie!" Zanna cooed.

Her mother emerged from the stone doorway, a festive jumper reading "Ho Ho Ho" in red glittery lettering. Greeting Shane first, Angela pressed her cheek to his. He bobbed down to meet her as she hinged onto her tiptoes in four-inch heels. Bronze and gold sparkling eyeshadow brought out the papery texture of her eyelids. Her lips were overlined and her hair was backcombed at the crown.

She turned to me, throwing her arms wide. "Paige," she said. "Pleased to meet you. Welcome to our home. We're so happy to have you." Her embrace was soft and pungent, a sugary fragrance hung to her, punctuated by caustic hairspray that stuck in the throat.

"Thank you for having me," I murmured, as she walked me towards the house. "My case," I said, gesturing towards the trunk of the car as Shane pulled it open. Angela told me not to worry about it. Dottie zoomed ahead of us through a high-ceilinged hallway with white and black tiles on the floor, smooth and shining squares laid in a diagonal pattern. The dog's paws slipped and clawed at it with a fervent scratching as it handled a corner into a room on the far left badly and narrowly missed a painful collision with the door frame. Angela and her frighteningly firm hands, with square gel nail extensions painted a festive glittery red, steered us behind Dottie. The house was old, but the kitchen was clearly renovated with white gloss cupboards and a fridge with an ice machine. At a kitchen island stood two young women, both the spitting image of Zanna but for slight differences, minor defects. One was a little bigger and smiled with crowded teeth; presumably

Zanna's original smile. Another had a slightly prominent nose that Zanna shared in earlier pictures.

"Hi," they said, both drawing out the one syllable in a high-pitched note, the way Zanna would. They chopped vegetables with synchronicity. The sisters were wearing matching jumpers, too. When their mother stood behind them nine "Ho"s bobbed over the counter.

"Have a glass of something, darling. I made a boozy punch from the Waitrose magazine. It's got fizz, gin with bits of gold in it, ginger syrup, apple juice and erm, something — Santiago, what's the name? It's like that designer . . ."

"Jägermeister," a low-pitched and yet thin voice with a discrete but discernible accent said. I hadn't noticed Zanna's father leaning against a counter, next to a double-door fridge. He didn't glance up from the magazine he was reading, even when Zanna trilled "Hi, Dad" and kissed him on the cheek.

"That's it!" Angela said, turning to me with a musical laugh, even her breath smelling sweet. "I can't remember it even though it sounds like Jaeger and I have a few bits from there. What am I like?"

She handed me a glass of the amber fizzy liquid and I took a sip, smiling as I tried to make an appreciative show of it. I smacked my lips, painfully awkward as six eyes were trained on me, faces cracked open by smiles. Zanna's laugh echoed through the hall and turned as she walked into the kitchen, while Shane turned up a winding staircase carrying two cases, mine and Zanna's, and a well-stuffed gym bag on his back. No one offered to help him.

"You know Paige doesn't like Christmas?" Zanna said, plonking a hand, as firm as her mother's, down on my shoulder.

"Well," Angela said, like this wasn't news to her at all. "We'll have to see about that. Which reminds me, why don't you two go and look in your room, Hannah? There's a surprise for you."

Zanna squealed and grabbed my wrist, pulling me up the first floor.

"Careful! I've just had new carpet laid on the stairs," Angela called.

I caught a glimpse of the poor old black lab finally making it to the kitchen door behind the rest of the family, tail wagging creakily. It was the ghost of a younger wag. A wag of Christmas past.

Angela shouted, "Shoes off!" behind us and Zanna called out "Sorry!" and "Come on, Pooh Bear" as she dragged me up the stairs.

Whirling into Zanna's childhood room, we penetrated a cream doughnut, the cold winter light outside now a warm glow. Fairy lights were fixed above a marshmallow bed with a white frame. Shane was putting the suitcases and gym bag next to double fitted wardrobes. *Vogue* magazines piled up haphazardly on a shelf over the bed.

Zanna took her shoes off, so I slipped out of mine, leaving them neatly by the door. In a silver frame, on a mirrored dressing table, was a photograph. I drifted over to take a closer look. The frame was embossed, reading "Summer Ball 1999". A younger Zanna stood next to a taller boy, a little spotty and smiling a closed-mouth smile of teenage insecurity. His hand placed tentatively on her waist, while she popped a hip and shot a smile at the camera with knowing eyes, not those of your average sixteen-year-old. In a long lilac halterneck dress, the pale purple turned on her olive complexion. And there was that nose, noticeably more severe.

"Paige, there's one for you!"

She brandished a package wrapped in gold in my face. I took it from her before she hit me with it. Squidgy and flat. Zanna had ripped her package apart. A bundle of green and red fell into her hands. Shane grinned as when he read "Ho Ho Ho" aloud from our jumpers after turning around.

"Do you think her mum knows?" he murmured to me, drawing a finger along his chest to indicate the lettering as we followed an exuberant Zanna bouncing down the stairs, alluding to the obvious double meaning.

"Who, Angela? Oh absolutely." I smiled back at him and he followed behind me. He raised his eyebrows suggestively and I giggled.

"Dirty bitch," he whispered, a laugh in his voice.

"Milf material?" I shot back. He grimaced and shook his head. I laughed again.

Were we flirting? The moment lingered between us milliseconds longer than it could have.

"What's that?" Zanna asked, waiting at the bottom of the stairs.

"I love this hallway," I told her, keeping my moment with Shane to myself. One more in a collection I was putting together, secretly, since I first saw him. There was a time he gave me a chewing gum and we agreed spearmint was the best mint variety. And there was the time I offered to read his horoscope from a magazine and it said something about "new horizons in love". I swear he looked at me funny.

The entire family traipsed through to the lounge. A large L-shaped plush grey sofa wrapped around one corner of the room, the walls also painted grey. Two armchairs in the same grey covered in soft, fuzzy cream blankets joined the sofa in flanking a fluffy rug on the wooden floorboards. I guessed at them being original. With my lino past, I'd never been able to really tell. A big smart TV sat in the corner of the room and in the middle of the rug was a large travelling chest repurposed as a coffee table. A real fire flickered away and three big windows opened out onto a garden at the front of the house, filling up with twilight. In one corner, of course, was a vast Christmas tree decorated with golden baubles and silver tinsel.

I took my cue from Zanna, sitting next to her on the settee and sinking deep into it. I tucked one foot underneath me. Here, every room was so big, you sat alone even when you were all together. Prematurely separated from Zanna, I was lost in the expanse of pure space. As if spurred on by a psychic act of pity, Blackie plodded over to me, putting her head on the sofa by my leg and sighing, wet pools of oil for eyes. Zanna laughed. "She wants you to stroke her!"

I obliged, gently patting her head, tentative. "Don't you like dogs?" one sister, Sophie, the slightly bigger one who had a soft, pretty dimension to her, asked with mild disbelief.

"Are you a cat person? We're such dog people in this house," Angela said.

"I never had a pet," I explained.

"You never had a pet?" Sophie was outraged.

"No." I shrugged. Blackie huffed and turned away from my inexpert hand, now plodding towards Angela. My hands were greasy after stroking his coat, must and meat emanating from them when I sipped my topped-up punch. I decided I didn't like dogs.

Angela leaned down and kissed Blackie on the muzzle. I felt ill, so I finished off the glass of punch, at which Angela immediately offered me a top-up. Zanna, her mother, her sisters and I imbibed the glittery punch, soaked it up like festive sponges. Only Shane put a hand up in protest as Angela tried again and again to give him a drink.

"So well behaved," Zanna said. "Anything for these pecs!" She giggled and squeezed his chest.

The Christmas Eve tradition at the Zagalo household was a Chinese takeaway, which Santiago went to the kitchen to order dutifully. He was a very quiet man, who observed in unimpressed silence as Angela, Zanna, Sophie and Claire spoke loudly, often over one another.

"Hannah, have you changed your hair stylist, it's looking a little . . ." She put her palm down on her head.

"A little flat?" Zan said. "Yeah, I thought that. Had a different stylist, wasn't that happy with it."

"Oh darling, you should make sure they let you see the right stylist next time," she said. Zanna's hair looked no different to me.

Plastic cartons full of steaming shredded beef with chilli and chicken and cashew nuts were popped open. Santiago set about shredding the duck removed from its paper bag — ordered at Zanna's request, one of her favourites — his sinewy hands clutching the handles of two forks with strange intensity. He put his whole upper body into it, his mouth grimly set. All of his quiet anger turned inwards on himself and downwards, onto the charred bird on the table. His wife and children ignored him, and bags of prawn crackers and chicken balls were placed on a tray on the chest. Plates were passed around. We were encouraged to eat buffet style.

Sophie, a children's fashion buyer, had recently bought a studio in Bristol. She was the perennially single sister.

"Men are so shit, I really need a break for myself." She sighed, reaching and pulling two chicken balls from the paper bag onto her plate. Angela sent a pointed look to Zanna, who raised her eyebrows at the gesture.

"Yeah, like focus on yourself, like be good to yourself, fuel your body with good things and, like, get into yoga or running," Claire suggested, Sophie nodding — not catching the implication.

"And how's the lovely Simon?" Angela asked, turning to Claire with such a doting expression that I thought Simon was a baby, or a child. But he was a boyfriend, and with the mere mention of his name, a smile of shy bliss spread over Claire's face. Her shoulders came up towards her ears in a mock coy pose.

"She's *so* loved up," Sophie cooed in a teasing tone. Zanna rolled her eyes.

"Well, we've been living together for a few months, it's going so well, I love it. We're both so busy with work, so we get that about each other." She beamed.

Zanna told me Claire works in finance, already making over £60K a year, a fact that made my head spin. It transpired she was renting a house in Richmond with Simon, whom she met at work. It was a very grown-up move for a twenty-three-year-old, but then Simon was thirty-three, a fact that made Angela puff up proud as a parakeet and left Zanna inexplicably annoyed, although she swore she wasn't jealous. While Claire was making a large salary, Simon was still paying for their rent.

"I swear to God if you get married before me . . ." Zanna glowered, shooting a glance at Shane, who had checked out of this conversation a while ago and was tucking into another huge portion of chicken and rice in a stupefied sort of state. As the oldest, Zanna would consider it an abject failure and humiliation to make it down the aisle after either of her younger siblings.

"She was so jealous when I got a proper boyfriend before she did, she broke out in a rash!" Claire said, pointing a finger at Zanna while chortling.

Zanna flushed, before retorting, "Oh yeah? And what became of that relationship, bitch?"

Everyone got another punch after Zanna's outburst was laughed off, except Santiago, who had picked up *The Week* and was reading it again, more content than he had been all evening. Claire showed us pictures from the new flat with Simon. Zanna was engaging Shane in a murmuring conversation, undecipherable. I spent the evening drinking whatever was put in front of me, smiling and nodding along with the girls and answering Angela's questions. What school did I go to? A local comprehensive. And what did my parents do? My dad works in a factory. Oh, a factory? You don't hear that much anymore, do you? How interesting. Must be nice to do something with your hands, so rewarding. And your mum? My mum's a cleaner. Well! Give me her number, we could do with one of those around here, couldn't we, Santi? She slapped her thigh in mirth, though Santiago barely looked our way.

"Oh Mum, come on, Paige isn't on trial, she's here to have a *nice* Christmas," Zanna said, rolling her eyes.

"Hannah, I hope you've brought us lots of those freebies you've been posting all over your Instagram!"

Zanna smiled coyly. I knew for a fact the bag upstairs was stuffed full of regifted goodies which we'd wrapped.

"How is it all going with the blog?" Angela over-enunciated the word. It was clearly a foreign idea to her, like it was to my parents.

"Good," Zanna said, glancing at her dad for any sign of interest. There was none.

"And Paige, you're Zanna's assistant?" she asked.

"I'm ghostwriting," I said.

Angela's smile faltered. She didn't understand.

"Alright then." Angela folded her hands in her lap, smiled a closed-lip smile, and shot a look at Santiago, who might not have been listening.

"Paige writes things for the site, captions and stuff, and helps me out," explained Zanna.

Angela nodded, but her brow creased, and her eyes glazed over with incomprehension. She changed the conversation.

"Oh Hannah, I bumped into John from school down the road, do you remember? He's passed his Bar exam, you know."

Shane and Zanna both shifted, small but noticeable. "Oh that's nice, good for him," Zanna said, shrugging it off.

A Christmas edition of *Top of the Pops* came on. Angela was transported back in time to the seventies by the appearance of a youthful Noel Edmonds and started swaying as the Rubettes sang "Sugar Baby Love". Her eyes were half closed and she lurched back and forth. Zanna rolled her eyes and grinned at me.

"Oh dear, it's that time of night," Santiago murmured.

"Aw, get in the festive spirit, Dad!" Sophie cajoled.

Santiago sighed again.

As the 2015 Kylie classic "Santa Baby" rolled around and Angela said, "Oh, I love this song," Santiago said, "I'm going to bed," and made for the door, clutching *The Week* under his arm.

"Oh Santi, could you lock all the doors and windows please?"

All three daughters exchanged looks. "Why?" Zanna asked, bemused.

"Well," Angela said. "Pamela and Wes had a break-in a few weeks ago. The bastard stole their Christmas presents and Pam's jewellery. Can you believe it? Since then I've struggled to sleep." She pressed a hand to her chest, which shuddered dramatically. "Then, I was taking the dogs out for a walk and I saw a young man drive past the house and I swear he slowed down to try and look through the gate. I could tell he wasn't from here, you know. I know all of our neighbours and, well, he was . . ." She gestured to her own face and went on. "He was a coloured gentleman. Not that I make assumptions."

Shane was stiff.

"He just didn't seem local," Angela went on. "And you know what, with Pam and Wes and the break-in, I just couldn't stop worrying. I thought, gosh — you know — the dogs are in the house all day, I don't want them being scared by a break-in. It would traumatise them."

The girls all nodded. Shane was unintelligible. I said nothing.

At bedtime I was shown to a spare room with a single bed. I settled down into bed, before realising I had left my trainers in Zanna's room. It wasn't too late to knock and get them, I figured, making my way down the hall to get them. Outside the room, though, the perfect profiterole cream puff room, harsh and hard voices came from within, enough to make me stop in my tracks.

"I look great in that dress, that's why I have the picture, for fuck's sake."

"Just seems weird to me. I don't have pictures of my exes in my childhood bedroom, especially ones who have passed the Bar exam now."

There were mocking air quotes in his voice.

"That's because you lived in your childhood bedroom till not long ago, when I had to practically force you to move in with me, which, by the way, I put up with, even though Sophie's new boyfriend is paying for them to live together off his own back."

"Oh, here we go. How did I know that was going to come back up at some point? I'm so shit and poor, okay, I get it. Get off my fucking back about it. Don't change the conversation, which is, why is your family still on about this guy you dated at school and why do you still have his picture?"

Shane's voice was unmistakable, but in a new form I struggled to reconcile with the laid-back man I knew. A whine, the stress in his hushed voice clear. Coarser, a sound of desperation. Zanna's casual flippancy, an attempt to play it all down, was undermined by a dry sound in her voice, like she'd been eating sand.

She spoke even lower as she said: "How can you even be getting at me like this? We've only just moved in, not even just the two of us. God knows if you're ever going to propose. My little sister's relationship is moving faster than mine. We've been together two years, why am I waiting around?"

"Why would I propose to you when you're clearly so unhappy with my lifestyle? Go and do better if I'm not enough for you. You only want it because you're worried Claire will do it first. You're so obvious. You make me feel like a fucking accessory."

"Come on, Shane." Her voice went a pitch up. "You know that's not true. We are a team. I want to build a life together, everything we talk about. I just want to know, are you in or are you out? Do you love me? Will you marry me? Do you even want to marry me at all?"

"Jesus Christ, I don't know. I'm allowed to not know if I want to marry you. And even if I did—" His voice dropped lower. "—why would I want to marry into this family?"

A startled silence from Zanna. Rare. She tried to catch her breath. Outside the door I tried to make no noise at all.

"What do you even mean? My family? What?"

"Your mum tonight, talking about the black guy stealing cars? You don't think that was a bit—"

"Don't you dare try to imply my mum is racist," Zanna hissed, sounding more assertive and acerbic, "again."

"Zan, they have a dog called *Blackie*."

"What the fuck, Shane, he's a black dog! And he's like fourteen years old. It was fine then! And actually I named him when I was, like, fourteen. Are you saying I was racist when I was fourteen?"

"All I know is I carried your cases out of the car and up the stairs and no one even asked or offered to help. Like, is this a plantation you're running around here?"

"Oh, for God's sake, Shane, they have you here for Christmas, I hardly think they are racist. You could be a bit more grateful."

Muffled commotion, Zanna yelping and gasping, the sound of snapping.

"Are you happy now?" Shane breathed.

Zanna fell silent and breathed in sharply. There was silence. Shane's breath heaved, then hitched.

"Baby, are you okay?" he asked, his tone sweet now.

"I think some glass got in my eye."

She sniffled and spoke, her voice cracked. "I don't want to go to bed on an argument on Christmas Eve," she said. It was a plaintive, hoarse and wheezy whine, like a squeaky dog toy being squeezed. "And my eye hurts."

"Okay, baby, okay. I'm so sorry. Let me get something for your eye."

I turned back to my room, moving quick and light on my feet, reeling. Zanna and Shane's relationship was perfect, that was the impression she had given me, the narrative I'd been told. But now, behind closed doors, I'd discovered all was not well. Sure, Shane was flirting with me a little and Zanna wished Shane had more going careerwise, but wow. It hurt me to hear my two dearest friends were so unhappy together. But now, having experienced this Christmas Eve, I understood it all much more. I understood all too well how Shane felt, that he'd never fit in with Zanna's world. Unworthy, the odd one out. I felt sympathy with his emotional outburst, identified with the pain in his voice. His anger was a disguise for how much he loved her. Zanna, on the other hand, she'd never really be happy with a man who didn't make her feel as though she was living up to her family's high standards. No wonder Shane and I were flirting, we were so similar. One and the same.

I struggled to sleep that night. A sore, irritating anxiety agitated my stomach, like I'd swallowed a large peach stone. I thought about Shane, imagining me sitting next to him in the front of the Golf, my hand massaging the back of his neck like Zanna's hand. His lips kissing my forehead like hers. I tossed and turned in bed, mulling over the idea until the pit settled and I knew what it meant.

I was in love with Shane.

*

Christmas morning I expected red eyes, but Zanna came and knocked on the door of my room in a full face of makeup, hair curled, bright and bushy-tailed like a festive squirrel from a John Lewis advert.

"Mum's going to expect you to wear the ho, ho, ho jumper you hoe, hoe, hoe. Now hurry up, it's time for hot breakfast."

Hot breakfast in Zanna's house meant full English, but with the best of everything. The sausages were plump, shiny and dark brown around the outside, perfectly crisp. The scrambled eggs were oozy with milk and butter. I feasted on bacon and drank a pint of orange juice, topped with champagne halfway through with a wink from Zanna.

131

"*We're rockin' around the Christmas tree,*" Angela sang. The Christmas cheer was in full force, but my alcoholic juice sat funny in my stomach. Guilt washed over me like the ice bucket challenge. Each time Shane smiled at me, my toes tingled.

Zanna was affectionate with Shane that morning, the cheer glossing over the chips like a few coats of paint. It was unsettling, how she smoothed it all over, how you would never know she was in pain, except a slightly red eye. But when I went to Zanna's room to collect my trainers, the Summer Ball 1999 picture frame sat snapped in half in the bin, covered with snowflakes of shattered glass.

Life of Zanna Documentary

Angela Zagalo Interview

AZ: Is my makeup, okay? I'm used to doing it myself, I said I could — you know — but they insisted.

PRODUCER: Hello, Mrs Zagalo, how are you?

AZ: Call me Angela, please. Not Ange, though. Ange, I just hate that. *Ange*. Sounds like a glandular illness.

PRODUCER: It's often a little nerve-wracking sitting down for an interview for the first time.

AZ: Well, anyone will tell you I know how to talk. And at my age, after what I've been through, losing my baby. I don't feel nervous much anymore.

PRODUCER: Well, no, quite. And we are so grateful to have you here—

AZ: I wouldn't have missed it for the world. After all, who knows Hannah better than me? A mother knows their little girl better than anyone else ever will. Hannah was my first, my angel. Sorry, Zanna. I know that's what she went by, but she was always my little Hannah.

It wasn't an easy labour. Oh no, no. I used to tell her, you made yourself known, darling. I'll never forget it, because I was trying on shoes and my waters burst all over them, so I had to buy them. She was a few days early, of course, she had to make an entrance. Twenty hours of labour. I told her, you were always wanting to do things on your own terms. We always knew she was special, the minute she lay in my arms for the first time and looked up at me. I said: "Hello, my little superstar. One day you're going to rule the world. And you owe me £200 for the shoes."

And she just looked back at me like, "I know, Mummy."

Sorry. [Cries.]

Yes, thank you. [Taking a tissue.]

Is my makeup running? Do we need a touch-up?

PRODUCER: You look great.

AZ: Thank you. So yes, what do you want to know about her? My darling daughter?

PRODUCER: Well we were curious to know, more so, about your relationship with Paige White.

AZ: Oh gosh.

PRODUCER: There were . . . harsh words at the charity event.

AZ: Not my finest hour. But I was distressed, and . . . well . . .

PRODUCER: What do you think of Paige White?

AZ: She was my daughter's friend. I thought she was fine. She wasn't a favourite of mine. She was very different from Zanna. Where Zanna was beautiful and natural, Paige, she had an air of nervousness. She was cold. Not easy to talk to. But it was fine. Nothing personal, until she took over Zanna's blog after she died.

PRODUCER: Why did that upset you so much?

AZ: [Sputters.] Because it was my daughter's work. Her face. Her image. It should have been laid to rest when she was. But Paige, she was all too happy to keep it going, in my daughter's name. It was ghastly, tasteless, tacky, but then what could you expect? Zanna made a mistake when she hired someone like that.

PRODUCER: But, to play devil's advocate, they were Paige's words?

AZ: But it was my daughter's face. Without my daughter, Paige would have got nowhere. And she still uses her name, her fame. Oh, it makes me so angry.

PRODUCER: And did Zanna really discuss firing Paige?

AZ: Yes, she did. With me. She said there had been disputes about whether Paige should get credit — publicly — for her contribution.

PRODUCER: Did you think she should?

AZ: Look, I don't want to talk about this in the documentary. It's in Zanna's memory. How amazing she was. It's got nothing to do with bloody Paige bloody White. Can I have some water, please?

PRODUCER: Yes, Mrs Zagalo, someone will get that for you.

AZ: Oh, please. I said don't call me that. I shudder at that name. I'm thinking of changing it but for my girls.

PRODUCER: Oh yes, I'm sorry Angela — your relationship with Santiago . . .

AZ: Well, they say it's common, you know, for parents of a deceased child to split up. And in this particular case, well, you can understand why I never wanted to see that bastard again.

Even though Hannah was an adult when she died, you never really see your babies as grown-ups — or I never could. Sometimes people say to me, at least she lived as long as she did, but that's no relief. Parents should never live to see their children die. Never. It's unnatural.

She had everything coming for her in life and was achieving everything I never could. And then it was all gone. Taken away.

Of course, I have my other girls. I moved closer to them after the divorce. I need my girls around me. And I'm glad Santiago is somewhere I never have to see him again. I couldn't bear to look at him again, that monster, after what he did to my little girl.

The Present

On a train to the London suburbs

Subconsciously I've dressed up for this. I'm on a train whirring towards the suburbs. Part burglar, part sleuth. Black jeans and leather boots, a black jumper hugging me, and a beanie hat. It's wintry enough, October has tilted the earth on its axis, nights draw drastically shorter as the mercury drops drastically lower. Wrapped around me is a Burberry mackintosh. It's one from the old days. I'd handed over £90 cash to the Camden Market salesman and it felt like a fortune slipping through my fingers. It felt like a fortune again now, after years of liquidity.

I'd muttered an apology, cheeks cherry-red from more than the cold, when my first card payment was declined at the train barrier and I fumbled, jostling customers behind me as I pulled out another card, from among seven or so options. I wore designer clothes I'd been given as gifts with handwritten notes from some of the most famous names in fashion, but had less money in some of my accounts than a single Underground fare.

I wished Zanna was here, to tap on the contactless card sensor and beam at me with an "I'll get it" like she so often used to do when she sensed that uptight panic in me.

This is why I need to do this documentary, I remind myself. This is why it's all going to be worth it.

I marvel at how fast this humming beast is zipping into deepest darkest suburbia, almost as far as Romford. It's been a long time since I've taken an overground train like this one (why would I ever need to leave London besides in a taxi to one of its airports?), but I couldn't hire a car. It wasn't inconspicuous enough, and it turns out I can't afford it. We race towards the documentary launch date with certainty and I hurtle towards my own personal mystery — who wrote that email? Now, two suspects top my list. Gianna, and Zanna's mother. Angela's words at the charity event echoed the second message but, for today, I'm trying to rule out the first, using my admittedly limited means.

I managed to find the address among thousands of WhatsApp messages. It was one of those sent after Zanna's death, but back when we were hanging on to the myth we were all close. Would stay close. Before, I suspect, Maggie, Sara and Gianna created a new group without me and the messages all dried up. Her excited update had come: "Guys, we bought a house. Here's the address. Housewarming soon!"

It was soon enough after Zanna died for us to still be going through the motions of friendship. But I didn't go to Maggie's housewarming. I was invited to a high street fast fashion event instead and, well, work is work. This is the first time I've visited Maggie's home, bought with an ex. She now lives in it alone. She was pleasantly surprised to receive my text suggesting I finally cross that boundary between London and Greater London to visit. It's a shame it has to be under false pretences, but here we are.

I've always considered moving to the Outer Boroughs as a sort of bowing out. Living in London is a battle of wills between you and the city. As you try to achieve your dreams, London is trying to run you out with rising prices, dating disasters, over-crowded Tubes and a general air of grey misery. Moving out is a surrender. Maggie's two-bed mid-terrace is somewhere I'd never live, both geographically and in terms of the architecture. A terrace-lined street, it reminds me of home. These houses side by side, squeezed so tight the brick might burst out into the front garden. The echoes of my parents' fights linger. I drag my fingers over the fluted glass of the front porch windows, and it makes me shiver.

The doorbell chimes with a synthetic seventies bell. My host pulls the door open, smiling and holding her arms out in excitement, ready for a hug. I let myself be pulled into it, although I'm sure we both taste the anticipation in the air. The strangeness of this — that I would announce a visit after so long — leaves a tang. We both wear lobotomised smiles to fend off that awkwardness. The nice bottle of wine I bought as a gift is heavy under my arm. I waggle it in front of her. She presses her palms to her chest.

"Oh Paige, that's so nice. You shouldn't have."

She takes it from me as I shrug and say, "Well, it's belated."

She leads me through a beige hallway into a front room painted a fashionable dark blue. That sort of carrot-hued, autumnal light comes in through the large window, lighting up velvet sofas in teal. Up one side of the room are shelves. A photo of Maggie and Zanna from uni hangs in a gold, gilded frame. On a low coffee table is a teapot and madeleines. Maggie pours the tea into cups that match the room. It's hideously kitsch, awfully basic.

"Wow, it's so beautifully decorated," I say. Maggie smiles. "And what a great location, really," I add. That's a lie too, but it's what you're supposed to say.

"So nice to move out of London proper," Maggie says. "It's so relaxing. Much greener and people are much nicer."

She talks like it's the Cotswolds, rather than a settlement focused around one of the Tube's most obscure stops.

"I don't think I could ever live so centrally now," she says. Of course she says this. No, she couldn't continue to live centrally in a hovel barely appropriate for students. Would she live centrally in a flat like mine, with river views and a Charcoal Mist kitchen? We both know she would.

"So, how are things going?" I ask, obligatorily.

"Great!" Maggie says. "Only a few months till the document-ary comes out really."

Eleven weeks, I think. Seventy-seven days. It sounds like so many, but it feels like so few.

"Oh gosh, I know." I rub my cheek. "I'll be so relieved when it's all over."

Maggie begins to tell me about her work, freelance graphic design stuff, which is picking up, she's happy to report. I keep my breathing steady. While her words fade in and out, I try to smile at the right points.

"You've not touched your tea."

"Sorry?" I'm yanked out of my panicked trance.

"You haven't had any of your tea?" Her inflection rises at the end as she gestures at the cup.

"Oh right. Yeah."

I breathe out heavily, flustered, trying to stop my hand shaking as I sip from the bland, hot drink. I try to gather my thoughts. *What am I even doing here?* I don't really know, except that I suspect Gianna of something. I'm trying to gather evidence to support my suspicions, but I'm floundering around. I know it full well, I'm horribly powerless.

"Did you have a nice time at the charity event?" I ask.

Maggie nods. "Oh yes, it was lovely. Well done for organising it again."

143

I nod and smile. It's not really me who organises it. It's all the charities. I turn up and do a little talk. I don't correct her, though — what would be the point? Let her believe it. I smile, nod and swallow.

"So," I say, putting my mug down. "I heard something at the event."

Maggie's brow wrinkles. It's so nice to speak to someone who hasn't used Botox to freeze their forehead. You get to miss those little expression lines in the world of influencers and PR girls.

"Oh?" she says.

"Yeah. Sheryl says Gianna's taking part?"

Now it's Maggie's turn to swallow. She puts her own mug down and adopts a smooth, meditation voice. "Yeah," she says, breathing out the word.

"I just thought she would tell us, if she was taking part. Or me," I add. "I guess you knew?"

Maggie nodded.

"Why didn't you tell me?" I ask.

Maggie sighs and leans back on her chair. "It just feels very difficult, Paige. I mean, after we all grew apart after Zanna—"

I cut her off. "We didn't grow apart, you guys started leaving me out."

I cringe as I say it. She blinks nervously. I sound like I'm eleven years old again, being bullied in the school playground.

144

Maggie's eyes widen, in a genuine sympathy. "It wasn't like that, Paige, really. I mean, I tried to stay in touch, didn't I? It was just hard with Gianna. She felt really strongly about stuff, you know, after Zanna died."

My pulse quickens.

"You know, there was speculation after Zanna . . . about me? Horrible stuff, like I had something to do with it?" I say, mouth thick — and not from grease and madeleine crumbs alone.

She nods and then shakes her head, showing an overt disapproval for the suspicion of me. I take a breath. "Well." My voice rattles. "I always wondered, got the impression, maybe, that Gianna thought that maybe there was some truth to it."

Maggie raises a hand to her chest and begins vigorously shaking her head.

"No, no, she doesn't. I promise you that, Paige."

I wipe my hair away from my face with a shaky hand. I had never thought I would find myself talking about all this, with Maggie of all people. Going live on my Instagram to millions of followers was easy compared to this real-life scenario.

"I'm so sorry you think that, Paige, it's not that at all."

"Then why? Why does she hate me so much?"

"Well, you know, you did sometimes butt heads; it didn't get off to a good start when you called her stupid at Sushi Samba."

I fight, hard, the urge to roll my eyes.

"But mostly, she thinks it's not right the way you and Shane got together after Zanna died. She thinks it's weird, like, morally questionable."

I open my mouth to defend myself, but Maggie interrupts.

"*I* don't, Paige. You know, a lot of people don't. But Gianna's like that. But I'm sorry it all got fucked up with the four of us. I am."

I nod. "It's okay. I mean, it happens. Life happens."

Possibly longing for respite from this conversation, Maggie goes to make another pot of tea.

"Are you okay?" Maggie asks, when she has again returned from the recess of her kitchen. "Besides this stress with the documentary, and everything. How are things with Shane?"

Why does her voice sound like that? Perhaps I shake my head too fast, too panicked, because I seem to wordlessly confirm something for Maggie, who looks down and swallows.

"Perfect," I say.

"That's good." She has the tone of a counsellor now, as she puts her teacup gently down. "Zanna told me, sometimes . . ." Maggie says, every word a foot on ever thinner ice.

I take a deep breath.

"Zanna told me, sometimes, Shane could be . . ."

Could be . . .

"Volatile."

Volatile, is that the word Zanna used?

146

"Oh."

My syllable hangs there, between my mouth and Maggie's concern-creased brow.

"I guess everyone has their moments," I say. I regret agreeing to stay for this second pot of tea.

"Are you two happy, though?" Maggie asks. She's not asking exactly what she wants to ask. She means, does he shout? Does he break things? Does he hit?

"We are." I smile. "We really are."

She nods, satisfied.

I go on, perhaps for my benefit. "I don't know what Zanna told you, but I suppose, relationships can be different, with different people. Don't worry about Shane and me, we are good. Great."

*

On the train, on the way home, I sit bundled into the corner of a four-seat cluster at the very back of a carriage, broken by the day. I forgot having friends meant you are expected to open up, crack like a nut. I'm smashed right now. Pulverised. If it's true, what Maggie said about Gianna, that she didn't suspect me of any-thing to do with Zanna's death, then she would have no reason to send the note. I can't be sure. But then, I try one more thing. Out of desperation. In case.

I hit reply to the last email.

Gianna, is this you?

My hands shake. A response comes back immediately.

You wish, bitch.

Life of Zanna Documentary

Gianna Henry Interview

PRODUCER: Hello, Gianna. Thanks for joining us.

GH: I'm happy to have been asked to take part, and pleased you managed to find my details, finally.

PRODUCER: Yes, well, it was a little harder to track you down than Zanna's other friends.

GH: You don't need to tell me why. Paige wasn't keen for me to take part.

PRODUCER: And why might that be, do you think? Can you tell us a little more about that? How did that friendship break down?

GH: Well, personal reasons. I was never that keen on Paige. At first I thought she was okay, but later Zanna told me some of the stuff she'd said about me. She said something about me at dinner once. Called me stupid. She always thought she was better, cleverer than other people. Me included, I guess.

PRODUCER: And when did Zanna tell you that?

GH: It was after things between her and Paige got tense, with the blog and everything. But I never warmed to her, even from the start. She was way too obsessed with Zanna. I thought she was in love with her, for God's sake. That was my concern. This woman who was secretly in love with Zanna had moved in with her and her boyfriend and she might do something to get in the way. I just wanted the best for those two, Zanna and Shane, I thought they were perfect together. That's what Zanna always said. I guess it's working out for Paige and Shane now. They're still together. But I just never saw those two together. I still can't get my head around it.

PRODUCER: You thought Paige was in love with Zanna?

GH: Yeah, I did. She came out of nowhere and, all of a sudden, she was always there. Always crawling around Zanna, getting dressed up in her clothes, copying Zanna, saying the things she said, adopting her mannerisms. After she turned up, it went from zero to sixty. It was hard to even get alone time with Zanna.

Paige was always there. So yeah, I came to the conclusion Paige had other feelings. Well, it was egg on my face because she only went and stole Zanna's boyfriend, didn't she.

PRODUCER: You take issue with that?

GH: Yes, I do. It's a bit . . . wrong, I think. Don't you? To be so close with someone and after they die start dating their ex? What kind of friend would do that? You wouldn't steal someone's boyfriend when they were alive, so why would you after they are dead? That's what I think anyway, but maybe Paige would have dated Shane when Zanna was alive. Maybe she did.

PRODUCER: They have always denied that.

GH: Well, they would, wouldn't they?

PRODUCER: What do you think?

GH: Look, I don't have any concrete proof. I'm just saying, it doesn't sit right with me. Paige was unhealthily obsessed with Zanna. Now her and Shane are apparently this loved-up couple.

PRODUCER: "Unhealthily obsessed." That's quite extreme, isn't it?

GH: Is it? You tell me. Moving in with your friend, working for them, running their business in their own name for five years after they died and shacking up with their ex? Doesn't that seem unhealthy to you? Doesn't it?

[A pause.]

Look. I really don't have anything against Paige. She's not my kind of person. That's fine, not everyone gets on. She said some nasty things about me, but personal things aside, it must have been hard, what she went through, after all of it and everything. It's just . . . not how the average normal person would act. That's all. But then, I guess Zanna wasn't entirely normal either, in a different way. Maybe you just can't be an influencer and be "normal", anyway.

My problem is that she carried on running the Instagram account after Zanna died, and that she began dating Shane. I don't think Zanna would have wanted either of these things to happen.

PRODUCER: And you say things got "tense" between Zanna and Paige. What do you mean by that?

GH: Well, I'm not sure it was that great a friendship. Zanna told me things, about Paige. They were arguing, living together was getting uncomfortable. Even Zanna was finding Paige smothering by that point. Even finding her a bit scary at times.

PRODUCER: Paige says their friendship was fine?

GH: I know things between Paige and Zanna weren't all rosy, no matter what she says. I can show you texts to prove it. I remember it well: it all started when the blog reached 100,000 followers.

PRODUCER: There has been a lot of speculation about the results of the case. Suggestions that Paige was more involved in Zanna's death. What do you think of that? Do you share those views?

GH: No, I don't. I mean, no. Things weren't always how Paige says they were, between her and Zanna. I know that. But I don't believe Paige would do that. Like I say, she loved Zanna, from what I could see, a lot. The police are the experts. If there were something, they would have found it, wouldn't they?

The Past

We went out for a night to celebrate, the three of us, when we reached 100,000 followers. We commonly did go out together, but this night was a little extra special. Zanna asked me to go to a party shop and buy six balloons, a one and five zeros, which she posed next to in a party dress for me to photograph and post. I couldn't help but wonder how many of those followers I was responsible for. Why Zanna had never asked me to pose for a picture at one of these events.

Zanna's brown eyes, liquid-lined, a perfect flick, bounced between Shane and me that night, celebrating the "Big 100K" as she called it. As he and I spoke, joked, laughed, her lids narrowed, pupils sharpened. She wrapped an arm around Shane's shoulder, pulling his attention with a needy arm, and when he turned to look at her, she smothered him with a pillowy, long kiss on the mouth. But after the kiss he looked straight back at me and continued our conversation, eyes barely meeting her own.

Her mouth set, I felt her gaze boring into me and smiled through it, acting natural. Yes, Zanna and Shane were already physically together, but Shane and I were a better match. We spoke more. We laughed more. We had more in common. Our outsider-ness. My loyalties lay with Zanna, my best friend, but it was becoming harder to hide the fact that I was in love with her boyfriend.

"Maybe people think we're all going to bang each other, like we met you off an app for swinger sex," Zanna had said to me.

I was the third wheel, and I knew people had started to think it was strange. That it was sad. It didn't help that I'd recently spent Christmas with Shane, Zanna and her family.

Poor Paige, why can't she get her own boyfriend? Weird Paige, why is she always buzzing around this couple like a wasp around a margarita?

"Here they come, the threesome," Gianna would snark, on any given day.

"The ménage à trois," Sara sneered.

"The tricycle," they said and laughed. At me. They always laughed at me. No one questioned Shane and Zanna, the beautiful poster couple.

"I wish I could have what you two have," Gianna simpered.

Of the many hundreds of compliments Zanna loved to receive, it was one of her favourites. Being chosen by a fine specimen of a man sets you apart from your peers.

Clingy Paige, so good of Shane and Zanna to tolerate her.

Two is the natural order of things. Couples are normal. So, the imposition was always supposed to be mine. It never occurred to anyone that perhaps I was wanted, filling a growing cavern between people drifting apart. Relationship Polyfilla.

"Please, get married already," Gianna whined mushily in the direction of the so-called happy couple.

She giggled at Zanna's exaggerated eye roll, a distraction from Shane's stiffening posture, the flicker of frustration in his eye, his jaw setting. Misdirection was the key to the magic, and I was the biggest misdirection of all. The elephant in the show, who allows the magician to set up the big trick. Shane palpably relaxed when I was there, something Zanna felt too. I eased the pressure on a relationship going slowly under. They were both unhappy, and I tried to help, I really did. I wasn't entirely selfishly motivated.

Maybe I became too bold in the way I looked at Shane, because it wasn't long after that night that Zanna changed. She changed towards work, and towards me too. Reaching 100,000 followers had lit a fire under her perfect upside-down heart-shaped arse. Her aspirations exploded with the catalyst — a sliver of success. She began to refer to herself as an "entrepreneur" and "media expert", a "creative director". Anything to avoid being called a blogger, which was too small for her now. It was now a "personal brand", she said. My role shifted too, from writer to live-in personal assistant.

Zanna and I had been "hustling", she called it. "Fake it till you make it" took on a new, all-too-literal meaning to me. We were sent free stuff and it got more and more lavish and we gained more and more followers. But Zanna pretended to be given a lot more besides. She bought a Chanel handbag, an "investment" she said, and posed with it. Sipping from a cocktail with a straw, the simple black flap bag sat, almost ignored, leaning against her thigh.

We wrote:

One mojito, two mojito, three mojito . . . and the rest is history. Thanks @chanel

It was ambiguous, I reasoned. It couldn't be called a lie, could it? Not outright. Let people assume the bag was a gift, or maybe we were thanking them for their great customer service, or simply for existing, I consoled myself, even while comments came in. Lies were not part of my initial journalistic ambition.

Being good at Instagram is not as easy as it looks; neither is building a following. It takes work even if, like Zanna and so many others did, you buy a few thousand fake followers to get you going. We still had to create the content. My boss invested in a Canon camera, which she instructed me to learn how to use. I stood outside Camden McDonald's, hands around the camera turned to claws by the cold, laden with bags full of glittery clothes for what Zanna was calling our "party edit" as she changed in the toilet. I kneeled on cold pavements to get the editorial, leg-lengthening shots Zanna wanted as the flow of bemused tourists and mocking teenagers moved around us, smirking or laughing. After we were finished, I was sent with the clothes, tags still on, to return them all to the stores Zanna had bought them from while Zanna called a taxi home "to warm up in the bath".

After my hands, stiff with chilblains, had warmed up on the Tube home, it fell to me to edit the images to Zanna's whims, remove blemishes, flatten her stomach and get rid of that little bit of fat under her chin she was obsessive about. The Zanna on screen smirked at me over a glittery, padded shoulder. She said, *I'm a cool girl and I'll teach you how to be like me. It's easy, don't you worry.* We sold a dream, and a lie.

You'd think we were at least good at the tech side of it all. But we weren't. Zanna spent £2,000 on a website redesign, complete with a tech expert to help us with any issues over the phone. All we cared to learn was exactly what we needed to do to gain followers on Instagram. That was always the heart of the business. To do that, someone had to be constantly working on the platform. That someone, of course, was me. My duties were to post the content, write the captions, choose the best hashtags, post the posts at the best time of day and respond to every single comment and direct message as though I was Zanna. I also had to constantly follow and comment on other, bigger bloggers' accounts to raise Zanna's profile. It was endless. There were no days off in Zanna's world.

Slaves to Instagram's algorithm, we jumped through the various — ever changing — hoops to boost our posts. The algorithm set the rules and we played catch-up and guessing games, which rippled through the blogging community. It was an arms race to boost exposure with the right content. Nothing drove engagement, though, like brand collaborations.

The more we worked with brands, the more the pressure to hit certain targets became a reality. They asked to know the stats, how many people saw our Instagram posts, the engagement, the clicks. And followers don't necessarily equate to engagement, something that was becoming a constant struggle for us. As brands became more clued up as to how to check the legitimacy of influencers, their real reach, Zanna became obsessed with these stats. We'd done a number of sex toy posts, feminist and sex positive, we reasoned. But the Instagram algorithm wasn't favourable to them, and for a while we suspected our account was punished for it.

"Urgh, why are people so shit? Why don't they like the posts? Dickheads," she'd say, hitting the arm of the sofa with her fist.

"We need engagement of four per cent, ours is like two. Ask more questions in the captions," she barked at me as she messaged friends, family and Shane, demanding:

Why haven't you liked and commented on my post?

Zanna noted who was quick to "like" pictures and who wasn't. She muttered, "Does Sara think I don't notice she never likes or comments? Bitch."

This was better than when the anger was directed at me. She would demand to know why engagement was down, why there were fewer comments. Why wasn't my writing engaging? she'd ask. She'd passively aggressively send me example after example of other Instagram captions that were better than mine, blog post ideas I should have had. Where she once was inspired by my writing, now it was never good enough.

It was always about the followers for Zanna, because followers meant money. Money meant success. Success was what she was trying to show her family — and her father — she could do. This success also manifested, for Zanna, in showing off her wealth. Being a "girl boss" for Zanna seemed to translate into hitting material milestones. I never heard a whiff about savings, but she bought Cartier Love rings, bags worth thousands of pounds, extolling their resale value and the "investment in her personal brand". Zanna couldn't separate signs of luxury from wealth, and being the subject of envy from happiness.

We churned out pieces about self-love, social media, being a "girl boss" and Zanna's (entirely fabricated) morning routine, in which she had me claim she included a morning sun salutation, mindfulness and a latte. For this we pocketed £2.5k from an alternative milk company. Later that company got exposed for dodgy palm oil behaviour. Zanna frustratedly deleted the post after followers commented on it. "Fucking cry-babies whinging over baby orangutans, who gives a shit?" she said.

It's hard, as an influencer, I learned, to maintain a high standard when it comes to who you work with. Zanna was after the Chanels, the Burberrys, the La Mer. She argued it back and forth with her agent, but the fact is, these brands pay less. As companies became more adept at finding the influencers with the high engagement, pickier about who they worked with, she was forced to lower her ideals. She ummed and ahhed over working with a brand of constipation relief medication, which was paying a huge sum.

As social media became a far more popular way for companies to advertise, stranger and stranger companies looked to get bloggers on board. Vegan cheese, kitchen disinfectant, even laxatives.

"I don't know if I really want people to look at me and think about shit," she said, as she assessed the proposal from the brand, sent over by Tom the agent.

"Can't we sort of put a girl-power spin on it, you know? Say you're being super empowering for talking about taboo subjects for women. You could be leading the conversation?" I suggested.

"I mean yeah, but ultimately, I'm still talking about shit. My shits."

Eventually, though, the lure of the cash was too overwhelming. I worked it into a euphemistic piece for the blog about routine and "feeling light". It was really the work of genius. Zanna posed for a picture with a morning orange juice, fresh and beautiful in the kitchen, the small packet of tablets tucked behind the kettle.

Still, I became concerned about Zanna's choices when it came to the blog. Hungry for money, for more, she would rarely turn down a brand for the right price. I gritted my teeth and wrote anyway. A paid post with an iron, all about looking after clothes in which, for the images, Zanna insisted ironing in her bra was perfectly appropriate. *This isn't what I would do with this platform,* I would think, and yet my ideas were rarely heard. She'd begun to be snippy with me. She pulled the camera from my fingers and demanded to know why I couldn't shoot images that met her *Vogue* spread expectations. If I ever retorted that I was a writer, not a photographer, she'd sneer that I wouldn't get anywhere without a photography portfolio in this day and age. Zanna was quite the expert in what my future career would require from me. Her expertise always happily aligned with whatever she wanted me to do.

The blog became more and about her, the images of her on it, than anything to with the content of the articles. Though I ground away at the content of the posts, she hardly gave them a second glance, only interested in the likes. And the likes were brought in by racier and racier pictures of Zanna. She instructed me to photograph her in her lingerie. She worked with a videographer to create an almost soft-porn-like video for

Instagram. Doing her makeup to sultry music in lace lingerie. "It's my body, I want to own it," Zanna said, pressing post on the risqué video. Soon, other people wanted to own it too.

As the content became more provocative, the responses to her content become more sexual. Men, popping up in the comments, offering to do things for her. Offering to pay for a membership to a private club after she posted an Instagram story about wanting to get in.

One man replied and offered to pay all her fees, just like that. "No strings attached," he said.

I said: "Those strings are about as subtle as Silly String."

One man, in his fifties with dyed black hair, and a wife and children, offered £20,000 over Instagram direct message to meet Zanna in a London hotel. "Just to meet, nothing has to happen," he said. It was the biggest offer she ever got.

Zanna whispered, "Should I?"

"Absolutely not!"

"But it's £20,000! I'll pay you £500 to be my bodyguard for the night."

"He's probably a murderer."

"For £20,000 maybe I'd risk it."

She said to me the next day: "Some Instagrammer is claiming she got offered £50,000 for five nights in Dubai with a guy."

I pulled a sick face. "Urgh, gross."

Zanna mused with a little "mmm" sound and nodded absent-mindedly. After a brief silence she asked, "Do you think I could get that much?"

While she told me the blog was about her ideas — *our* ideas, and *my* words — I was working on little less than a vanity project for Zanna, whose main interest seemed to be only to see herself in pictures, and have strangers respond positively to them.

What hurt most was how Zanna changed towards me. Shorter, brusquer. As she leaned into being my boss, she twisted further from being my friend. My mind drifted to my work experience at the newspapers, where I'd been treated like nothing when reporters heard my regional accent and unremarkable last name, as Zanna barked orders at me across the kitchen table or when, at an event, she shoved her handbag and iPhone at me, demanding, "Take my picture, keep your shadow out of the shot."

I asked her, "Do you ever wonder what the point of what we are doing is?"

She replied, "Paige, if I ever thought about that, I'd never do anything."

*

We were in the living room, getting ready for an event to launch a new "healthier milk chocolate" when she found it. Zanna was being paid to be there, and to post the event to her socials. I was prepping captions at the same time as steaming the dress Zanna wanted to wear. Shane had smiled sympathetically at me crouching as I worked on the cuffs. The heart leaped a little, as it always did when he met my eyes, and hurt a little as it always did when he left the room.

"Fuck, fuck, fuck," she'd said, staring at her phone. Her face was wan, features wiped clean of emotion by pure shock. "Oh my God."

Zanna's outburst rang out over the blasting music. She said nothing further, staring at her phone agog. I got up and moved over to her, where she'd been sat painting her nails while I worked, and tried to get a glimpse past her shoulder at her screen. She held the screen reflexively up to her chest.

"What, Zanna?"

Zanna had jumped up from her chair and was gasping for air. Her chest went red, a crimson rising up to her face.

"What the fuck," she shouted again. Shane came back into the room at the commotion, looking at Zanna with a mix of confusion and concern. She very rarely lost her cool like this, gulping airless at her phone like a fish. Shane, taking control, took Zanna's phone roughly from her hands and squinted at the screen.

"It's not real," Zanna whined, trying to take it back.

He held the phone above her head and furrowed his brow. "I don't get it, what's Dahlia Duchesses?"

I was on my feet, arms hanging helpless by my side. I ought to be doing something.

"I'd never even heard of it," Zanna whimpered.

Shane read aloud: "Dahlia Duchesses is the foremost London escort agency for gentlemen who anticipate the best. Our British escorts are fun-loving, engaging and open-minded."

"What on earth," Zanna muttered under breath, sitting on the sofa with her head in her hands. She shook her head in confusion.

Shane fixed his gaze on her with a face like thunder.

"It's not real," she cried again, this time with indignance. "Seriously, Shane."

"Well, can I be sure?" He was tense, eyes boring into her.

"Oh, for fuck's sake," Zanna said. "Paige, look at this."

Animated now by irritation, she took the phone from Shane's limp arm and handed it to me.

It was a website, the words "Dahlia Duchesses" in lush, curling letters on the top. Underneath it read: "The fastest growing escort directory in the UK! Rated 'Excellent' on Trustpilot!! Free Sign Up!!!"

"That's a lot of exclamation marks," I said.

"Scroll down," Zanna barked. I did. There, among a number of clickable profiles with pictures, names, ages, and accepted sex acts listed, was a profile for Zanna.

"What the fuck?" I said. There was a picture of Zanna, one in a bikini taken from her Instagram.

"It's already on fucking Prattle," Zanna said. It was true. Zanna's thread was inundated with new posts, all of them mocking.

Lol can't believe one of them has finally been caught out, how stupid to use your own blog pictures. Well, we all knew these girls were doing it.

I think we all know where Zanna's latest Celine bag came from.

I knew she was looking for a sugar daddy the minute she started posing those lingerie pics. So glad she's finally been caught out.

"You're escorting?" The words left my throat, almost a breath. Shane raised his hands to his head as if about to tear his own hair out.

"No!" Zanna protested, throwing both her hands up. "Honestly, why would either of you even think that?"

Shane and I looked at one another. I said nothing. I looked from her to Shane. My gut cramped.

"Why would someone make a fake profile of you?" he asked.

Zanna spluttered. "I don't know — some loser, for fun. I don't know. Shane, come on, please."

She stepped towards Shane, who took a step back, massaging his head.

"This is ridiculous," she said, storming into the bedroom, and slamming the door behind her as she shrieked, "Ridiculous!"

Life of Zanna
Documentary

Paige White Interview

PRODUCER: Let's talk about the escorting profile.

PW: Oh gosh, yes. That caused mayhem. That was a nightmare. Zanna was upset, very upset. It was a shock.

PRODUCER: How did Zanna respond?

PW: Well, she cried. She denied that it was real.

PRODUCER: How did Shane respond?

PW: He was supportive.

PRODUCER: Really?

PW: Yes, we both just wanted Zanna to be okay.

PRODUCER: Did you think it was fake?

PW: I didn't know. But I wanted to be as supportive as possible, no matter what.

PRODUCER: Did you ever have any thoughts about who was behind it?

PW: Honestly, it could have been anyone. Most likely a sad Instagram follower who decided to mess with Zanna. These people do strange things. Having experienced it first-hand now, I know the bizarre things these online stalkers will do all too well.

It was devastating to Zanna, and of course, it went on to have catastrophic, irreparable effects. If I'm honest, I think it was that profile, and the fallout from it, that was the catalyst behind Zanna's kind of breakdown, and all the decisions she made next.

The Present

In Paige and Shane's flat

I don't wake, because I'm not asleep. I can't sleep with Shane's body next to me. He breathes, and I count the breaths, not dozing for the dread taking up residence in my stomach. It wiggles and agitates, like a family of mice have set up in there. I'm not hungry. I haven't been hungry for days. A diet of Coke Zero sustains me.

Giving up on sleep entirely, I take two diazepam from the bedside table. My anxiety is the worst it's been. I'm running out. It's going to be a hard sell on my GP to get more. I pace to the living room, put my head against the window. Why are some stragglers on the way home singing *I Wish It Could Be Christmas Every Day?* Ah, yes. It's the 25th.

I've been up since 4.13 a.m. Bad dream, though it hardly needs to be said. When are my dreams not, you know, bad? Blood and black hair, gold jewellery. Hyperventilating sobs that aren't mine. Zanna's voice calling for someone. Shane won't be up for another half an hour or so. He went out with some gym friends last night, so he told me. Merry Christmas.

Six sleeps until the documentary goes live. I've been waiting for the other shoe to drop, for something to appear on a blog, in the news, something about me. I've been playing pen pal with my anonymous correspondent. They send back short replies.

Why are you doing this? I'd asked.

Cus I fucking hate you.

Going mad, I've guessed all sorts of culprits, even — during one evening when perhaps I'd taken one too many diazepam — Zanna's ghost, emailing from beyond the grave. But Zanna would never write "cus". Angela wouldn't either. I wonder if perhaps I don't know this person at all. Perhaps a complete stranger has made a shot in the dark. Here I am, worrying over nothing. Maybe I'll laugh about this later. Still, I wait for a response to my last email.

What do you want?

Nothing. No response so far. It's like a taunt, being kept waiting for news I don't want.

I check Prattle, another daily obsession, a ritual of self-flagellation. Of course, there are some positive comments, but I only ever focus on the bad. The wild theories flew back and forth, strangers discussing my innocence.

I know the police timeline checks out, but I wonder if there's another way for Paige to have done it. To have killed Zanna for the blog. After all, Zanna's mother said after she died how

Paige was asking for more credit on the blog. That Zanna wanted to fire her. I call that motive.

We've got no evidence Paige knew Zanna wanted to fire her, though. It's hardly enough to claim someone is a murderer.

I think she did it for Shane. Maybe she killed Zanna and emotionally manipulated him in his time of grief?

I think it's weird no one looked at Shane a bit more. I thought the partner was always the first suspect.

You guys, the killer was literally there, caught red-handed. Some people just don't want to accept the facts.

I shower the bad dream feeling off my skin, buffing myself with sugar scrub in oil, like a plum fairy. I'm still learning to enjoy this day, Christmas. It more often than not goes down like a lump of coal.

Oliver Bonas decorations hang on the tree, a real tree with spines that have all but destroyed my cordless vacuum cleaner. Tongue-in-cheek baubles hang on it, a little bottle of Moët champagne on a gold ribbon, a teeny bottle of rosé wine. A red lobster model sits in the branches, festooned with white pom-poms glowing with the warm light. A gold "P" and "S" nestle in the branches. It isn't the traditional tree, but brands tend to send more novelty decorations and I make do. Dangling in the spiky branches are small Swarovski crystal trinkets, sent over in a box by the brand. The filter I'm using to film them accentuates the light the snowflake shapes throw around the room.

@swarovski thanks for bringing the Christmas cheer to our merry little home this year #gift

The room is the result of hours of work. Our six-foot tree stands in the corner of the living room against the huge windows. Shane and I went to choose and collect it together, and to take pictures for Instagram. We got it free for tagging the tree company. The reflection of the glittering baubles and lights from the tree mingles with the lights of the Albert Bridge, of the flats opposite the river, of the headlights and taillights on the cars tootling along the Thames. We are suspended in an eternity of lights around us, living in a Yayoi Kusama installation. I never want it to end, him sleeping safe in the other room while I keep watch over this tiny kingdom, our slice of the world, but I know the sun will rise soon. At least it will rouse Shane, so we can open our presents.

Shane has been generally miserable about Christmas ever since we've been together, but just because he's going to be a Grinch, it shouldn't stop us from trying to have a nice day. Beneath the tree lie the gifts. One large one for me, a black box with a white ribbon and camellia flower. I don't need to read the boxy writing on the top to know what this means. Chanel. My stomach drops. But Shane doesn't know, couldn't know, that we can't afford this.

Smaller gifts sit around it, wrapped by me in brown paper, this year finished with black ribbon. An #itsawrap Instagram post was followed with copious heart-eyes emojis.

When I was little, with my mum and dad in the terrace house, I thought the bigger the gift, the better. As I've gotten older, since I took over the blog and the numbers seemed to multiply on their own like rabbits, I learned the smaller the present, the more precious. I'd be lying if I said I didn't fantasise one day a small, squarish box would be heading my way, with a glimmering promise inside, tiny but huge. Christmas is the most common day of the year to propose. Who knows what Shane has planned? But I calm myself. I never bring it up, marriage or babies. Men don't like it. I won't make Zanna's mistake, that's for sure. Men don't want to propose to a woman who's begged for it. Hopefully Shane will do it on his own, soon.

Before Shane wakes up, I do my makeup quietly in the ensuite bathroom. I smooth first primer and then foundation over my face, buffing it over the flaws. A little dimple scar on my forehead from chickenpox, dark marks dancing down the hollows of my cheeks from spots I picked in my early twenties. Soon, I'll be the age Zanna was when she died, thirty-two. There's a sick thud in my stomach.

Padding through to the kitchen on tiptoes, I get started on a healthy egg-white omelette breakfast. Healthy, for Shane, and lavish, for me. We have it every year with champagne. It's our tradition. I've tried to create a Christmas that is just ours, unmistakably. One that doesn't remind me of my parents and doesn't remind me of Zanna either. Later, after I clean the dishes away, we settle on the sofa and take turns to bring presents over in the order we want the other to open them. Opening my Chanel handbag, I hold it like a baby. So much more precious to me because I really shouldn't have it. Perhaps I'll return it to pay money towards the credit card bills, or our overdue rent. I should, but I won't.

"It's the Hobo! How did you know I wanted it?"

"I saw the hints on your Instagram stories," he says, rolling his eyes in an exaggerated manner.

"Well, it is beautiful."

"You can put it with the rest."

"Oh yes! I'll have three. Mummy, Daddy and baby," I laugh, stroking the bag. Maybe I'll sell the whole family, though I'd have to find a convincing reason if Shane ever asked where they were. I lovingly lay down the bag like Mother Mary did Jesus in his manger, and fetch a gift from under the tree for Shane. A heavy box that I hold out to him in both hands. As he unwraps it, I bite my nails. Unable to resist the compulsion to start explaining before he's reacted to the gift, I say, "I thought you'd want something for everyday, you know."

"Oh my days, Paige."

He prises open the wooden box with a hinge on the back. I read the name of the brand upside down. Even the wrong way up it reads "wealth". It's a watch I caught him lingering over in a window on the King's Road. At least I hope it's that one. My stomach turns over looking at it. For under £5,000, I'd bought it as a celebration when I got the documentary, before the email and despite the bills, celebrating riches to come. You can't live with a scarcity mindset. That's one of the key rules of manifestation.

"They said I can return it," I say, but he is already reaching over and grabbing my neck with his huge hand. He pulls me towards him and plants his lips against mine.

"No way, it's perfect," he says, smiling, easing the black watch out of the box, eager to put it on. A little boy with a remote-control car.

"You're perfect," I say, smiling, having earned my kiss. Shane puts the watch on. He reads through the manual, working out how to change all the settings while sipping on champagne. Then there's another tradition of ours, opening cards. Though we celebrate alone, this adds a little more festive spirit. Shane's friend from school sent a card with a picture of his baby. Shane's family, his aunt and cousin, sent a card too. I have a card from Sissy, which fills my heart with a warm feeling. I open a number of cards from PRs with promises of drinks in the new year. These are who most of my cards are from.

Shane opens one and says: "Aw, Mr Mazur. What a legend."

Mr Mazur, the old flat block's supervisor. Such a sweet, older man, he was always so fond of Zanna, and nice to me too, though she got all his kindest attention. That was generally the way, but she was better with him than I was. I struggled not to wrinkle my nose; his breath had that nicotine tang.

He constantly showed us videos of his little girl and wife on his phone, playing in the park or doing something otherwise cute. It was inescapable, happened every time we spoke with him. He glowed with pride as his phone screen lit up his face, scrolling for the most recent adorable thing his daughter had done.

"You remind me of my girlfriend," he would say to us and wink, jokingly flirting. Zanna handled the clumsy and sometimes, to my mind, off-putting flirting with ease, with unsuspecting good heartedness.

After we open all the cards, Shane shows me the tricks his new watch does. While my face is close to his over the watch, he kisses me, and then we have sex on the sofa. Afterwards, I wriggle out from under him to go to the toilet and put my dress back on. I sigh. He's ripped the lace. He's too rough. Still, Christmas is going quite well, isn't it? For once I have high hopes, or is it simply the effects of champagne before lunch?

When I come back through to the main room, where he still sits on the sofa, I smile. He frowns. I stop in my tracks. There's something in his hands. My phone.

"Do you mind—" he begins. His voice is as controlled, cold and hard as the weights he lifts in the gym. "—telling me what the fuck—" his voice rises to a military, sharp, loud shout on "fuck", and I flinch, "—this is."

The Past

The holiday was Zanna's idea. Ibiza, the boutique villa. She said we needed to get away. Or, really, she needed to get away.

"This fake escorting profile has really stressed me out," she said. Her and Shane's tense behind-a-closed-bedroom-door arguments had increased in frequency. He chastised her for posting too many pictures in lingerie and bikinis. Her trim body brought in as many likes and follows as her fashionable clothes, and so she upped the sexy content considerably. "Women's empowerment," she said.

He'd said, "No guy wants his girlfriend posing in their lingerie on the internet. Anyone would think you were escorting, how am I supposed to know you aren't?"

She'd fire back, "If I wasn't the only one pulling my weight financially I wouldn't have to be posting pictures on the internet."

It was a low blow, and not entirely honest. Zanna would have chased the feeling the likes and followers brought

181

regardless of whether Shane pulled in a six-figure salary or beans. I felt for Shane; all those men commenting on Zanna's posts, asking her to message them privately. There had been tears, things thrown and nights where one or the other of them had slept on the sofa. The escorting profile was only deepening cracks that were already there, magnifying them till they were yawning and cavernous.

"Won't Shane mind us going off on holiday without him?" I asked. In truth, I'd miss Shane punctuating my time with Zanna. Coming to terms with being in love with him had become easier: I'd learned to enjoy what time I did have with him, the friendship we'd built. I'd loved him from a distance, even if the yearning never totally went away.

"Oh, forget about Shane, he's being so annoying recently. I want fun. You and me! Getting dressed up, dancing, pulling. You pulling, obviously. But I'll be your wing woman! Anyway, I'm your boss. I'm saying you're coming, so you're coming."

Zanna also saw the holiday as an opportunity for content and set me the task of searching for Ibiza outfit inspiration for her to wear, before I'd even had time to think about what I'd pack. She also asked me to arrange the booking of flights and airport taxis, throwing a bank card onto my laptop keypad. I was a lackey, but reminded myself how lucky I was. The lucky lackey, surrounded by boxes of freebies, booking airline tickets for myself on Zanna's card.

The way she threw a white thong bikini into a suitcase, with aggressive finality, made me nervous. Zanna had managed to talk her way around the escorting profile with Shane eventually, but she had steam to blow off, and she blew into the Balearic Islands like the Chattanooga Choo Choo — if the Chattanooga Choo Choo had prosecco in the airport, three gin and tonics midair, and was relentlessly filming the whole thing for its Instagram stories.

"Hi guys," she slurred and giggled, camera phone pointing at her face as she tripped over the bottom of the plane door leading to the tunnel taking us through to baggage claim. The air hostesses feebly waved, but Zanna, who was a jangling blur with her Prada bumbag falling off her hips, an expensive digital camera bashing against her Louis Vuitton tote and vintage Fendi sunglasses bouncing on her head, rarely saw employees such as air hostesses or waiters at the best of times.

"We just landed in Ibiza, baby!" she squealed.

It was a short drive to the catered apartment. Zanna had ordered me to email the company with our media pack, asking for a free stay in exchange for coverage. Eventually we'd settled on a half-price deal with a personal rep, a new service they were running with an English-speaking Ibiza "nightlife specialist" who would arrange the details of our entry to clubs and beach clubs. The half-price deal left a bitter taste in Zanna's mouth.

"Don't these idiots know the value of coverage like mine? They should be paying me," she'd fizzed with indignation. But finally, she had agreed.

The evening we arrived, we were awkwardly greeted by a chef who was preparing to cook linguine. Zanna dashed over to film the cook and I pulled the two large suitcases into the main bedroom with the holdall swung over me, so I had to practically crawl out of the pile of luggage I'd been carrying — mine and Zanna's too — after putting it down. The flat was beautiful, jaw-droppingly so, on top of a large white complex. As much as I'd been exposed to fancy things so far, with Zanna the driving force behind it all, there was something about this view in particular that set my soul aflutter, like a flock of seagulls stirred up by a running dog. Through wide glass doors was a glass balcony with a view of the ocean fading into a turquoise sky, smothered with pink kisses by a horny-drunk sunset.

"Oh my fucking Jesus." Zanna wrapped her arms around me from behind. "This is the fucking dream," she breathed, and put a pointy little chin on my shoulder.

"Yeah, it's amazing," I said, smelling the sweet scent of her and the bitter gin and tonic-y breath.

"Want a cig?" She unwound herself, digging into the £600 bumbag with a feverish hand, then emerging with a twenty deck of Marlboro Lights. "Love you," she said, as she held it out to me.

I echoed her, "Love you."

She went inside, came out with her Polaroid camera. She loved the thing. The bright flash was flattering. She posed together for a picture, her arm held out, the flash creating an aurora on my eyelids when I closed them.

It was a short trip, and it was intended that we would make the most of every night. Criminally, while Zanna was a lightweight with alcohol, she never suffered from the debilitating aftermath like I did, your body trying to turn itself inside out. Despite full prior knowledge of my unfortunate intolerance, I drank vodka and slimline tonic like I'd never heard the words "hang" and "over" in the same sentence. We were choosing between silver sandals and black espadrilles for Zanna when the doorbell rang.

"It's the personal rep," Zanna said, without looking up from the troublesome shoe quandary. "Get it."

Please had been dropped from Zanna's vocab when it came to me, unless it was a derisive, "Oh, Paige, *please*."

Mild irritation vanished, though, because of the striking man at the door. He was an undiscovered teen idol. He mouthed "Hi" and his watermelon pink lips pulled apart in a grin with edges sharp enough to cut.

"Hi," I said, real life coming back into focus.

"It's Zanna, right? Cool name."

He possessed a level of male beauty that did something truly, horribly physical to me, like standing in a wind tunnel at the edge of a cliff.

"It's like Harry Styles and Jesus had a baby," Zanna said to me later. She was totally on the money.

"I'm Paige," I said, "that's Zanna."

I opened the door, and Zanna looked up from the floor. Without missing a beat, she asked this man, "Silver or black?"

He walked past me, hair curling to his shoulders and a swallow tattoo on his hand.

"Black, it's sexier. By the way, this is my pal and colleague, Antonio," he said as a gangly Ibizan shuffled through the door. His strong Mancunian inflection mangled the local's name. "I'm Mason."

*

An hour later and it was getting pretty clear I was stuck with Antonio. It wasn't really like there was anything wrong with Antonio, but it's always difficult to get excited about the consolation prize. There's an extra air of desperation about the second friend, more off-putting than bad breath. But it wasn't any of that offending me. Not Antonio's hand crawling closer to mine in the back of the Uber like a tarantula with alopecia and the sweats, or the defanged, timid smiles he kept shooting my way, desperate to keep my eyes on his longer than a second or so to initiate flirting. I moved my hand away. No one compared to Shane, certainly not this loser.

It was the way Zanna threw her head back and laughed when Mason made a joke that was starting to irk me. She was teasing him, aping the overly pronounced vowels hanging fat and round in his Mancunian accent like ripe plums and the loose "eh" sound he made at the end of words like "party." He said, "C'mon girls, let's par-teh. I'm gaggin' for a bev."

I decided I didn't like Mason, no matter how good-looking he was. His crocodile eyes fixed on Zanna. His lizard body, too cool, too relaxed, too self-assured. When his eyes locked with insipid sidekick Antonio's, they shared a disquieting secret. That night we drove to Cova Santa, a long drive up to a sprawling club cut into the hills of the island, surrounded by palms, hidden by jungle-like green until the bright red lights of the sign came into view.

"This is an old-school hippie Ibiza place," Mason was explaining to Zanna as we traipsed towards the entrance of the compound. It climbed up multiple levels, with many bars lit up and staircases falling down it like waterfalls.

There was performance art taking place inside. A drum circle, by the looks of things, with performers in rainbow ribbons and masks.

"Let's get a drink," Zanna said, and we climbed up to a bar on another level. From there, the lights of Ibiza town twinkled in the distance. Zanna leaned against the bar, where Mason propped himself up like James Dean, leaning on the elbows. She put a hand, with cayenne pepper red nails ("Orange hues pop with the tan I'm going to get") on Mason's tattooed hand, an old-school swallow.

"I love men with tattoos," she said.

I remember it clearly, because I bristled when she said it. As Mason was languishing under her heat lamp of compliments, I was going cold. Not, "I love tattoos." But, "I love *men* with tattoos."

"What does it mean?" she went on.

"It's a sailor tattoo," he said, looking into her eyes and curling his lip, dimples folding up in both his cheeks. "I like to travel, so it's for luck. If I drown at sea, the swallow will carry my soul to heaven. I need all the help I can get going there."

He brought a bottle of San Miguel to his lips and winked at her with sparkling eyes. How often had he pulled that line out of his arse?

"Well, I hope you don't die," Zanna crooned.

The words jumped from my mouth, sounding less light-hearted than I had hoped them to. "It would be irritating to have to book another guide at short notice."

Mason smiled with one side of his fanged mouth and said, "I think Antonio here would be able to help you out."

The two men fell into conversation and Zanna caught my eye, leaning over and asking, "Are you tired?"

"Yeah," I said, as breezily as I could muster. "Shane would love it here, I think."

Her eyes flared wider, disco lights reflecting in the dark brown orbs. "Shh," she mouthed, like a schoolteacher. So that was it then: whatever she was doing, it was more deliberate than she wished to let on. Red-hot fire burned down my throat and in my eyes like an inexpertly taken shot of tequila. Her flagrant flirting with Mason undermined my relationship, my friendship, with Shane. She was shameless. She hadn't blinked when he said he was twenty, eleven years younger than her. She kept running her eyes over the taut, hairless skin under his shirt, hanging saucily open at the chest. Why should she think I wouldn't tell Shane? Why did she assume my complicity? The idea brought a bitter taste to my mouth, like taking a paracetamol for one of those Ibiza hangovers and having it only go halfway down.

We danced that night, after a few more drinks and a shot. Zanna whirled across the dancefloor in her sparkling gown and became her own disco ball. Her whirling became manic, out of control. She laughed as she tripped over her own feet and fell about the place, stiletto pinning my foot to the floor. Her eyes sparkled. She huddled towards Mason's chest, chiselled nose dangling over a small plastic bag full of white powder, a key disappearing up a surgically enhanced nostril. He watched her with spring-loaded-jaw threat, a ticking clock in the belly. Zanna frolicked around him, an ever-young, Botoxed, moronic Peter Pan. He gestured towards the bag when he saw me looking, offering the key and powder towards me. I shook my head.

"Zanna, please be careful," I whispered, shrill and wobbly. She shrugged me off, glancing around to find Mason.

Antonio tried to dance with me, engaging in conversation, moving his head to catch my eyes, trying to stare deeply into them. But I kept an eye on Zanna, teetering on her heels around Mason, swaying as they talked in each other's ears against the loud music. His claws were creeping around her lower back; she didn't notice. He continued to offer her the drugs, buy her drinks, and lean his face ever closer to hers.

Mason and I shared the same sense of surprise when she didn't invite the two men back to our apartment for drinks later.

"I want to be fresh when you take us to the beach club tomorrow," she said, beaming at Mason with those stunning veneers. "We need our beauty sleep."

*

After six hours of restless sleep in the huge bed, I woke with a shock, taking something sharp and cool to the face.

Zanna stood topless in bikini bottoms, holding a coffee. She'd done her hair and a face of no-makeup makeup. She'd got the jump on me. I had yet to scrape the dried dribble off my face. I'm not a very attractive sleeper. I stain a lot of pillows. I looked down and saw a blue shiny packet to my right, the source of the cool and sharp from seconds before.

"It's a sheet mask," Zanna said. "Put it on. It'll help with the puffiness from the alcohol. I've got two cold spoons in the fridge for your eyes and coffee in the pot. Do you want eggs?"

I obediently applied my sheet mask and padded into the kitchen area, where Zanna poached eggs and sautéed spinach. I was still wearing an old, grey pyjama shirt, while Zanna had put on the top half of a white bikini, the bottoms of which cut high on the hips, eighties style. The bandeau top stretched tight across the chest, flattening her a little, but pulling her tits up and close together. Stunning, no surprise.

I was going to be sick, the taste of cigarettes and alcohol still in my mouth. My hands shook as I eagerly gulped down water in an attempt to soothe my head. My stomach contracted at the invasion of a foreign liquid, like a slug doused with salt, my temples beating either side of my head.

"We're leaving for a beach club in half an hour. Mason's driving us," Zanna said. She brought her phone up, the lens on me.

"The Ibiza turn up is getting to Paige," she cheered as she filmed me. I laughed and brought a hand up to my face.

"No, I'm gross!" I called back, matching her energetic tone despite my self-induced bout of poor health, thankful for the sheet mask, currently hiding my wan pallor. Zanna laughed and put the phone down. I peeled the face mask off and dropped it on the kitchen counter, now slightly limp and warm, crumpled there on the counter, flat and sad like a dead thing.

*

We bounced along a road through Las Salinas, the Ibizan salt flats, in Mason's car. My stomach churned. Fucking Antonio grinned at me from across the back seat. In no mood, I pulled my large dark sunglasses over my eyes.

"Oh Paige is a little worse for wear." Zanna giggled, embarrassed, explaining my behaviour when no explanation was needed. "You can't get the staff these days."

A huge pile of salt lay ahead of us. A flock of little white birds with black wings and long, skinny legs pottered around, disturbing the otherwise cool blue and still water.

"So pretty," Zanna said, looking serene with a printed headscarf and winged sunglasses. "We need to pick up some Ibizan salt before we go home. Paige, can you make a note to remind me?"

I focused on her profile as she gazed wistfully out of the window, my proverbial gears grinding. Despite Mason's crappy car bouncing like the drop tower at Thorpe Park, Zanna managed to stay still and statuesque. I attempted to sink back into the car's fabric seats and avoid the direct sunlight streaming in through the window. *Oh God, my stomach.* It clenched and spasmed.

"If you come out here at sunset, it's really nice, the glow reflects in the salt flats," Mason said as he operated the machine torturing my guts. "It's really nice to come out on the motorbike, too."

"Ohh, could we do that?" Zanna cooed, turning her head to meet Mason's gaze.

"I feel sick," I moaned from the back seat.

Zanna turned her head to glare.

I ran to the fancy beach club toilets and held my own hair up, trying to keep my white cover-up off the floor, as a semi-digested mixture of tequila, Cointreau and poached egg flopped into the toilet from my mouth. I shut my eyes as toilet water splashed up at my face.

When I staggered back outside, Antonio waved furiously at me from a row of four white loungers. Making my way over, the sun bounced off every element of this beach club, blinding me. It ricocheted from the all-white furniture, the parasols, and off the oiled-up bodies of people I clumsily navigated between.

"Have some prosecco," Antonio said, handing me a prefilled glass, which had presumably been poured from the open bottle tucked up in a bucket with ice.

A wave of warmth towards Antonio washed over my stricken body, but only because I craved the sweet and refreshing fizz. My stomach settled as the delightfully cool and tickly fizzy liquid titillated my tongue.

"Where is Zanna?" I asked, and followed Antonio's bronzed, Ibizan-native arm as it extended towards the sea.

Zanna and Mason were already in the sea, up to their thighs in the sparkling water. You didn't have to be a genius to tell that whatever they were talking about, however minor, was a front for the mere thrill of being stood in the water next to one another. Their bodies faced out towards the horizon, but their heads were turned towards one another, conspiratorially. Zanna threw her head back and laughed; I could see the dazzling Crest-white of her teeth from my place higher up on the beach.

My phone buzzed. As I lifted it from my bag, I saw the message on the screen, from Shane.

Hey. Haven't heard back from Zan. U girls okay? Land safe?

Not really checking up on me, but checking up on Zanna, whom I could only assume hadn't texted Shane since we set off. It's the pretend-concern text that really means, *What are you doing?* and *You better have a good excuse as to why it's more important than me.* A little part of me, which had grown given my foul mood and hangover, rankled at being used like this, a go-between for this couple, especially while Zanna misbehaved. But then I softened when I thought of Shane at home, worrying over Zanna. In comparison, she cavorted with a tattooed almost-stranger — technically an employee. Unlike

Zanna's family, I'd never had staff but I was sure fraternising was not *#muybien.*

Yeah, we're okay. Pretty busy. Hope you're good :) I sent back, glancing again at Zanna and Mason.

They were standing like before, but she leaned a little towards him, and her arm bent at the elbow, fingertips dancing in the air by his arm. The ghost of a flirtation, a whisper not decipherable on the wind, the silhouette of a vague promise. I wanted to send Shane a picture.

"So Zanna says you're, like, her assistant?" Antonio feebly tried to make conversation with me. When would he get the message and stop?

"I'm a ghostwriter," I mumbled, although I wanted to scream. I threw myself down on the beach bed and hid my face from the sun, and Antonio, with a towel.

While I disapproved of Zanna's flirting then, I never imagined what would happen next. We drove back to the apartment around three to get ready for dinner at a restaurant. I was wiped out by the sun and a number of glasses of prosecco.

"I'm going to have a nap," I called, collapsing into the large bed. "Will you wake me in an hour?"

I waited for her to call out yes before I let my body relax. I fell down into the soft bed and slipped seamlessly into unconsciousness.

*

I woke cold, in the dark. Confused. Momentarily trapped in the limbo between consciousness and unconsciousness, when the world is utterly new and infinitely strange, before the memory of our life reloads. I shot up in bed, totally aware of the silence and lack of light around me. Where was Zanna? We were supposed to be up hours ago for dinner.

Lights of clubs and bars, and the glow of the Ibiza strip, glimmered tantalisingly in the distance through the sweeping floor-to-ceiling windows of the apartment. On the kitchen island a note read:

You looked so peaceful sleeping, I didn't want to wake you, so I'll let you have the night off. Went to the salt flats with Mason. Sleep well x

I got out of bed and poured myself a large vodka and orange juice from the fridge. I sat on the balcony, sipping it, boiling up with red rage like an electric kettle. Not only had Zanna abandoned me while I slept, hopping on the back of a shitty moped, without even the nerve to wake me up, but she had taken the cigarettes. She'd given me "the night off". Each time I thought of those three words, I wanted to smash something. Why was she doing this now? Treating me like an employee when I was supposed to be her friend, her *best* friend. I sulked on the balcony, the lights flickering across the island, occasional hoots from revellers wafting up to the balcony like an empty baggie on the breeze. Eventually, the Balearic breeze stole any soaked-in sun warmth from my skin and forced me inside. I took a bottle of red wine from the side fridge. You had to appreciate great service and I made a note to write it up in "Zanna's" review.

Her laptop sat open on the side, charging. Notifications pinged silently, and I couldn't resist. I crossed the apartment and leaned down. Messages from Shane blinked one after the other in quick succession.

Where are you?

Why aren't you texting me back?

I'm calling you.

Missed call

Missed call

Missed call

I'm so fucking done with this, you selfish bitch.

Missed call

I poured another drink and sat out on the balcony until it got cold. I turned on the TV and propped myself up on the white sofa. I kept topping myself up, watching music videos with glassy eyes until the door opened behind me. I seethed. 12.30 a.m.

I turned my head to meet Zanna's slightly shocked gaze. She quickly recovered.

"Hi, sleepy head," she sang, beam on full wattage. I didn't smile, and hers didn't flicker; she evidently hoped I wouldn't be standing up for myself tonight. She put her Fendi baguette bag down on the table, wearing white hot pants and a black tube top. Her hair was in a messy ponytail, wrapped with a white tie with little pink flowers in a haphazard bow, like an American 1950s ingénue having a summer romance before the last year of high school.

"Why didn't you wake me up?" I asked. Having not spoken since far earlier in the day, the sounds came out of my throat in a thick croak. I sounded more wounded than I had hoped and less like a slick detective or authoritative headmistress.

"You looked so cosy, I thought it might do you good to have a little snooze," she said, with the nerve to act both hurt and surprised.

"Don't you think that's up to me? You didn't even wake me up to ask me." I had a bitter tone in my voice, but Zanna wasn't ready to let me have my anger just yet. Her brow didn't move, of course — it couldn't — but her smile faded and her jaw fell, allowing her thick lips to fall into a confused pout. If you look closely at someone who's had too much filler, their lower lip actually dangles, weighed down by the sludge injected in there.

"You were so hungover, I thought you should rest up for tomorrow so you could be on form."

"Oh, so I need to be 'on form' now for you to decide what I get to do?"

"Well, to be honest, Paige, this whole trip was arranged on the back of me, maybe I didn't want you there being hungover and gross."

Arranged on the back of her? I'd been the one sending the emails, steaming her clothes and carrying her bags.

"Mason and Antonio are being paid to take us around, Zanna, we hardly have to be in the best form for them. If you didn't want me to come, you should have just said."

I allowed my bruised feelings to seep through into my face and posture, my voice getting slow and quiet and sad. How could she counter that one? I didn't really want this argument to go on. I wanted to make my point and go back to normal. All she had to do was apologise, come over to the sofa and promise not to leave me out again. But Zanna didn't do what I expected. She rarely did. Her face contorted. A spitting harpy came for my jugular with her talons in an unexpected verbal assault.

"You don't get to come everywhere with me just because I let you have this job."

It stung, and the argument wasn't about me being left alone here anymore. My mind wandered to where Zanna had been. Mason's offer in the car from earlier in the day, soaked in unconsciously by osmosis in my still half-drunk state, played back in my mind pure and crisp.

"It's really nice to come out on the motorbike, too."

Pictures of a sunset reflected on still waters swirled into clarity like in a fortune teller's ball. A motorbike parked up, silhouetted by the sun. Only two seats. Then, my long-overdue realisation.

"Was Antonio even there?"

A shifting of the feet. "What does that matter?"

"What the fuck are you playing at, Zanna? Have you totally forgotten you have a boyfriend? A boyfriend who is my friend too?"

Her eyes narrowed. "You are pathetic. You think Shane is your friend?" She laughed. "That's cute. You don't have any friends, Paige, besides *me*."

I sprang up from the sofa, to make my rebuttal, but displaced the red bottle of wine I'd tucked between my thigh and the sofa, too lazy to reach down to the floor each time I filled up my glass.

"Oh shit," I gasped, grabbing the bottle by the neck but not before a considerable amount of Malbec had gushed onto the couch with a heavy flow, like the first day of your cycle.

I held the bottle up and stared down at the sofa, irredeemable.

Zanna smirked. "I'll take the cost of those damages out of your wages, shall I?"

I was shocked by the threat. Not because it was bitchy. Zanna had long been a bitch. No, it was that this was the first time Zanna had ever made a comment about money to me.

It was so unlike her, to even mention money in the context of our friendship. As people don't generally comment on each mouthful of air they take, Zanna never noticed money changing hands, generally from hers to mine in some sense or another. I was so conscious of that enormous gulf between her and me, but Zanna never acted like it mattered. Loaning me that designer dress to wear to Sushi Samba that night, letting me wipe her Givenchy lipstick against my mouth. Small things, like paying for Ubers, drinks. She never blinked.

Now I winced. I could pretend, before, that Zanna never saw that difference between us. That gulf. How I wasn't the same as her in one enormous, important way. I didn't have the power she did. Didn't matter like she did. Now she held it over me, threatening me with it, using those numbers in the accounts — hers and her father's — like weapons. She glared at me from across the holiday apartment, eyes flashing as she let it sink in, before she clattered to the bedroom.

Later I lay in the large bed, resigned to let it go. What choice did I have? I let a tear roll down my cheek. It was gentle, almost silent, as it hit and then was absorbed by the pillow.

*

As we got through security and headed to our gate to fly home, a stony silence between us after last night, both waiting for an apology neither would ever give nor receive, Zanna froze. She dropped her bag of duty-free on the floor, holding her phone with both hands closer to her face, squinting, moving the phone, shaking her head and then squinting again. Not much in the mood to tend to such a dramatic display from Zanna, I carried on walking to the gate until I looked about for her and she wasn't behind me. Turning, I saw her figure, still, duty-free carrier bag on the floor, phone pressed to her ear.

I almost turned to head for the gate again on my own, but her mouth moved large, round and fast, and travellers walking past her glanced back over their shoulders. As I reached her, she said: "I don't understand, can he even do this?"

Her mother's distressed voice came down the line, tear-stained, shout-swollen.

"Darling, I'm sorry, but we think — he thinks — it's for the best. You know how he feels about the blog and now this . . . He's embarrassed. And we want you to stand on your own two feet. He's doing what he thinks is best. Oh, I don't know."

Her voice contained all the concern for her daughter, echoes of what were, I presumed, Santiago's words; confusion and anger, pain and confliction. She made matching sounds of despair down the phone as her daughter did.

"It's not me," Zanna said, her voice rising to a shout.

Her mother's voice was a little muffled. I only caught fragments. "He said", "he heard", "he thinks" and "Sophie".

"She showed him?" Zanna's voice climbed through the octaves. "Fucking bitch! I fucking hate her," she screamed the last two words out.

People walked past, some concerned, some laughing. Two girls about our age covered their smirking mouths with their hands, locking eyes.

"I'm going to kill her," Zanna growled, voice low like a cornered wolf. She shifted slightly from side to side on her feet, rage rocking her.

She hung up the phone on the rising and falling voice of her distraught mother. She looked pale, dead behind the eyes. Otherworldly, for a moment. Then her demeanour, face and voice cracked.

"My dad cut me off. The escorting profile. He thinks it's real. He cut me off."

She fell into my arms.

I felt terrible for her, I really did. In the airport toilet, I dabbed her face with paper. She was red, blotchy, eyes swollen, everything swollen, her overfilled face now almost comic. She'd fall quiet for a while, her chest settling, before thinking of it again, her breaths ratcheting as the panic came over her.

"What am I going to do without my allowance, Paige? It pays my rent. I mean, what the fuck?"

I wasn't even aware Zanna received an allowance. Or any adult over thirty, for that matter. I had been paying my portion of the rent with my wages from her. The rage of unfairness bubbled under my skin, but I bit the side of my mouth so as not to snap in answer.

She oscillated violently between complete despair, indignation, and rage, ricocheting from one to the other, a blur sometimes, muttering and murmuring.

"Sophie showed him because she's overweight and jealous that she doesn't have a boyfriend and has got absolutely fuck-all going for her."

Slowly, she lost the energy for it. We sat down, slumped by the wall, waiting for the gate to board the plane taking us home. Side by side, shoulder to shoulder, Zanna slumped like a deflated balloon, totally defeated. It dawned on me that now Zanna and I had the most in common we had ever had.

I smiled.

"Paige."

A small voice, like that of a child's, a totally helpless thing.

Brown eyes stared vacantly ahead out of eyelids swollen by tears. Then those lifeless orbs fixed on me. She asked me for one of the few things I did have power over.

"Please, don't tell anyone. Not Shane. No one. Please."

And so I promised her.

Life of Zanna Documentary

Santiago Zagalo Interview

PRODUCER: What did you think of Zanna's career, Santiago?

SZ: [Clears throat.] It's strange to try and explain to people what Hannah, that's what I named her and so have always called her, did. And when they google her, they find bikini pictures, walking around in miniskirts, sex toy reviews on her blog.

I'm from a Catholic family, so, for me, where I come from, that is not considered to be an . . . acceptable form of work.

To me, it was not a real job. Not like my other daughters, who worked hard at school, studied for many years. They are private girls, modest. Hannah . . . [Sighs.] We spoiled all of the girls, but Hannah perhaps the most.

Hannah and I had stern words numerous times about what she was putting online. Bikini shoots. Suggestive pictures with nudity. Videos dancing in clubs in Ibiza wearing tiny clothes. Swearing online. Any father would be displeased. In my family, making money is not reason enough to disgrace yourself. To put your body on show. However, Hannah was not entirely self-sufficient. She asked me for more money, to "invest" as she called it, on her website. At first, I helped, but when I saw what it led to, I was displeased.

I was angry, but she refused to listen to me. So, eventually, after many warnings, I cut her off financially.

PRODUCER: What prompted this decision?

SZ: Firstly, she wanted my help to buy a flat for her and her boyfriend to live in. I said, where is all this money you claim to be making from the website going? She told me, well, it's not that much, she still couldn't afford the deposit, all this. But I saw her boasting about the money she was earning from the blog online. There was a never-ending stream of designer clothes at her house. Her hair cost hundreds of pounds for all these Brazilian treatments, whatever ridiculous thing it is. She had an £800 pair of trainers. And yet she still felt entitled. She always seemed to feel so entitled. I grew up without so much money. It shocked me. It offended me.

I said, Hannah, no. You've had enough from me. If you want this flat, you'll have to buy it yourself. And then of course there are the tears, the swearing, and finally I said, you are ungrateful. Enough is enough. No more money from me.

These girls, these days, see something online and think they can just have it, like that — [snaps fingers] — no hard work. I worked hard for what I have.

Secondly, there was the business with the profile online.

PRODUCER: Did you think it was real?

SZ: I don't know. Hannah was always a dark horse, the daughter I understood least. When she was growing up, I was afraid of her. Always so grown up, even as a child; I was always afraid of the things she might do. She had an appetite for danger. I hoped for her sake it was not real, but it did sound like her. Like my daughter. It broke my heart. I was disgusted. I said, this is where all this blogging brings you, to be accused of selling your body online? It was the last straw. I said, Hannah, I don't want you in whatever business this is. I refused to support her financially anymore, until she changed her lifestyle. It was a humiliation for me. Do you know what it is like to have your own parents ask you what your children are doing, only to find sexy pictures online? Business partners and old school friends, who took an interest in my family life, laughing behind my back at my daughter's antics. It called into question my own parenting, my own values. Hannah reflected badly on me.

PRODUCER: Did your ex-wife support the decision?

sz: To an extent, initially she did. We both wanted our daughter to rely less on us for money. But Angela was much softer on the girls. If she hadn't spoiled Hannah quite so much, it might not have been necessary. Of course, this is not exactly how she remembers it. She blamed me and we never moved past it, well, as you can see.

[Holds his right index finger up to a bare ring finger on his left hand.]

She calls me a monster. I say, I did what any parent would have done with a daughter like Hannah.

PRODUCER: Do you regret it?

sz: My regret is that I did not teach Hannah the value of hard work earlier in her life. I attempted to give her business advice, but evidently it fell on deaf ears. She never spoke to me again, and hardly to her mother, in that short time after we cut her off, before she died. I regret that, too. But ultimately, that was Hannah's choice.

The Present

In Paige and Shane's flat

"What the fuck, Paige," Shane shouts, making me jump. He holds my phone in his hand, the pads of his fingers white from the pressure of his digits on its case. It could crack. Shane's eyes are locked on mine. He's breathing in and out through his mouth, like he's about to pounce.

Shane walks towards me and shoves the phone into my chest, pushing me, sending me careering three steps backwards towards the kitchen counter. I'm nearly knocked off my feet by the controlled movement. This is a fraction of the strength Shane wields. I fall back and reach behind me, to put my hand on the counter to steady me, knocking a glass of water onto the floor.

As Shane steps closer to me amid the commotion, I step back onto glass and I yelp. Slipping on the water, I nearly tumble but Shane catches me with his hands.

"Oh baby, oh no baby," he says, changing in an instant, as he lifts me and carries me away from the glass and water, and sits me down on the sofa.

"Shane, Shane, the carpet," I squeal. He picks up a piece of Christmas wrapping and holds it under my foot to catch the blood. My blood is still pounding in my neck, and my foot, apparently.

"Oh baby, okay, hold still. I'll sort you out."

My head is spinning. My foot is throbbing. I couldn't care less. Shane could have cut my foot off. All I'm thinking about is, what has he seen on my phone? Emails and messages from the banks chasing up on me? The blackmailer? Perhaps they'd sent some evidence.

Blood is on the Christmas wrapping, blood and glass by the kitchen counter. It brings back horrible, dark memories, the ones that slip away from me as I take my pills every morning. Convulsing heart in overdrive, the claustrophobic pressure of a panic attack closing in. I'm slipping again. Shane takes a small shard of glass from the bottom of my foot. He looks up at me.

"Paige? Paige."

My heart pumps so rapidly I could lose all ten pints though my foot. I'm woozy, feeling the room compress in and expand out as my temperature rises and falls. But I can't lose consciousness. Shane moves manically around me. What has he seen?

Shane puts a cushion under my head and throws a blanket over me. I check my pulsating foot, and his hands are wrapping gauze around it. His personal trainer emergency first-aid kit is emptied on the floor beside him.

"Are you okay?" he asks, bringing his face close to mine. His breath is hot and acidic. I nod. Shane moves back and holds my leg up to stem the flow of blood.

I search his face for signs of anger. It's not the first time he's gone through my phone, my accounts. I never know what he's looking for. I'm not sure he does either. But still he looks. It's a reflex that comes naturally to hurt people, I suppose. He's never found anything of interest, till now. He massages my foot with the hand holding it up. With his other hand, he lifts my phone up and holds it a few inches from my face. His thumb trembles, a little firmer. His hand on my foot begins to squeeze.

"What's this, baby?"

I pull myself up onto my elbows and focus on the text on the screen. There they are, the words that have been haunting me.

I know what you did.

Shane is a deadly still but buzzing ball of energy, a chilling quantum fluctuation. Swallowing, I open my mouth.

"I got this email."

"I can see that," he says, still crouching on the sofa in front of me. His voice is so quiet, but his neck is thick, stiff and tense.

"It's just some mad person, Shane. You know how it is. What those people are like. I used to get them all the time."

"Yes." I flinch at his raised voice. He makes a trembling fist, composes himself. He starts again, shaking from the effort it takes to control himself. "Yes, but not recently. And not that you haven't told me about."

"I knew you would be angry because you didn't want to do the documentary, and—"

"You're fucking right I didn't. I don't want to invite all those strangers back into our lives again. I just want to go on living happily, the two of us, with none of—" He gestures with the phone hand, the other one still holding my foot and tightening like a vice, "—this anymore. I wanted to move on. But we always have to do what you want — don't we?"

He pants, mouth open, eyes wet with panic. His hands shake.

"Well, we can't move on right now, Shane. And right now, strangers are our livelihood. At least, they are how I pay for things. How I make money."

His mouth pulls in a straight grimace. It sounds like Zanna's words in my voice.

"I don't mean it like that," I say quickly.

He sighs. Nods. Puts my phone down on the sofa and rubs his temples, moving a large, barbell-calloused hand across his forehead. He realises he is squeezing my foot and lets it go, moving the hand now to run across his eyes.

"I think," he says, deliberate and quiet, "you should have told me. We should share things like this."

"I'm sorry," I breathe. "I was scared."

He shakes his head and gets up. Within moments his jacket is on and he has his gym bag over his shoulder.

The flat door swings shut behind him, and I'm alone.

*

One last interview with the documentary team before it's a wrap. I can't believe how quickly they've created this thing. A hivemind of sound engineers, camera operators, script writers, wardrobe and exec buzzes around. There's a festive mood. The wrapping of the huge project is like a present, the last day of filming. A glass of fizz or two are being enjoyed by some and even Sheryl is smiling. Of course, she would be. She's had some personal news. On Christmas Day, her boyfriend got down on one knee and presented her with an engagement ring. Interviewees and employees alike coo over it like a baby as she holds it up for them to see. It's small but perfectly formed, and she glows from within, lit from somewhere else by an antiquated display of a man's love. There's that sting and lingering irritation, a mosquito bite of jealousy.

"It's gorgeous, congratulations." I smile.

I wish I could enjoy the sequin sparkle of joy, but I'm unable. Emails, worries and bad dreams have sucked at me like Victorian creatures of the night. My appetite, gone. Any semblance of positive feelings between Shane and me, gone. He's been ignoring me since he found the email. A passive-aggressive ball of coiled energy.

I hardly sleep. I'm rail thin. And I know people are noticing. My followers, and even Tom, are telling me how good I look.

"Did you get fillers? Or Botox, or something?"

Oh no, it's this new product, it's called despair.

After wrapping on my last interview, Sheryl hands me a glass of fizz and I take it. It couldn't possibly hurt. Some of the younger staff members are on their second or third, smiling wide smiles and standing a bit closer. I find Jessica, who is also wrapping up some interviews today, speaking with two employees of the streaming platform.

"I guess there's some detective-y elements to it," one is saying. "You know, finding interviewees, researching."

"So, it's just like your job," the other jokes, gesturing at Jessica. She smiles indulgently, despite the tension in her neck and the dark round her eyes. Late nights, crime schemes, taxpayer money. It's not quite the same.

"I bet you see some wild things, though," I venture, muscling in besides Jessica.

The girl goes a little red, and her male co-worker says: "Don't mind her, she's a fan."

I smile and turn to her. She blushes, shrinks self-consciously into herself.

"I follow you," she says, sweetly. I feel a warmth towards her. "I loved Zanna."

Squeezing out my response is painful. Fighting my face to maintain the smile, wrangling my mouth. "Thank you."

She beams. I drink my fizz in one gulp and put the glass down before I break it.

"We see some wild stuff, even with this one," the male co-worker is saying.

"I bet," I say, rolling my eyes as my stomach does a similar motion. I press my sweaty hands against my jeans. It's hot in here. So many bodies.

"Oh gosh, all those obsessive true crime fanatics," the girl says, rolling her eyes too.

"Yeah, or that woman that called up saying she knew you from a while ago." He gestured at me, face red from sugary booze. "I thought that was kind of interesting, but she kept asking for money and there wasn't any budget so—"

He's elbowed by his co-worker, who blushes. Was it confidentiality about budget issues, or his implication there was something "interesting" in it?

"Trust me," Jessica says in her police voice, now thick with authority. "There is nothing 'interesting' about this case."

His voice is tinny through my ringing ears.

*

Jessica grabs me on the way out.

"Fucking get a load of that guy, Mr Honorary Detective. God, I hate people like that. Every member of the public thinks they can do my job better than me." She's red in the face with irritation.

"What a dick," I say. Meaning it. His smarmy little face saying "interesting" lingering in my mind. I wanted to slap it.

"Well, fuck 'em," she says.

She notices me biting my nails, my chest rising and falling fast, my eyes, dulled by stress, darting in their sleep-deprived, dry sockets. She's trained to notice.

"Oh Paige." She puts a comforting hand out and strokes my arm, like she did all those years ago. She's a stern, upright, solid sort of woman, used to showing curt sympathy while wearing the uniform. She's got a sure, forthright voice that's comforted many a victim, or even perpetrator, but it's still comforting. It's how I'd

216

imagine a boarding school matron or a kind Second World War army general would be, had I ever experienced anything like that.

"Don't let them get to you."

It's an instruction, and I respond like a student or an officer cadet. I stand up straighter, nod and blink away my despair, for now.

"Paige, I forgot to say last time I saw you. You mentioned getting some malicious messages."

I nod.

"If you have concerns about any of them, you can always send them to me to take a look. There are things the police can do to find out who is sending them. IP addresses, that kind of thing, technical stuff."

I thank her and say I'll think about it.

I turn her words over in my head in the paid-for taxi home, chewing on my lower lip until it bursts, tracking every turn the driver takes, counting down the seconds to get home, as I am afraid to try anything in the taxi. This driver could be anyone; he works for the documentary after all, there could be cameras.

As soon as I'm back in the flat, deserted by Shane who is still performing his act of protest, his daily walkout to the gym, coming home later, drunk and silently fuming. I search it in Google.

Find out email IP address

It's all there. Instructions on how to do it, and it's so simple. I pull my hand up to my face, laughing despite myself, tears in my eyes. I've been so stupid. Of course I couldn't ask the police for help, but I could do this. I'd never been good at the technical side of the website. All I ever concerned myself with was how to copy and paste words and pictures into boxes on blogging sites, how to use the simple Instagram interface. Had Zanna not had the cash to outsource the technical stuff, I may have known this all along.

Heart shaking in my chest like a broken tumble dryer, I take the IP address, extracted from the data in the email — a click away all this time — and paste it into a website. I click, and then it's decoded. Disbelieving, I blink at all the information in front of me. An internet service provider, the town, even the longitude and latitude.

Bordsfield South.

I know exactly who lives here. Now it all makes sense.

The Past

Two weeks after we came back from holiday, I returned to the flat after another Bella Italia lunch with Mum and Dad. These lunches were becoming fewer and further between, with less and less to say. I was surprised to find Mason in my living room, sitting on the settee as natural as anything. He smiled as we locked eyes, bold as brass, his lips curling back in a Joker smile. I froze. It didn't help my mood that I'd been in for another tense line of questioning from Mum and Dad over a personal pepperoni pizza with a soggy base. *Why wouldn't I come home for my aunt's birthday? Why, in fact, did I never come home?* I shuddered with memories of that town and the people who lived there.

Unwelcome guest Mason said, "Hey," holding up an open bottle of beer and tipping the neck towards me. It wasn't Shane's beer, because Shane didn't drink beer at all. He drank cider, if he drank, which he rarely did. He's gluten intolerant. Did Zanna ask him to bring his beer? Or did she buy it? How long had she been planning this visit? No one turns up announced with beer, do they? That's presumptuous and then some.

I asked her, when she came into my room a few minutes later, after I walked away in a timid protest of the scene unfolding in the flat.

"Mase says you weren't very friendly," she said. It was Mase now, apparently.

"Why is he here? I asked pointedly. "Did you invite him?"

"Oh no, don't be silly." She sat down on my bed next to me, ruffling my hair which was haphazardly affixed on top of my head with a rough hand, gel nails digging into my scalp. "He texted me saying he was in London and that he was coming over. It was only this morning, otherwise obviously I would have told you. Don't be angry with me." She stuck her lower lip out.

It felt convenient Mason had arrived this weekend when Shane happened to be working away at a convention. With his personal training business thriving under Zanna's social media marketing tutelage, he had been invited to a convention by a big protein powder brand in exchange for free travel and accommodation and exposure on their account. Zanna had masterminded the details, squealing, "I'm your manager now, I'll be taking a cut soon," as she snatched his phone to email the PR back on his behalf.

Zanna, still playing with my hair, said: "Look, I know Ibiza was a miscommunication and I'm sorry you got upset, but

220

Mason really likes you. He thinks you're cool. We're going to London Fields to the pub; he wants you to come and so do I. It's been a shit time with my dad and everything. Come with us. The weather is nice, let's do it!"

I still stung from the holiday, despite the fact Zanna had been sweet to me since we'd come back, probably to ensure I kept her now less fortunate financial standing to myself.

"Zanna, seriously," I said. She took her hand out of my hair as she listened, to prove she meant business. "Did something happen between you and Mason?" She shook her head in protest and I held my hand up to stop her, persisting, "And *is* something maybe going to happen?"

Zanna switched attitudes. She stiffened, then softened. She set her eyes wide, looking directly into mine and pursed her lips, painted with what I suspected to be the new Baharani Brown from Revlon sent in a pack for review yesterday morning. She then pulled them apart (I observed cakey-ness we would not mention in the glowing review) and said, "Paige, absolutely not. I have not cheated on Shane and I never would cheat on Shane, or anybody. Stop giving me such a hard time and have some fun with us."

"Look." Her voice changed. "He just turned up here, it's a bit intense. I want you with me, please?"

My pepperoni pizza lunch sat heavily in my gut. But despite the fact I didn't approve of Zanna's relationship or friendship or whatever it was with Mason, this was the first time she had addressed the argument in Ibiza so directly, and I wanted to put it behind us. It had been hugely difficult to keep up my resentment towards Zanna for the past two weeks, my life was so entwined in hers. I craved her infectious laugh and her smothering, controlling love, like before.

"Zanna." I grabbed her hand. "Do you swear?" Like a little girl tying a friendship bracelet around a wrist. "Do you swear," I said, searching deep in her wide eyes for truth, "that nothing's going to happen?"

She smiled, and half laughed in a way that said, *Paige, you're so silly.* "I swear."

"And you swear," I went on, tears prickling my eyes at how horrible the last few months had been, how far Zanna and I had careered off track, "that we're best friends?"

"Oh Paige," she said, grabbing me and pulling me in for a tight hug. "Of course we're best friends. I love you more than anything. I swear, and you can trust me, forever. Now, get in the shower and I'll find you an outfit — ten minutes."

As I dried off, eight minutes later, Zanna smiled holding up the ensemble.

"You'll look great in this, because you have nice small boobs," she said.

Within twenty I was dressed, sitting on the Overground on the way out with Zanna and "Mase". It was three o'clock, and a mature yet mellow Cathedral City sun beamed into the carriage, creating dusty spotlights.

Shifting about in the scratchy, uncomfortable seats of the train, the tight crotch of the shorts let me know I'd made a mistake. The sweat on my inner thighs made them stick together, if I peeled my legs apart it would make a sound.

Zanna made every effort she could to bring me into the conversation, and Mason nodded at every word I said, replying enthusiastically with a, "That's sick, man."

It turned out Mason and I had more in common than I'd supposed originally, and certainly more in common than he did with Zanna. I learned this as we sat on a sun-soaked bench table in a pub garden surrounded by beautiful young people, the kinds that committed to normcore because they look best when their natural, healthy beauty is undiluted by the frippery of fashion. Mason wrote poetry. He liked Jack Kerouac and "Having a Coke with You" by Frank O'Hara. He hadn't read any Sylvia Plath.

Zanna zoned out of these conversations in a rude manner, but at least it was honest. She was not one to waste time trifling in matters she had no interest in. She slumped forwards on the bench, tanned arms propping up her head, heavy with boredom. Her breasts fell out of her sundress a little, one of those cheap wrap dresses with floaty sleeves and a ruffle around the hem. Layers of delicate gold bracelets dangled around her forearm and she held her phone to her face, listlessly scrolling through

Instagram and drinking with more than her normal gusto. Since the holiday, though, she had been drinking more, I noticed. Shane noticed too, wordlessly watching her bring home a bottle of wine every night.

"Guys, stop this lame talk. Unless it's Ariana Grande, I'm not interested. Things don't become inherently good just because they're old, you know. And you aren't cool for not engaging in the zeitgeist."

She sat up and put an arm around Mason, pulling him in around the neck, their bodies still apart. He stared down at her chest in the dress.

"I would like a margarita," she said, gazing deep into his eyes like a fake hypnotist.

He laughed. "Alright, this round is on me — again — but next time one of you is getting it. Paige, what do you want?"

"Erm, a white wine? A white wine spritzer, please."

"Coming up."

We let the sun go down, ignoring its pleas for attention as it lingered on the horizon, throwing pink and orange shades into the sky. Conversation had become increasingly silly and I had warmed to Mason. Where there'd been an aggressive poser before, now there was someone else.

Zanna said to me, as we went to the loo together, "You and Mason are getting on, aren't you?"

"Yeah, he's nice." But he was no Shane.

After hammering through three pints and ordering a whis-key, Mason was running his fingers around the rim of the glass and telling us how he grew up with his father in jail.

"Dealing drugs and aggravated robbery, but that last one was bullshit. He was just asking a guy for his money. He had a knuckle duster, but it wasn't even in his hand. The police wanted to put him away for as long as possible because he was a troublemaker, like me."

He nudged Zanna with an elbow and gave me a wicked smile. We both giggled. Find me a middle-class woman who doesn't swoon at romantic notions of petty street crime. He went on.

"My mum, she was involved, kind of. She hid drugs and she had guys over sometimes, who were involved. I took my first ecstasy pill when my brother and I found them in my mum's bedside table. We knew what they were and what they did because we'd seen Mum and Dad take them before."

"How old were you?" I asked.

"Eleven."

"Oh my God," I exhaled.

"Smoked my first spliff with my dad aged ten. Mum has a lot of stolen jewellery," he went on, ignoring my breathy outburst. He sensed it excited Zanna. "A whole hoard. Diamonds worth loads."

He spread his tanned arms out across the back of the bench. Alpha. Potent.

"Oh, I want to try them on!" Zanna cooed.

"Can't say you'd fit in round my ends," he said, smiling at her warmly. "You on the other hand," he added, turning to me, "a life of crime is right up your street, I reckon."

I swallowed, self-consciously.

"So, why did you leave Manchester then?" I asked.

"Crazy ex-girlfriend," he replied, smiling wolfishly and running his hand through messy hair that erred on the right side of tangled. "Tale as old as time. She got obsessed. Wouldn't leave me alone. So I had to skip town."

Zanna sighed. "Urgh, I hate girls like that. So pathetic."

We were shivering when we finally ordered an Uber back to the flat.

I lay in bed, drunk, legs and feet alight with tingly static, zipping from my toes through my thighs. Creamy silver moonlight mingled with the amber glow from streetlamps like the few bodies left entangled on London Fields as we departed. It was as quiet as East London gets, the whir of a passing car, the occasional whoop of a late-night drinker under the window, the buzz of a number of sirens far away.

I imagined Mason opening the door to my room, the slow creak of the hinge and his curls filling the space between the door and the frame. His taut, muscular, lizard-like body next to mine between the sheets. I imagined kissing him, his hard body and harsh language both softening. But then I thought of Shane, and my stomach filled with something else, more consuming, more painful, gentler than simple lust. The creaking went on. I lifted my head off the pillow. It wasn't in my imagination. Something was happening outside my bedroom door. Soundless as a reflection, I made my way across the room and opened the door, holding my breath. There was more irregular creaking. I stood in the sliver-crack of my door. Our main room was lit by an eerie mix of silver, amber light, both moon and street. It lit Zanna's hands in Mason's hair as she straddled him on the sofa, bouncing in his lap and they both quietly gasped.

*

I woke the next morning, head hot and pounding as usual after copious drinks, blood running cold. Mason tucked into a plate of huevos rancheros whipped up by Zanna. She stood at the hob, wearing tiny, skintight workout shorts and a large white T-shirt tied in a knot above her belly button, one of those cute ones that is pulled into a perfect fleshy circle by the taut skin on her stomach. She fried more chorizo and poached an egg.

"This is for you, sleepy head," she cooed as I entered.

I shook my head, glancing over at the sofa, flashing back to last night. It turned my stomach.

"Aw, hungover?" Zanna asked, smiling. "Maybe later."

She shimmered, radiating a good mood. Mason grinned as he chewed avocado and crunched toast. Her words resounded in my head, repeating on me.

"Of course we're best friends. I love you more than anything. I swear, and you can trust me, forever."

She had sworn to me, and she'd lied. *Could I trust her? Could I ever trust her?* I stayed in my room until Mason left. Then I stayed there longer, even as Zanna knocked on my door.

"Want to watch a movie?" she asked, voice cherry sweet.

"I feel sick," I croaked.

"Why have we got beer?" sweetly incredulous Shane asked on Monday evening when he came home. I heard him from my room where I sat sorting through some bags of clothes we'd been sent.

"They're Paige's," I heard Zanna reply.

From then on, not only did I come to not trust her — I came to hate her.

*

I dated other men despite having fallen in love with Shane, seamlessly, easily, thoughtlessly. It's amazing how healthy your relationships are when you aren't at all emotionally invested in them. I marvelled at it. Before I met Zanna, and therefore Shane, I was constantly searching and consistently failing to find a man who was interested in me beyond a string of dates and a couple of nights together. Each time was like clockwork. A few heady dates where I would nervously tug at hems, tuck hair behind my ear, giggle at lame jokes I would genuinely find hilarious and overdrink, allowing myself to enter that place between blushed and flushed; tickled pink, they'd call it.

Kissing in the Tube was always a favourite moment, my back against the wall of the Northern Line station at Old Street. Their mouth against mine, their backs to the Tubes that we'd allow to go past. Many different men, the same dates. The same sex. The same slow petering of the text messages, so much like clockwork it didn't even hurt anymore.

All that changed after my heart was committed to Shane. The texts didn't slowly dwindle away to nothing like water from a dripping tap. Men know when women couldn't care less for them, and they like it. I learned no man wants to date a woman who is grateful to have him, especially when the biggest compliment one man can pay another is to imply the woman he's with is too good for him. All the men I've met ascribe to the Marx manifesto, Groucho, not Karl.

I don't want to belong to any club that will accept me as a member.

Or:

I don't want to belong to any woman who will accept my member (or not straight away at least).

The change in me was marked too. Without desperately wanting approval, I was given it without question. I dated a few men that summer, sometimes overlapping. A history lecturer at King's with red hair, who wore desert boots and made references I never understood. I was sure he knew this, but I didn't care enough to ask what he meant, and he didn't care enough to check I understood.

Another, a "musician" and "poet", lived in Highbury and took me to pubs in London where everyone was beautiful and more people spoke German or French than with a regional British accent. His godfather was Nick Cave and his dad was a TV producer. He lived in a maisonette inherited from his grandparents. Had I loved this man, I would have wanted everything about him to change. Mostly the way he spoke over everyone else, including me. As it was, I could smile blithely through it all, letting irritation wash over me, like the prosecco washing over my tongue.

That, at least, was the situation unfurling when Zanna encouraged me to invite a date to Shane's birthday party. Then she implied maybe I wouldn't be able to get one, and so I brought Mr Highbury along. She was throwing a "cocktail soirée" in honour of Shane's birthday at the flat. That's what she was calling it in the Facebook event she had created for it and the WhatsApp invitation where she coordinated plans like Anna Wintour for the Met Gala, held a few weeks after the night of Mason's sleepover.

A collection of her friends — not Shane's — were on the unofficial organising committee. Membership was by appointment and non-negotiable, a mafioso style of party planning.

You come into my flat on the day of my boyfriend's cocktail soirée . . .

Gianna came early, allegedly to help with party prep, although she leaned against the kitchen worktop, touching up her makeup in the reflection on her iPhone screen and telling us about her boyfriend who'd be coming along later as we worked around her. They'd not been together very long, but it was moving fast, propelled solely by Gianna, by the sounds of it.

"I've asked when I can meet his mum but he's not sure. I'm thinking of dropping round with his jumper so then I have to meet her."

I wondered why Gianna's boyfriend, in his early thirties, lived with his mother as I put liquor on the counter. Jägermeister, Tanqueray and Bacardi, a number of Shane's favourite drinks. I didn't ask, though. I didn't care.

Zanna put some crisps in bowls. Carefully premade nibbles, blinis with smoked salmon and mini Scotch eggs, were on plates in the fridge ready for guests. She'd tidied. She'd hoovered the sofa, leaning over the cushions where Mason's naked buttocks and her knees had been. Did she feel any shame? Huge helium-filled balloons, the number thirty-two, danced around held in place by string tied to weights. They swivelled back and forwards, never quite staying the right way round. Zanna would move across the room and set them right, they had to be right for the pictures, only for them to move back again.

She was wearing a white slip dress with nude strappy heels. I was wearing a backless funnel-neck jersey dress that fell to mid-calf, with black sandals tying around the ankle.

"Oh yes, you look fucking amazing," Zanna gushed when I came out of my room. I smiled, forcing my face so it gave me a cramp.

Since *that night* she'd been sweeter than pie. I'd been full of an unstemmable flow of hatred. Hatred for her, hatred for Mason. Hatred for the way she betrayed Shane, and lied to me.

I couldn't imagine how she'd respond if she knew I was dressing myself for the benefit of her partner. Of course, she believed it was for my date's benefit, as would anyone else, including the birthday boy himself.

In fact, Zanna was more excited to meet my date than I was to spend time with him. But I didn't see the harm in inviting him, letting him bounce jovially around the room. It'd be entertaining to witness middle-class Zanna come up against someone of such an aspirational background. He was the type of person born with a free glass of fizz in their hand. Wrinkled and covered in blood and waxy stuff, he would have been offered a tea-stained egg and liver foam canapé. Later, after Shane had come home from the gym, showered and changed, we — Zanna, Gianna, Shane and I — waited for Mr Highbury to arrive at the flat. Shane said, "Have to check this guy's good enough for our Paige."

He said it like a joke, but I saw his muscular chest puff out like a cockatoo. If he had a feather on his head, it would have been pointing skyward. It was like someone had dropped an effervescent vitamin C tablet in my stomach. Little things like this let me know everything I needed to. No matter what Zanna said about Shane not being my friend, he cared about me, more than she was willing to accept.

Guests arrived in dribs and drabs, some of Shane's gym friends who wore everything a little tight and sported shaved chests beneath V-neck T-shirts, Tom the agent. With each ring of the doorbell, Zanna looked excitedly at me. When Mr Highbury arrived, he said, "You look amazing," and kissed me on the mouth.

I turned to Zanna, his hand still on my face and said, "Well, here he is."

I let him talk Zanna's ear off, as she nodded with rapture at every word he said. If I didn't hope it would work out in my favour, I'd be suspicious she was trying to flirt. I barely spoke as the two effused together, before Zanna clapped her hands and said "Presents!" I grabbed the rectangular item I had wrapped for Shane in blue paper with a green ribbon from the desk in my room. Inside sat a beautiful, sleek navy diary from Smythson with the year ahead in it. Personalised with his name, "S. SEACOLE", it cost £80, above and beyond what was necessary or expected. My grip on it was feather light, so my fingers couldn't soil the paper, as I waited for when I was called forward to present the gift. As I handed it over and Shane slipped the ribbon off and gently tore the paper, he pulled out the book and smiled at me.

"Paige, wow, thanks, it's lovely. Look, it has my name!" He held it up to some of the boys standing by his shoulder and they said "Ooh" appreciatively.

"That's quality, that is, mate," one of them said, and my cheeks heated. When I locked eyes with Zanna, she was looking at me strangely.

"It's for all your new PT clients," I said, and Shane nodded at this appreciatively.

"You remembered." A wide smile crinkled the skin around his eyes. "I said I wanted something like this ages ago, it's mint that you thought of it."

We looked at one another. I was compelled to step forward and wrap my arms around him.

Zanna took the book and put it on the table where other presents, mostly vouchers or alcohol, had been placed. "It's lovely," she said. "Such good quality. I think most people settle for Google Calendar these days but this is very sweet. Who's next?"

Another present was passed forwards by one of Shane's gym friends. It turned out to be a pack of novelty miniature condoms.

Zanna grimaced as the group of men jumped, bellowed with laughter and slapped each other on the back, risking sending the now served blinis clattering to the floor from the side table. She pulled it together though for her present, to be handed over last, topping the bill. With a coy smile she handed over a gold envelope to him. The guests waited in hushed silence. Gianna was filming, ready to capture Shane's reaction on her phone as Zanna had asked. He pulled two tickets out of the envelope and narrowed his eyes to read them.

"Las Vegas," he said with a gasp, which went around the room. "Oh my word, babe. This is amazing." He stared at the tickets, a huge smile across his face.

"All expenses paid, five nights," Zanna announced to the room, more than to Shane.

"How did you afford this?" he asked. She shrugged coyly. I couldn't understand how she had afforded it either. Since Santiago had cut her off, she had told me we would be tightening our belts, that any raise was off the cards. My skin stung with betrayal. Zanna in her white dress, and Shane showing the tickets to Las Vegas to a friend. I had a queasy feeling. She looked bridal. The idea of Zanna leading Shane down the aisle like a lamb to slaughter, I couldn't stand it.

After the excitement of gifts died down, Zanna pulled me to the toilet with her. "Shane's going to get annoyed if he thinks you're doing coke, you know," I said.

Zanna ignored me and said, "He's really nice, Paige."

"Mmm?" She meant Mr Highbury. My mind was still on Shane. When wasn't it?

"Yeah! He's over six foot and his family's rich. He's a great catch."

"Mmm."

Zanna pulled her dress up and peed. She wasn't wearing underwear. In the mirror I picked some flecks of mascara from where they had fallen on my cheeks.

"What do you think?" she pressed me, a twang of irritation in her tone.

"I don't know. Don't you think he's kind of annoying?"

"Shhh," she chided me, "what if he's walking past the door? And no, actually, I think he's fun, chatty! And he's interested in you. He seems really keen."

"He doesn't work, though. Like, not properly."

"That's great! If he's rich enough not to work, that means he's really rich. That's the only proper kind of rich there is. I'm jealous."

She wiped, contorting her arm behind her as she wiped front to back, before standing and flushing too. She jostled me out of the way to wash her hands and turned, putting a still damp palm on my arm.

"Paige, tell me you are going to give this one a chance."

"What do you mean?"

"You know what I mean. You date so many eligible guys and you never give them the time of day. I don't get it. I want you to get a boyfriend and be happy."

"Who needs boyfriends?"

"Paige, the three of us can't all live together forever. Shane and I are going to buy together soon. What will you do then?"

My stomach dropped. "You're buying soon? How soon?"

I was hot. You could fry an egg on my forehead. I put my hand on the sink, the cold porcelain like an ice cube.

I was dazed. "Zanna, hang on a minute."

She turned back.

"Oh by the way," she said, "it was so cute of you to spend all that money on a little present for Shane, but honestly, I wouldn't bother. He wouldn't do the same for you. Save your money."

She unlocked the door and strutted out into the busy hallway, now humming with all the expected guests. "Cake!" she called, a little cheer going up among the crowd.

My head spun. I couldn't stomach cake. Zanna was planning to move out with Shane, despite all this with Mason, despite the fact she was cheating. She was going to take Shane away from me now, leave me with nowhere to live. Desperation made its way through me like a hot rash. I felt the bodies at the party rushing past me in the blur, while I stayed fixed in place, processing it all. How would I afford to live without splitting the rent? Where could I go? I couldn't let this happen. I had to do something.

*

I woke in the arms of my date, but my mind was in the other room, where Zanna and Shane were. After a nightcap, we'd separated to our own rooms, me like a puppy being led away from its mother and littermates. After a passionless session of morning lovemaking, at least on my part, my guest and I headed to the kitchen, where Zanna was up to her usual displays of culinary expertise, like whenever we had a guest in the house. Always a proud host, watching guests enjoy their food with an almost psychotic attention and air of victory. Oddly determined to excel domestically.

On that morning she had cut fresh avocados and fanned them out, with smoked salmon and capers on sourdough. She beamed at us, and Shane smiled too. My heart burned. I ate my slices of creamy avocado but tasted ash. Through a shell-shocked ringing in my ears, Zanna and Mr Highbury were chatting away.

"So what exactly is the set-up with you two working together?" he asked, fascinated by all aspects of blogging, as most were when you met them. *So you just post pictures and get paid? How much do you make?* Young men like Mr Highbury in particular, incredulous and a little hostile to the idea of women making money in this unconventional way.

"Oh it's great. Paige is the best little employee," Zanna said, "couldn't have built my empire without her as my assistant."

"Zanna," I asked a few days later, "do you think I could be credited somewhere for the blog? You know, since you said you couldn't have built it without me."

There was nothing to link any of it to me. Not on the blog, not on Instagram. While most of the ideas were mine, the words were mine — tens of thousands of words, all mine — there was no evidence. I would need that evidence to get a job, if I was to rent another place of my own.

She turned to me, brow furrowed. Her hair was swept in a bun, slick wet with coconut oil. She was wearing a sheet mask, and the wet tissue kept slipping down. She was never not attending to some part of her beauty. She cocked her head to the side. "What do you mean?"

"Well, like." I'd rehearsed what I wanted to ask, but stumbled over the words regardless. I rested my sweating hands on the keyboard of my MacBook Air, by far the most expensive thing I'd ever bought myself, paid for with the wages Zanna was paying me. I'd never had a raise since the blog was founded. I'd never even asked for one. A labour of love, it was, for the lifestyle it gave me access to, for the glamour and beauty, for writing itself, and for Zanna, of course. But some love wears thin.

I pushed on. "I was just wondering if the words could be attributed to me somewhere on the website. Like on the about page, or something. So people know it's me."

Zanna smiled, but shook her head. "That's not how it works, stupid. Ghostwriters don't get named credit."

She looked back to her phone screen and kept scrolling through the *Mail Online* website. I was dismissed.

"I wonder," the words squeaked out. It was a cheek to push it and pushing Zanna on anything made my heart beat faster, "how is anyone going to know it's my work?"

"Paige, listen, I'm the brand, okay? Me. It's about me. People come to the page for me, they are interested in me. It's Life of Zanna, okay? Not, Life of Zanna and some person called Paige who no one's ever heard of. You're like my shadow, okay. You're like the swan's feet under the water. No one sees you. No one knows you're there. They're not supposed to. No one ever sees you. So why would you get a credit? It's Life of Zanna. Just Zanna. Just me.

"You want to do Life of Paige, go ahead, good luck. But I think you know you need me, so drop it."

I stared at the back of her head as she scrolled through Net-a-Porter, through bags, stopping to enlarge images of huge black holdalls. Pain and rejection twisted into hate projected onto every fine, shining strand. There it was again, that smarting sting and bitter mouth taste. She wasn't the Zanna I knew anymore, my Zanna, who took me under her wing, gave me her new dresses, told me her secrets, said I was beautiful, that I was a writer, that I'd do anything I wanted, that I was going to make it. She had turned off her warm, radiating love glow, the one that held you, supported you, made you worthy.

I stared at her back, the only part of her I knew these days. She was leaving me, moving away from me. The rejection seared and blistered my heart. The pain expanded with every beat, a billowing mushroom cloud of blood in water. Hot. Red. Simple. It called for action. It called for justice.

The Present

A suburban Birmingham home

"Alright, Pooh Bear," she says, on the doorstep. The "r" is slightly rolled, the "t" is sharp as a pin prick. I'm back in Brum, no doubt. I depress an involuntary shudder.

However well my mother claimed Talia was doing as an estate agent all those years ago, she clearly wasn't doing well now. Once a pretty girl, with a turned-up nose and a sweet, chipmunk-like grin, now she's gaunt. Chipmunk cheeks chiselled out. Her hair is pulled back off her makeup-less face and the sore pink of picked spots sets a path across her pallid cheeks. But she clearly still remembered the name my mother called me when she played round my house, and then even later at the school gate. She and Sophia had mocked me with it. Mocked me and my slightly round tummy in my school uniform. *Paigey Poo*, it quickly became. *Pooey Paige*. Stupid, but still cruel.

"I tracked the IP address of the email."

She nods. "Well, I suppose you had to work out it was me at some point."

I nod too. She lingers on the door and I shiver, exposed outside this squat, square, pebbledashed house, built within a finger's length of the other in this overcrowded estate. Clapped-out cars in overgrown front gardens, children's toys discarded there so long they were becoming a part of the soil.

"Well, want to come in, then?"

She sighs, her words full of frost and distaste, as though I'm the imposition here.

"Yeah, I guess."

Behind Talia, a narrow corridor with threadbare carpet stairs is adorned with sad, plasticky tinsel, sellotaped to the wall, now a memorial to Christmas, two days behind us. She leads me to a kitchen bathed with sallow light through an open back door. Cigarette smoke leaks from a fag recently dispatched on the doorstep. It's stale here, through and through.

Talia was my old school friend, till she wasn't. It had been a difficult time for me at school, because of girls like Talia. Pretty, popular ones. I've always felt a twinge of pain when I've thought back to those times. Talia, or Tee-Tee, or Lia, as I called her at the time, has changed beyond recognition before my eyes. Formerly a high-school babe in a rolled-over skirt, butterfly clips in her honey hair, this woman in an aged, once-white tracksuit in front of me is an anaemic husk of the girl I remembered — like a tick has buried into her, sucking her life force away. Thin, dry lips, rough skin with spots both spent, crusting, and fresh, red and shiny, dappling her chin. She scratches at her flaking scalp, white under hair straining in a tight ponytail. I wonder, do I look different to her too? Sat either side of a table that has turned since our youth, I am the pretty one, with my deep-conditioned hair, my expensive makeup, my designer clothes.

Talia's blue eyes are filmy, yellow round the irises. Cigarette stained, maybe. Colourless and emotionless. I wait, in nauseous head-spin, for something to happen. She gestures to a chair, one of two opposite a tiny kitchen table. I sit in a cold, hard chair furthest away from the open door, letting in the cold air, so I'm wedged between the table and a washing machine that is whirring. Talia doesn't notice the cold, even though her thin fingers with yellowing nails are mottled in various shades of red and blue.

"Nice of you to visit," she says, with mocking smile and laughing intonation; it rises at the end like mine used to.

She smiles, exposing teeth the same ashy colour as the whites of her eyes, and it's horrible. She sits down opposite me.

"Talia, what is going on, why are you emailing me like this?"

"Hark at that," she says, pulling another cigarette from the packet on the table and lighting it. She doesn't ask me if I mind. I guess we aren't dealing in pleasantries here. "You don't sound Brummie at all anymore. Wouldn't even know you were from here."

I shrug, unsure what to say.

"Not got much to say to your old school friend?" She laughs again, putting the cigarette in one side of her mouth and dragging on it, eyes fixed on me.

"Why are you emailing me all this shit?" I ask, the stress and worry clear in my voice.

She laughs. Chuckles, skinny shoulders in a men's grey hoodie bouncing.

"Ah man," she says, wiping her eyes. "It was funny." *Fun-nay.*

It was a game, like the bullying games at school. I was that fifteen-year-old all over again. A powerless plaything, a stray kitten being kicked by thugs. This is like a nightmare. I'm so cold deep down to my marrow, and not simply because the back door is letting in the December climate.

"Well," she goes on in her speech like a Bond villain. "At first, anyway."

The way she's looking at me, like a street fox eyeing a caged canary through a window. "But then I saw the story in the papers a few days later. Doing a documentary, are we?"

It gets even colder.

"About a friend that died?" She flicks ash from the end of her cigarette into an empty plastic Coke bottle on the table. Some of it misses and floats down into the waxy, cheap tablecloth. She licks her front teeth, eyes on me, and then leans back in her chair. "Interesting."

There's that word again.

"You know," she says, after a deep inhale. "It's been sixteen years since she died?"

We lock eyes. She taps her cigarette again.

"I know." My voice is so thin. It's a lie. I didn't know. In fact, I'd pushed it to the very back of my mind. That school business all those years ago. I'd moved on, and never looked back except by accident, even then closing my eyes and keeping it out. Now, in the shock of remembering, I can feel my face flushing.

"You didn't have a clue, did you? God, you are self-involved. Well, you should know." *Tap tap* on the top of the Coke bottle, more flakes of ash in the air. "You killed her."

I blink. Shake my head. My hands are shaking too, from more than the cold.

"You made Sophia kill herself," Talia says.

"I did not *make* her kill herself."

"Oh, but you did."

She sings it, confident and sadistic.

"I did not. I had nothing to do with what happened. It was tragic. I was as devastated as anyone else."

Talia scoffs.

"What does this have to do," I say, "with you harassing me? All that what happened with Sophia—"

Jesus, I'm slipping back into the dialect.

"Which was horrific and tragic—"

247

Talia rolls her eyes.

"Is in the past. So why are you emailing me now? It's a crime, you know. It's called electronic harassment. I could go to the police."

"You know, I think about it every year, on the anniversary. Go to her grave. And this year it just got me thinking, sixteen years. Her whole life span again. And it seemed suddenly so short to me. Things change over that period of time. I got a new perspective. It made me realise even more so what you'd done. And I looked at your Instagram, and your life. One you don't deserve, and I don't know why but I just wanted to mess with you. So I sent the first email. It was a surprise to see your name in the news a few days later. A documentary about that Zanna."

She toked on her cigarette and itched at the side of her neck.

"A pretty lucky coincidence, I thought. I rang the documentary company. Thought they might want my intel, for a little bit of cash, like."

So it was her, the caller the young employee of the producers had mentioned.

"Didn't seem to want to listen to me. Maybe it's the accent. Maybe they don't think a person like me has anything of value to say. Maybe they think I'm mad. But I'm not mad. Am I, Paige? I know what you are."

I swallow. "Maybe you ought to listen to them. If they think you are being unreasonable, I imagine the police will think you are too, when I go to them about this ridiculous harassment."

"You see, Paige," she draws out my name like parents and school friends used to do. "I don't think you will go to the police. Because if you were going to, you'd have done it already."

When I don't respond, she smiles.

"I'm betting you've got some more skeletons in your closet. That would be just like you, Paige. Maybe something to do with your pal Zanna?"

Again, I say nothing. She laughs.

"When you replied to my email, asking for — who was it — a Gianna? I knew there were something more. Oh Paige, what have you done now?"

I'm not debating this with her. So, I get to the point.

"What do you want?"

"I need money," she says. *Mon-ay*. "You've got some."

I shake my head, but she interrupts me before I reply that I don't, in fact, have much money at all. I have negative money, in fact. Who'd have thought we had something in common. Our key difference, I suspect, unsettlingly, is that Talia has much less to lose than I do.

"Don't fuck around with me, Paige. Look at your designer bag, look at your hair."

"Don't you work at the estate agent?" I ask, curious, more than anything. How do things change so much for someone?

She shakes her head.

"I can't work. I've got chronic illness," she says.

"What illness?"

She's glacial and hostile, pursing her lips. "A chronic one."

She pauses. Then, "How 'bout this. You give me five grand, and I won't go to the papers about Sophia, or this visit, for that matter. How's it going to look when they print that you had another girl die, linked to you? And that you came here to talk it all through? I think the papers will be rather interested in that, after the big documentary and all that. And what might that provoke? Think the police would be interested to know you took those emails seriously? Thought they were about your pal Zanna? Came all the way here, instead of reporting them? Oh, they'll know you had something to hide. And then they won't be paying you to post pictures of shit anymore."

My stomach sinks. If I'd not been so concerned with tracking down the sender of the email, I wouldn't be here, giving justification to its accusation. Eyeing the heavy ashtray on the table between us, I imagine grasping it, its cool heft in my hand, bringing it down on Talia's flaky scalp until it's a bloody scalp. It'd bring colour to this kitchen. But no. I'm not the violent type. I'm not a murderer. I'm not about to start now.

250

A pregnant pause between us, and then, at this moment, a baby begins to cry upstairs. It's then I notice the baby bottle by the sink, near to where an empty pack of a fags, a lighter and a quarter bottle of vodka linger on the counter by the kitchen door.

Talia's "new perspective"? A baby. A child to look after, a child, like Sophia was.

Talia sighs and rubs her eyes, the sleeves of her too-big hoodie falling down, and she stretches. It's obvious, I can't believe I didn't put the pieces together before. No wonder Talia needs money. How different our lives have become. Can I say I wouldn't do the same?

The Past

Zanna had been making a lot of bad choices lately. Shane and I were in danger of becoming her victims, victims of her reckless, selfish decisions. He would lose his love, I would lose my livelihood and lifestyle, all because of Zanna. What gave her the right to make fools out of both of us? So, I decided I would expose her affair. I'd meted out justice before, and I'd do it again. If I lost everything too, I reasoned, at least she would lose Shane.

Espionage, then. I used the same old method I'd used before, with Sophia. Rudimentary hacking. It wasn't hard. Zanna was so sure she was safe, that she had nothing to hide from me, regardless of how badly she treated me. Well, despite her obvious beliefs, I was not defanged. I knew Zanna's password. It wasn't hard to piece together after a few glances over her shoulder. *Ch4n3l5*. Basic as fuck. Zanna left her Mac on her bed. I covered my hands with my jumper to gently take it and prise it open. You can't be too careful.

I went for the good stuff straight away. WhatsApp messages. No, no. Archived WhatsApp messages. That's where the juice would be. Guilty people like to hide things away. And there they were, Zanna's shames, in order of last opened. Of course, Mason's name appeared. The last chain of messages to be deleted were from him. His last message, not what I expected.

He'd written: *I love you*

Resentment, negroni-bitter, caused my lip to curl. What was it with this woman? She made everyone fall in love with her. It was unfair. All so damn unfair. As I scrolled through the messages, their relationship came to life backwards — unfurling passion in reverse. The beginning was sweet, the end so sour. As it turned out, they had slept together in Ibiza.

And she had sent the first message.

Thanks for everything — and making me forget the world for a moment.

Major eye roll. Oh yes, Zanna and her appalling "world". What was she running from? Only the love of a good man and a devoted friend.

Perhaps she had meant for it to end there. But Mason clearly had not. He responded. And then responded again. Soon he charmed her with flattery, of her face, her body. Flattery never failed when it came to Zanna. She rewarded him with pictures of that body, explicit pictures that shocked even me. She held a phone in her hand for a selfie, leaning over in front of the

254

mirror, exposing her back end and looking over her shoulder. Shaved pudenda on show. My stomach lurched at the images, to which he responded with requisite aubergine emojis. He sent a picture of his own genitals, unappealing and unhygienic above what looked like a public toilet floor. I shuddered.

He had invited himself to London after all, like Zanna had said.

I'm right by your place. Let's hang out. Don't let me go back without having seen you, he wrote.

Okay. Don't tell Paige though. About us. She doesn't know.

It stuck in my craw. The idea of Zanna keeping something from me so overtly, though she had already lied to me. To see her write it out like that. Betraying me.

So, they'd slept together that night, most likely at the salt flats. I'd always suspected it.

Last night was amazing. I want to see you soon, Mason had sent, shortly after he'd left.

She'd tried to let him down gently. First in the polite way. The pauses between texts lengthening, the length of her responses shortening. Like a lot of men, Mason carried on belligerently. Resorted to sending explicit messages in an attempt to get a response.

I miss you sexy.

I want you.

I want to . . .

He described some heinous sex acts I can't bear to name. Zanna eventually responded:

My boyfriend and I have decided to try and make it work. I'm sorry, we need to end whatever this was between us.

This enraged him.

You're back with that asshole? The one who treats you like shit? Shouts at you and pushes you around? What the fuck?

You led me on. I love you. You used me.

How would that psycho boyfriend of yours feel if those pictures you sent me got around? The pictures I have of you (. . .) on my phone. How about that?

He described another intimate act in terms too rude to repeat. She responded:

Do you really have pictures of me?

He sent one, as described. I saw his chiselled torso, her head of shining, onyx black hair and his hand on it, swallow tattoo and all.

Oh my God, Mason, what the fuck? Delete those!

He responded.

Why should I?

Zanna changed tack.

Okay, I'll meet you. I want to see you. Come over tonight. Shane's at a convention. I'll work a way around Paige.

I checked the date on the messages. Tonight was *tonight*. My head swam, woozy. It was a lot to process. Zanna had slept with

Mason, and he had taken photos without her knowledge. Now he was blackmailing her. My heart sank. Regardless of the way she had treated me, I pitied her. My fists curled into a ball thinking about it.

Next, I searched for my own name, in Zanna's messages. Call me conceited, but I couldn't help it. Who doesn't want to know what is being said about them? My so-called friend and boss had been discussing me in messages to her mother and to Gianna. Hot, red prickle panic rose from my chest to my neck and around my ears as I read them, followed by fizzing outrage.

She's so weird, Zanna had written about me to Gianna. *She's obsessed with Shane. I'll be pleased when we've moved out and I don't have to deal with her anymore. She wants to be me. Maybe she's in love with me. The fucking freak.*

Like a dagger to the heart. But the messages to her mother were worse again.

Zanna: *I'm firing Paige as soon as we've moved out. She's getting way too much. Maybe I need someone more professional who'll get it, and won't keep asking about credit. Someone with a degree. I'm going to hire properly, you know.*

Angela: *Okay darling. Your father knows an employment lawyer you can speak to, make sure there's no legal issue.*

I blinked away tears called to my eyes by shock and indignation, rather than sorrow. My hands shook, the taste in my mouth was bitter. The world whooshed around like a washing machine and I had to catch myself on the floor to prevent my fall. An implosion of wrath knocked me reeling, physically, mentally. Blind rage saw Zanna and mine's past flash before my eyes. As she'd held me and told me to throw away my university degree to support her business. Abandon it all for a job as her lackey. Discard my own future to be the woman behind the words she would claim as her own.

She had promised "they'll hire you in an instant" as she pried me away from my hard-won university place. Well, none of the job applications I had fired off since Zanna had refused to credit me for my work — and had unceremoniously told me I'd soon be homeless at Shane's birthday party — had been responded to instantly. They hadn't been responded to at all. I was not surprised: the job applications asked for experience I didn't have for any position that paid what I needed to stay in the lifestyle I had become accustomed to, which I had helped to fund with my words. Now that same so-called friend planned to fire me. Zanna would leave me with absolutely nothing. I blinked through livid tears. And then I caught myself.

Perhaps it didn't have to be this way. Zanna was under stress. She'd been cut off, blackmailed, in a tailspin. Drinking, sleeping around. Thinking of firing me. All bad decisions. I could be, once again, that support she needed, when no one else believed in the blog, the website. And I'd save myself and my job in the process.

Either way, I needed insurance. I went to forward the messages to myself, and then I stopped. I couldn't leave a digital paper trail for Zanna to discover and give her a legitimate reason to fire me. I took pictures of the conversation on my own phone. Click, scroll, click, scroll, click, scroll. Then I sat on the sofa, where so many movie nights, face masks, popcorn and nail-painting sessions had taken place, now defiled by Mason and Zanna's indiscretion. What to do next. My flesh tingled.

This is where Zanna found me, when she walked through the door smiling, carrying shopping bags, looking like a million dollars. She couldn't distract me from the pain behind the smile and panic behind the purchases. No wonder she'd been drinking so much, seeing more of Gianna and staying out late. Stressed, living under duress, losing her father's money — and acceptance — made her fragile, vulnerable to bad ideas and outside influences.

I smiled, fawned over the new purchases she showed me from her bag, holding them up to me like a child bringing toys to its parent, hoping for approval, and admiration, her major vice, her one addiction. We smiled and laughed, a little bit like old times. I even asked how the flat hunt was going, for the home she intended to take Shane away to.

"Oh fuck, Paige, this one is in the wrong size." She held up a shirt. "It's a six but I want an eight. Oh balls. Paige, would you mind going to return it tonight? I want to shoot it tomorrow. Please! I'll let you keep it after if you do."

She was trying to get me out of the house to sort things out with Mason. Her eye twitched. It hurt to see her like this. I wanted to reach out and hold her, soothe her. Make her my Zanna again. I really tried.

"Zanna, I'm worried about you." My voice was cashmere-jumper soft.

She started a little and blinked at me. If her forehead could have creased, it would have.

"Zanna. I know about you and Mason, I've seen the pictures."

She was still as marble, frozen with first incomprehension, then creeping horror. Behind her blusher, her face paled.

"What, how?"

I sighed, wet my lips. How to approach this? A step ahead of me, she said: "You hacked my messages?"

I bowed my head, a half nod. Zanna sputtered. I waited for her anger to give way, and it did. She breathed and sank onto the sofa, hands shaking. She let me sit down beside her and hold her, her body stiff as she processed it all.

"He's a scumbag," I said, as Zanna's tears came thick, her face wet and her voice viscous and nasal.

"I didn't know he was taking the pictures," she whispered.

"I know, I know." I held her and patted her shoulders, shuddering with her small sobs.

"I don't know what I was thinking. Honestly Paige, this is the biggest mistake of my life. I just, since my dad cut me off and

Shane's so — so aggressive. I just feel like it's not working out. Nothing's working out."

Sparkling pearls of pain fell down her flushing cheeks.

"We can manage this between us, Zanna. Let me help you." I took her hand, leaning towards her and trying to placate her with a gentle, honeyed tone. Droplets fell from her thick, dark lashes — expensive mink extensions — with each blink. She looked at my hand, holding hers, and then at my face. So reticent, afraid, like a baby deer.

"Let me help you," I implored her. "We'll report this guy to the police. We won't let him intimidate you. You can take some time off. Let me run the blog for a while. We have enough content to last a few weeks at least and I can take it from there, while you sort out whatever is going on here. It will all be okay. I can be like, a partner in the blog, or something—" *How to make it sound like I hadn't been thinking about this for a while?* "—and we can manage the fallout of this together. Think about it — you can be a feminist icon, talking about it all — it's an important story, you can share it with people. Women will respect that, and I'll be right there helping you."

Her body swayed as she thought about it. Her head must have been spinning. She leaned towards me, towards the idea, but then she leaned away again. She shook her head.

"No, it's okay. I can handle it myself. But thanks. Thanks, Paige."

She pulled away, breathed in deeply through her nose. She pressed her hands to her wet face and smoothed her hair back. She wrung her hands and pressed them into her waist. She nodded, to herself, and spun around to face me again.

"You're right, I can handle this myself. I'll go to the police."

"I'll help you," I yelped, jumping to my feet. "I want to help. I can help run the blog while you—"

She put out her hand and I fell silent. "Seriously, thank you, Paige, but I don't need your help."

I couldn't believe it. After everything I offered to do for her, to help her out of this mess she had got herself into, and she still pushed me away. I'd given my life to Zanna, without question, and again she cast me aside.

"Zanna, I really think you need my help. I mean, I know everything that's happened with Mason, you know. I know a lot of stuff."

What was I saying? I didn't even know. I was desperate. Desperate not to lose her, or my job.

Zanna looked at me like how Talia looked at me, with Sophia whispering in her ear. *She's weird. She's creepy.* My stomach sank. I was losing Zanna. No, I'd lost Zanna.

She rankled. "I'm not going to let you gaslight me into giving you the blog, you freak."

I exploded. "How can you do this?" I said, voice high-pitched with pain. "How can you treat me like this? You want to fire me?

After everything I've done for you. Getting you the following *I* deserve for *my* work. Covering for Shane. You don't deserve any of this. It's all me. It's all off my back. You don't deserve anything you have."

Hot tears slipped down my face and my stomach cramped with suppressed bawling. It was so unfair. Zanna's massive house, her money, her beauty, her boyfriend, all her fancy bags and her friends who loved her. My parents' tiny house, bullying in the hallways, everything I'd had to work so hard for, the uni place I no longer had, the fact a man had never really loved me, the fact that no one knew who I was and, if Zanna fired me, no one ever would. So unfair. My whole life. Unfair.

"Paige." Her voice was high-pitched, shocked, almost like a mother admonishing a child. She was treating me like an infant, her junior. Old habits die hard, even when your dignity hangs in the balance. "This really isn't appropriate."

There we go. From friend to boss. Another person, pushing me away. It was over. We were over. The dream, dead.

I spun on my heel and left the flat, grabbing my bag. Zanna didn't deserve anything. I had just one thing I could take away from her. One way to serve justice, however small.

I typed.

I'm sorry, Shane, I have to show you something.

The Present

A screening on New Year's Eve 2021

I'm in the holiday apartment we rented. I know I need to find Zanna. My heart is racing, I can't breathe. I want to shout but I can't. I can't muster the breath. I try to scream out, but my chest is feeble. There is a sound, a phone. It's pinging over and over again, aggressively.

I move quickly from the hall to the bedroom, but my feet hover above the floor, it's like the room moves around me. I'm trying to find the source of the noise, the phone. It's Shane calling, I think. He's found something. He's angry. I feel afraid. It's dark outside. Wind howling. The pillows, duvet, even the fitted sheet, have been strewn around the floor. My body aches. The balcony windows are open. The white curtains are being pulled nearly off their fixings by the weather, a storm raging on a sea outside the window, miles away beyond the lights. Nothing but blackness outside. The wind screams in pain.

The door bangs. I turn around. I can't make out the voice behind the door. Who is that? I look back at the bed. It's stained

265

bright red. Blood? No. Someone's knocked a wine bottle over and it's pouring out onto the sheets. I turn. It's Zanna. It was her in the doorway all along. She begins to scream at me, her mouth wide open, a terrible angry scream.

I know it's a dream before I wake. Relieved, I leave the bedroom behind me and head to the kitchen, like I usually do. As my eyes adjust, the dark corner of the kitchen created by dark cabinets isn't so empty. A shape is moving, a dark shape. A grey hoodie, a sullen face. She screams, raises a knife. The world around me begins to crack. Reality fracturing, terrifying voids where the atmosphere breaks apart, defying physics. My knife flashes in Talia's hand as she screams an angry, metallic, multidimensional scream.

I wake again. This time it's real. I'm comforted by Shane's heavy body on the mattress beside me, but I know I won't be sleeping again.

My blind hand reaches out in the dark, fumbling to pull open a drawer. I tentatively search through different packets of pills, like reading braille. The little many bumps of the contraceptive pill, large bubbly Nurofen. Then I find them: a number of packets held together with an elastic band. In the living room I stand with my hot head leaving an oily patch against the cool glass. Across the river, the lights of London glimmer like they did in Ibiza.

Today's the day.

*

We settle down in a cinema theatre in the basement of a private members' club in Soho. The seats are plush, blood red velvet, with little tables for your drinks. Matching velvet curtains hang around the screen too. Not old, but meant to look so. This is the premiere. What we've all been waiting for. The streaming service has opted for a more respectful occasion than attendees shivering on a red carpet. This is boutique and quiet. After all, this subject matter is serious. Death is serious. My situation is serious. Talia's threats hang in my ears.

How's it going to look when they print that you had another girl die, linked to you? They won't be paying you to post pictures of shit then.

But this circus, these kisses on cheeks, these champagne flutes, this midnight blue dress I'm wearing, they're not serious at all. Everyone tells me how stunning I am because I've lost a stone I didn't need to lose, whittled to my bones by anxiety. It's amazing how this sign of suffering is a success, at least when it's women who lose their body mass. Since visiting Talia, my dreams have been full again of other memories, more deeply repressed. Ones I'd never returned to since leaving those suburbs.

Sophia was a girl in my class. She and Talia were joined at the hip, after Talia abandoned me. We had been friends on and off during primary school, and for a few weeks at the beginning of secondary school, until Talia found a better option. Sophia set her sights on my friend, took her by the hand. Took her away. It happened gradually. We were a crowd of three, for a while, until the crowd thinned out on my end. Sophia didn't understand, or didn't care, that I wanted to be her friend. Instead, she took Talia's hand and ran — literally, sometimes. That hurt.

I tried to resist the robbery of my best friend. I attempted to speak to Talia on the school bus. I brought in her favourite sweets to share. I will admit, it became a little unhealthy. When fury, rejection and love meet, people take strange actions. I stole little things of Sophia's and Talia's. Pens, scrunchies, whatever I found. I was never caught, but the girls knew. So Sophia called me a stalker, she called me a psycho, a lesbian, spitting out the last word, as though it would be such a terrible thing. Soon, everyone else did too. I sank into a deep depression. Home and school, both torture. Reading, again, my only solace, where I retreated, and learned to write. Write stories, narratives. A skill that has come in useful for me.

For years, they laughed at me. Every day I attended that grey block of a comprehensive school, imposing, with its small windows, full of sadness and violence. Relentless. Can you imagine how that makes a person feel? Merciless cruelty. Water poured over my books, my work smeared before hand-ins. Compliments on my shoes, backpack, new hair clips, were all lies dangled like bait before me. After giving me a kind word, they'd wait, like barracudas, for me to smile a feeble acknowledgement — what else was I supposed to do, encourage them with anger? Then they'd reveal sharp demon teeth and laugh. Laugh, laugh, laugh. People who act this way should be careful. When you're laughing, you're too busy to watch your back. But I push those memories down, away. It's in the past. It's going to stay there. I'll do whatever it takes to ensure that.

Here we are, a low-key premiere, moments to go. I've done interviews with *Grazia*, the *Guardian*, the *Independent* in the run-up to it all. Thoughtful think pieces about male-on-female violence, stalking, the dangers of social media, the state of the world. I've sat on the white sofa and poured my heart out, offering my tears, my memories. I've carefully curated my social media to lead to this, I've watched every word, every action in the press interviews. I've done my part to make it *perfect*. I've endured the negative comments whipped up by the press. I've been harassed and blackmailed. I've been waiting, desperately as time went on, all for the moment when this is finally over and my problems are solved — money, exposure, debt. And now, the darkest part of my life — a part I thought long dead — has come home to roost.

It all hangs in the balance now, and the next forty-eight hours will dictate how those scales land. Doom or triumph. Victor or villain. All of it.

I'm already thinking about the hole paying Talia off will burn in my pocket, and the incriminating nature of it. But I think I have a better way to deal with the issue. I glace over at Jessica, and she flashes me a trusting smile. She could believe I was a victim of another malicious rumour. Perhaps she might caution Talia for me, stick up for me if any questions are asked.

I'd pacified Talia's threats for now, with promises of money once I'd been paid for the documentary. Five thousand pounds, more than any paper would give her for her bullshit. Her threats will be less worrisome to me when the documentary comes out. The absolute worst scenario would be for the documentary to be delayed. I can't have that. I need the money, I need the exposure.

Shane is with me tonight, of course, close by my side. His palms are sweating like mine. The whiskey he drank before we arrived is on his breath. I've taken half a diazepam. I need my wits about me. We were both nervous in the silent Uber ride over. There's a lot on the line.

The place is decked out with advertisements for the documentary. I stand face-to-face with Zanna's flat visage on a poster. She judges like once again she's not satisfied with my outfit. Sheryl is in the front row, where Angela and the two sisters are sat. Santiago is nowhere to be seen, despite taking part in the documentary. He never went in for any of it, really, Zanna and her mother's aspirational semi-showbiz dreams. Now he and Angela are no more, I hear he's living back in Portugal. It's tragic, he's estranged from his daughter even in death. I wonder if he feels guilty.

Gianna is here, sitting at the very front. She is showing, pregnant for a second time, and she's got that superior look to go with it. Pregnancy really deludes some women into thinking they are goddesses incarnate, rather than any old breeding sow with leaking teats. In a printed silk dress, she's like a sofa, especially next to razor-thin Sara in her "oh so high fashion" all black. Maggie, who wears a pink jumper, waves at me. Trying to fan the flames of a friendship she considers recently rekindled. I smile and wave back, if only because it annoys Gianna, who scowls. Angela pretends not to see me; perhaps she is embarrassed after that outburst at the gala. Well, she really ought to be. Gianna whispers into Sara's ear. *Sticks and stones, bitch, sticks and stones.*

I sit with Shane at the very back. He's been quickly quaffing the champagne offered out on trays, one after another. I silently will him to slow down.

"Thank you for coming," Sheryl says, standing at the front of the room and holding her hands together in front of her. I spy a flicker of humanising nerves.

The lights go down and a Maroon 5 song starts playing. On the nose, if you ask me. Pictures roll down the screen in a fake Instagram interface, the pretend "like" button pinging, hearts flying around the screen. It's the real pictures of me and Zanna I sent over to Sheryl scrolling down the screen, one big WeTransfer containing the sum of my precious memories with my old friend. There's Zanna posing with a bottle of prosecco,

271

a fag dangling out of her mouth. Angela shifts in her seat. Hah, I'd hoped Sheryl would pick this one for that very reason. Not so perfect now, is she? I remember that night. Zanna spiked our drinks with MDMA. I didn't get to sleep till 7 a.m. and I ground my teeth so hard I carved little notches on the front two. They're fixed now by a private dentist who did composite bonding, free in exchange for an Instagram post. But that's not the point. Zanna never even asked before she put the mandy in my drink and she never offered to pay to have the grooves fixed, even though she pointed them out enough times.

A re-enactment shows two girls on a bus holding boxes with our names on. This didn't happen; we didn't move on a bus, Shane drove us in his friend's van. Creative licence, though. I understand that, I've given myself a huge proportion of it. Then, there's my voice. I wince with every hint of the regional accent I've run from. I close my eyes, a little dizzy. I breathe and count to ten. When I open my eyes the text on screen reads "Life of Zanna". What comes next lays out the tale, as the public knows it, of the life and death of Zanna.

Life of Zanna Documentary

Jessica Baines Interview

JB: Zanna's body was on her back when police entered the property. Her arms were by her side, her legs straight out. She died there, like that, on her back, after — we believe — being initially pushed and hitting her head against the kitchen counter — hard.

I was not first at the scene, but I was there shortly after, as the most senior officer on call at the time. It was a truly shocking scene. Every scene stays with you, but this one I do remember as harrowing. It looked like any young woman's dream apartment; to see those dreams snuffed out so violently . . . I was immediately sure we had a big case on our hands, and I was put in charge of said case very quickly. It was important to us, to the Met, to have a woman at the forefront of this case, to handle it sensitively and seriously, given the nature of it. Unfortunately, the Met has had, and did have especially at that time, a bad reputation of failing women in the face of male violence, of failing to take stalking seriously as a crime.

Not only was Zanna's death itself shocking, such a young woman having lost her life, it was relatively high profile, what with her status as an influencer; someone many young women looked to, idolised, following her day-to-day life on their phones, feeling as though she was almost a friend or member of the family. It was clear how much this was going to shock not only the victim's family, but many, many people in the UK and internationally. I don't think it's going too far to say that at the time it was the biggest case I had ever worked on, and it still is the defining case of my career.

I had to get ahead of the press, and fast. You want to avoid journalists getting to witnesses before you, publishing the elements of your case in the newspapers and online. Not only can the media compromise a trial — and it frequently does — but it's intrusive and undignified. And besides the press, with a case like this, there are many moving parts to manage. The suspects, the family and friends of the bereaved, even fans, and those God-awful true crime enthusiasts. Nothing can screw a case like an amateur detective. So, as you can imagine, I was anxious to find a resolution as quickly as possible, for the sake of the investigation and Zanna's dignity in the press.

Time of death was estimated to be between 12 p.m. and 3 p.m. This laid out our enquiry parameters. There were a number of suspects, and of course one was far and away the most obvious.

The Past

I went to the café, a familiar independent near the flat, still fizzing and lightheaded. On autopilot, I had to sit down. The barista Zanna always asked me to flirt with waved at me as I came in. I breathlessly sat down and pulled my laptop from my bag and put it in front of me on the table, not even turning it on. What had I done? I'd jumped from a ledge, I'd taken the fucking red pill. Nothing was ever going to be the same again. God, I was high. Colours brighter, sounds louder, the light so bright. Everything and nothing whizzed through my head. I chewed my lip. I jumped out of my skin when the barista appeared, by my side.

"The usual?" he asked, a smile highlighting those rugged cheek lines.

"Yes, please," I breathed.

"You good?"

He was always so cheerful.

"Oh yeah, swamped with work. Do you mind if I get through some of it here?"

"Mi casa, su casa," he said, opening his arms out and winking. "Take as long as you need."

I waited till I saw him, Shane, leaving the Tube station. Like I anticipated, he'd left the bodybuilding convention after receiving those texts, his heavy gym bag swinging from his shoulder with the momentum of his pace. I waited a while, but in the end, I couldn't resist. I followed him. I wanted to be there, to see it all implode. Let's see her talk her way out of this. I wanted to see Zanna's life crumble like mine. Not to see it come to an end.

It was quiet in the flat. It wasn't unusual for it to be, but in this circumstance I was not expecting silence. The peal of emptiness rings clear in my memory of that day now. Where I expected shouts, there was nothing at all. Not a sound.

What I found instead of a couple in meltdown, a breakup taking place soap-style. Shane, so pale his lips were practically purple, stood in the hallway, stock-still, petrified.

"I didn't mean it," he said. All at once it felt cold in the flat, shockingly cold. Like when clouds pass overhead on a summer day and the colours of the world fade, a moody Instagram filter of greys. I moved down the hall, elongated like a nightmare tunnel, slowly.

"Shane." It wasn't a whisper. I couldn't breathe. "What is it?"

He sputtered, sudden, explosive, uncontrolled spittle and tears on his chin. He shook his head, eyes squeezed shut like a child. I think I knew what I would see. No, I knew. I knew the moment I saw Shane in the hall. Still, like that. Terrified, like that. He was never like that. Not even after he had shouted, lashed out, thrown something, broken something. That was embarrassment. That was contrition. *This* was pure fear, and nothing frightens more than that primal, gasping, muscle-tensing, hair-on-arm-erecting fear in someone else's eyes.

I walked a couple of steps across the hall and opened the kitchen door. My brain carried on with its usual functioning as my stomach sank. When you see a dead body, you know instinctively exactly what it is or, at least, your body does. Deep down in a part of us kept separate from our intellect, older and far more powerful, fear and threat can stop you in your tracks as the beast seizes control of your circuitry. It takes a while for your brain to catch up.

On her back, Zanna looked like she'd been laid out there. So perfectly beautiful, even in this moment. It was hard to imagine anything about her wasn't by design, difficult to reconcile anything about Zanna being outside of her control. Calm, almost composed, she could have been napping or sunbathing on a billionaire's yacht. Except for the blood that seeped from her head, turning her hair into squid ink linguine. Snow White pale, with a glass case around her, she could have been waiting for true love's kiss.

On legs not at all like mine, I moved over to Zanna. She wore her wishbone necklace, given to her by her mother. Symbolising luck, it still glinted in the sunlight, unaware of the irony, sitting innocently in the little hollow dip above where the collarbones meet. It took some time for it to feel real, to feel anything other than ice cold. All my faculties came back into play at once. My body tingled.

Shane breathed in a deep, shuddering breath, huge barrel chest in overdrive.

"Is she dead?" he asked.

"I think so," I said.

At the sound of my voice, Zanna's flickering eyes opened. She defied expectations once more. Her eyelids fluttered like bird hearts and her chest rose and fell, if unsteadily. She gurgled, her chest like a drain. She wheezed my name. Hardly audible. But I heard the "P" as her fading pink lips formed it, and the rasp of the vowel. For a moment, it was as though a patriarch called me to his bedside for the final time. I was compelled to step forward, closer, five steps with my numb feet. I stood above her. Deep brown eyes darker than ever, voids endless, wells without bottoms.

I stepped out of the way of any blood. She spoke to me.

"Paige," she tried to say. Her eyes oozed tears, tinged pink by her blood. She smiled. Blood seeped between and around her teeth, her perfect white veneers. She must have bitten her tongue on the way down. She saw behind me and Shane, and tried to raise an arm to point. I shook my head.

"Zanna, don't move. Don't move."

She dropped her hand. Closed her eyes and tried to breathe. She moved her mouth to form more words.

"What, Zanna?"

"Ambulance."

I got it the second time, despite the hiss of her fragile breath and slurring, bleeding tongue.

Her jaw shuddered with cold; she was losing blood rapidly. Shane shook his head. Tears fell from his eyes as he struggled to take shuddering breaths. "Oh my God, oh my God," he repeated to himself, under his breath. He held his arms around himself, using muscles for comfort now, wrapping his hands around himself for relief.

"What did you do?" I ask.

He sank to a crouch, his back against the wall, cowering in the dim hallway, out of the sunlight. His voice a crushed whine, he struggled to speak.

"I didn't mean to," he said. "I'm sorry. He spoke through huge, constricted breaths. "She said she didn't. She said she would never. She lied. I showed her the pictures you sent me—" He paused here as his whole body shook. "And then—"

He let out a groan like an animal. Preverbal. His wet face turned inside out with sorrow. As grief cracked Shane in half,

279

the multi-note sound he emitted a song of grief — but for Zanna or himself? It hit me like a kick in the gut, and my body responded. I put my hands to my face, and a sob came up like vomit. I wiped tears away and waited for Shane to catch his breath, which was getting away from him. He took little gasps of air where he could, coming up to breathe from dark water. When he'd regained a semblance of control, he squeezed out the words.

"She said she did, so I—"

He mimicked the pushing. The push that did this. How hard must it have been? Then he sobbed again, lost to the agony.

"Jesus, Shane," I breathed, to no one.

Zanna held on to life. Her shivering intensified, lips bluer and bluer with each of those elongated, mutilated, freak of physics moments. So long and so short. So tangible, and yet they slipped through my fingers like glitter. In that way, this, the last moments, were like those early days of our friendship. Her breathing quickened and shallowed as she watched me, panicking. Her brow furrowed and her lips pulled down at the sides.

Her eyes said, *Paige, what the fuck are you doing? Call me a fucking ambulance.*

She said it again, this time with more force, defying her ebbing body.

"Ambulance."

Even as she needed me, she looked at me like that. With a sort of incredulous, sneering frustration. Like I was an idiot, or a child doing something wrong. I rocked back on my heels and breathed. I could call an ambulance and save her. Or, save him. I looked at Shane. He looked back at me.

"You'll go to prison," I told him.

He shook his head. "I can't, I can't. Oh my God, Paige, I can't."

Zanna's brown, endless, fathomless eyes. Her face. Her lips, all filled with Juvederm, so white; her tweaked nose, so small, almost juvenile; her sharp jaw, model-like. Her eyebrows, creasing at me. Her eyes narrowed. She realised what was happening, and those brown eyes flashed unconcealed hate. She wanted to fire me. She wanted me out of her life. And even if I saved her now, I would never get what I wanted. She would never, was never going to, give me any credit for the blog. Still, I looked between them. Zanna and Shane.

"Please," he said. "Help me. Help me, Paige, I'll do anything. Please."

He came towards me, hands like a prayer. "Please." He blinked, wet his flips, frowned, and then said: "I love you."

My head spun. My heart fluttered. Tears came to my eyes.

I shook my head.

"I'm not calling an ambulance, Zanna."

Her breathing picked up, as she panicked.

"I wish you'd been a better friend," I said, gently, trying to be conciliatory in my tone, "We had some good times, though. I'll always cherish the memories. I did love you."

She laughed then. Blood sputtered from her mouth like a fountain, landing on her smooth cheeks, little red, wet freckles. Her laugh was still pretty, even as she wheezed and struggled. Shane gently wept.

"Fuck you, Paige," she whispered. She bit her lip and chuckled. Then, she settled down again, her breathing slowed, slowed and slowed. She cried. Tears fell with abandon.

"I want my dad," she whispered, squeezing her eyes shut, diamond globelike tears sparkling as she opened them. She said it once. Then again, a mutter, a murmur or a prayer. Then it was on her breath. Then her breath was gone, and so was she. Unmistakably dead. Zanna. Once my best friend. Now, gone.

We waited a few minutes. Then I licked the back of my hand and held it over her mouth. No cool breath. No movement. No time to lose.

Shane fixed his manic sight on me, calmed by my presence. I loved how he turned to me. I felt butterflies. He held his hands out to me like a child. Those big bear mittens were shaking. I grabbed them.

"Take your bags, go to your dad's right now, fast. On the way, destroy your phone, smash it to pieces and distribute those pieces as you go, bit by bit. Till it's gone. Say you left the bodybuilding convention to help your dad with the house, or something, something like that. Tell your dad, if he needs to, he has to lie."

"What are you going to do?" he asked, afraid.

I said to him something I've said to him so many times since — and I've never broken my word.

"It'll be okay. I'll handle this."

Thankfully, I remembered that last secret message on Zanna's phone.

Okay, I'll meet you. I want to see you. Come over tonight. Shane will be out.

Life of Zanna Documentary

Sissy Thomas Interview

ST: Zanna wasn't to know how dangerous Mason was. His criminal family background, his previous police cautions for stalking. I was not remotely surprised when the police investigation found he had been hit with a restraining order after stalking and harassing a previous girlfriend in Manchester. Sending her frightening messages, threatening to publish intimate photos he had taken of her under the understanding they would remain between them. This is likely why he left the city for Ibiza, where fate would bring him into the path of his next victim, Zanna.

But poor Zanna, she could not have known any of this when she started her affair with Mason, that this romance would prove deadly. And of course, Zanna would have faced the stigma of that too. We are so quick to judge women for their personal lives. We have seen victim blaming in so many cases, including this one. These misogynist views are the very same ones that prevent women like Zanna from being open about what is happening to them when their love affairs turn sour.

Sadly, Zanna did what I, and any professional, would advise a victim of a stalker not to do. She continued attempting to pacify her attacker's behaviour by responding to texts and messages. Stalkers know that the vast majority of their interactions with their victims will go ignored, like a lottery player knows they will rarely, if almost never, win. However, the occasional tiny pay-out and the promise of a huge prize at the end is enough to keep them playing each week. Even the smallest acknowledgement from a victim is enough to spur a dangerous stalker on, even if to the mind of any reasonable person a message asking them to stop is embarrassing or clear enough. In the obsessive mind of a stalker, this sort of thing reinvigorates the whole process of harassment all over again.

Women are conditioned from a young age to be seen as likeable and agreeable, and to be very sensitive to the pain or disapproval of others, particularly men, whose emotional suffering is perceived as far greater than women's, even when they have shown little outward signs. We call it male fragility, the idea that men's emotions are so volatile, women must be especially careful not to upset or anger them with harsh rejections. Zanna demonstrated this so clearly. Despite the fact she was being blackmailed by a man she was trying to end an affair with, she went so far as to invite Mason into her home to try and settle their differences.

Mason fell into one of the most dangerous categories of stalkers we recognise: the rejected stalker. This is a person who will sometimes seek reconciliation, a relationship, the romance they are misguidedly dreaming about. But when this inevitably does not happen, they want vindication, to punish their victim. However, Mason also shows, at times, some signs of the intimacy-seeking stalker, a person who is delusional, mentally ill, and believes their victim is in love with them, or will be in the future. In some ways, this makes him more sympathetic than the typical predatory stalker, who intentionally uses threat to strike fear in their victim, and more often than not this fear is at the crux of sexually violent fantasies about the victim.

It appears Zanna invited Mason to her flat, maybe to try and end the relationship for good in a way that would finally make sense to him. Sadly, he did not have reconciliation on his mind, but something much darker.

This is why I do what I do. The red flags of a stalker are missed so easily, mistaken for devotion, obsessive devotion to the victim, what we call "love bombing". This is the scary thing. It's so difficult to predict who might be dangerous.

The Past

With Shane gone, I worked fast. My plan fell into place seamlessly in my mind. It's amazing how clearly you can see things when everything is at stake. I took a millisecond to look down at Zanna's face, her blood-soaked teeth as a kind of reverent moment. A mini vigil, a matter of human decency. I took in her hair, her lustrous hair, for the last time. Her beautiful face, as colour drained from it. And then there was no more time. I found her phone, opened it with her thumb print. Then, holding her limp, still warm hand in mine, I used her forefinger to open WhatsApp.

Thank the Lord, a message had been sent by Mason in the past twenty minutes.

I'm close, tell me when the coast is clear.

Zanna's forefinger clumsily typed.

Come now.

I left the flat, and I lay in wait in the alley tunnel without the CCTV. I thought of that poor lady with the big head piled with braids and her mournful voice asking for locals to sign her petition. I'd wished she'd had more signatures, I really did, but I was now thankful she did not.

Come soon, come soon, come soon, I begged, repeating my mantra, manifesting it. I tapped my feet and chewed the skin around my fingers. Less than ten minutes later, my heart fluttered with relief. Mason had arrived, his face stern and full of purpose, ready to talk his lady love out of reconciliation with her boyfriend. A moment later, Mr Mazur headed outside for a cigarette. I waited till I heard the sirens, and then I left the other side of the alley and stopped at a corner shop, where I bought a bottle of wine and some popcorn. I'd planned a movie night, innocent enough. I walked the long way round, like any sane woman would to avoid, "Stabby Alley" as Zanna had so nicely put it. I walked towards the flat block, heart pounding.

I entered the flat, contorting my face into the right level of concern for police cars outside your building, and police in your flat. I furrowed my brow at the officer when she said, "Ma'am, please don't go in there."

The police officer held a steady and authoritative arm out, and I stopped.

"What is it?" I asked. "What's happened? Is everything okay? Have we been robbed?"

The officer maintained a sense of stern blankness. "Do you live here, miss?"

"Yes, I live here. Is everything alright?"

"Please, come with me, miss."

I shook when they told me, so they put a foil blanket around me, which I clutched. I didn't cry at first. I tried to make myself, thinking about Zanna's last moments, then our first moments of friendship. It didn't work. I tried to think about Shane, about losing him, him in prison. That didn't work either. Then I thought about myself, myself in prison, never being able to claim my words, to write again. Then I cried.

The nice police officer put a hand on my shoulder. She said, "It's common to feel numb at first and to cry later, you're in shock."

At that moment police frogmarched Mason past me in handcuffs, wild eyed, afraid.

"Paige, oh my God, have you seen what he's done?" he said.

"You're a monster," I shouted, holding my finger out towards him, letting my hand shake. "You're a psychopath."

They took the baffled Mason away.

Then they took me to the police station to help the investigation. I went willingly, desperate to help my friend. Before they even asked me the question, I said, "Mason Hicks, he is obsessed with Zanna, he has been threatening her."

The police officer who questioned me, Jessica Baines, the kind person who had wrapped me in foil like leftovers outside the flat and who later became a friend of sorts, nodded.

"Yes. He's in custody at the moment."

I shuddered a sigh of relief. I reached inside myself and pulled tears forward.

"I feel so bad. I didn't help her. I didn't help her more."

A hand with a tissue extended towards me. I took it and dabbed my eyes. I imagined myself lying in that pool of blood instead, and it helped.

I explained that Zanna had been getting threatening messages from Mason. That he'd tried to blackmail her into being with him with explicit pictures. She showed me the messages on her phone. If the police looked, they would find them. He had always been a bit obsessive with Zanna, following her to London after the holiday. I kept her secret, like an exemplary friend, but now, oh how I wished I hadn't.

The police wouldn't need anything from me for the time being. I asked Jessica to please keep me updated. I picked up my bag, popcorn poking out the top.

"I thought we could watch *Clueless*. It's her favourite."

The officer touched a kind hand to my shoulder. She was very, sweet, very professional. I'm glad she got her promotion after her case, and it's always nice to know someone in the Met. I couldn't go back to the flat whilst they were carrying out their investigation, so I rang someone who could generally be depended on.

I listened to Maggie's shocked silence on the phone as I explained the situation. She shakily said she and her boyfriend would pick me up soon. Maggie and her boyfriend owned a one-bed flat on the outskirts of Battersea then, before they bought the home in the suburbs, which Maggie came to own on her own after their split. I slept, sort of, on their sofa that night as the police dealt with the scene at the flat. I would sleep for what felt like an age to wake and learn from the large kitchen clock on the wall that it had only been four minutes. I'd lie awake with nothing but the whirring sound within my brain and it would have been forty-five minutes. Eventually at about 4 a.m., I got a chunk of sleep all the way through to quarter past seven, but it felt like I closed my eyes for two seconds just to be transported three hours into the future. My mouth was dry, I'd sweated into the T-shirt I borrowed to sleep in, and my head throbbed as though waking to a particularly severe white-wine hangover. Shock. The sight of Zanna's body had frozen me, and I thawed throughout the night.

All throughout the night and the next day a hellish cycle replayed, as if I was temporarily forgetting the events of the previous day, like when your stomach drops as you realise you might have left your straighteners on. Then I'm remembering the blood, Zanna's rigor-mortis face lurching at me, dislodged from the debris of my subconscious, hurtling sickeningly to the surface. I couldn't look at myself in the mirror. Zanna loomed like Sylvia Plath's terrible fish, getting older now far from my greatest fear. They haunted me and only stopped with my prescription, acquired shortly after.

I stayed in the old flat. Not out of a desire to, but I couldn't face a move. I had nowhere to go. All evidence Zanna had been lying dead on the kitchen floor had been swept away by the police, some things in plastic bags for the police to examine. The open-plan kitchen and living room looked so clean. There were things untouched still on the low, glass-top coffee table Zanna had bought off eBay. "Antique," she had told me when Shane carried it in for her, "a steal." She liked to tell people when they came over, even if they'd heard it before. A bowl of crystals Zanna had bought from an Etsy shop and "charged" under the light of a full moon when they arrived sat on the glass next to some sage she burned to "send away negative spirits". If only it had worked.

I travelled back to my parents after the funeral. It didn't look right, to immediately take Zanna's mantle. So I waited it out in the suburbs of Birmingham. But not a part of me wanted to return to the cold terrace house with electric heaters and bad memories. I hated it there. It reminded me of the past. The traumatic bullying, the horrible feeling of sadness and death. Victimised by my peers to the extent I became a shell. A shivering, twitching mass of nervousness, flinching, waiting for the next jeer, insult, or prank.

I was only a little girl really when I started secondary school and Talia and I were torn apart by the cruel transition from primary. And I was only fourteen when an opportunity for revenge on Sophia reared its head. One I couldn't pass on after so long. It does things to you when you grow up with no one. In a household that neglects you, parents more concerned with their fights than they are with you, in a school cohort that abuses you, bounced from cruelty to total indifference. Malnourishment stunts growth, physical and emotional. I experienced both.

I'd learned to stay away from the places it was worst, and the computer lab offered a place of refuge, quiet. Sophia had left herself logged into her school computer account one day and, as I sat down at the keyboard, I couldn't believe my luck. It was too good, too fortunate. In her MySpace messages I found the flirty messages she'd send to boys in the class. Boys with girlfriends, boys who weren't her boyfriend. I found pictures of vodka, weed, Sophia enjoying them all on school property. Finally, I'd found a way to make her pay. The messages were all printed — at a computer café in town, not the school, I'm no fool — and left somewhere they would be found.

While she and Talia told teachers it was me, where was the evidence? The school didn't have cameras. Even if they had, the teachers wouldn't have sought that evidence. I had always been known to be a good girl. Quiet and sweet. Teachers liked me, especially sweet Ms Quinn, who brought me the *Sunday Times* supplement each week. She vouched for my good character most of all. Sophia was simply not believed. Well, she'd brought the ramifications on herself, hadn't she?

Sophia was expelled, but more than that, the pictures were shared far and wide. Immortalised. Unbeknown to me, she had very strict parents, who were mortified by her behaviour, moved her away from the town, and sent her to a stricter school. She couldn't handle it, apparently.

Of course, I hadn't wanted Sophia to take her own life. But I had wanted her gone. If she couldn't cope with her come-uppance, I rationalised, that was on her. People shouldn't do in secret what they couldn't admit to in public, shouldn't do things the ramifications of which they couldn't handle. Like the journalist I had always wanted to be ever since my unwitting accomplice Ms Quinn put the newspaper in my hands and the idea in my head, Sophia was my first exposé. I'd revealed the truth about a corrupt actor, every laugh, every snide sneer in my direction, unpacking my whole self, my skin, my clothes, my soul. The victim finally found the strength to fight back. And I did. I made my choice. Sophia's suicide was hers.

Sophia was gone, like she evaporated, and with it, for a time, so did my torment. School paused for a period of mourning, and we were so close to our GCSEs that Sophia's death scattered the school cohort. I overperformed in my exams and took a place at a nicer college on scholarship. I never saw any of my school friends again, or I made sure they never saw me, ducking behind bushes or down gullies to avoid them.

Now, Zanna was gone, too. But, no matter what happened, I knew I couldn't stay there, in my family home, even though I was scared. Scared of the police investigation going right, and, strange as it sounds. scared of going on without her. I sat on my parents' navy blue sofa, my toes digging into an ornate but threadbare rug left to Mum by her grandparents. Life was dull, grey, there was nothing there for me. Time, like the night after Zanna's death, remained amorphous. There was nothing but time. Time to think.

Did I kill Zanna? Did Shane? It depends where you fall on the scale of personal responsibility. If a man whips a horse, and the horse tramples another man, did the first man kill the second man? I debate philosophical questions like this at night.

I was so dreadfully lonely at university. I'd hoped for what everyone hopes for when they start life over, something better than before. Why else had I worked so hard, revised and studied till my brain fried, to get a place at uni? To get away from the drab grey terrace, my parents, crass and too consumed by their own unhappiness, with each other, with what the world gave them. In a series of cigarettes, arguments and tears as regular as *EastEnders*, they never learned to change the channel. Whereas I, on the other hand, had the remote in my hand and desperately pressed the buttons. I craved friendship. I longed to meet someone who would see me, make me feel loved. It was a flop with my first flatmates in halls. They soon worked it out, they smelled it, sensed it. I was undesirable. I had been as far from the "in crowd" as can be. The door would slam at night after the raucous of their pre-drinks. Drinks I had never been invited to. If I ever tentatively opened the door to the kitchen as they got ready, the girls, daubing makeup on each other's faces, wouldn't meet my eye. So, after they left, the flat now tauntingly quiet, I turned to social media to not feel so alone. I started with my current flatmates, searched through their friends, looking for — I don't know. Something interesting.

Then I came across her. A profile different to the others. Her magnetism shone through straight away. And that unforgettable name. Zanna. She was gorgeous, but a little naughty. Beautiful, but a little trashy. Night-out pictures with blurry brown eyes ringed in glitter, Marlboro Lights dangling from full lips. Always surrounded by friends like a chorus of angels, a gorgeous, gorgeous boyfriend. I found myself revisiting that profile again and again, until I could describe each photo in order, tell you each caption.

I'd been burned so many times in the past by so-called friends, Talia and her bitchy alumni, the new university crowd, but I still dreamed. So I learned the names of Zanna's glossy friends and family members before our first introductions. Yes, I'd fantasised about Shane. I'd seen the interior of Zanna's family home long before that Christmas. Beige interiors and kitchen islands became an element of my fantasy life, modelled now on Zanna's.

I dreamed of sitting in that living room in one of the matching jumpers, part of the lavish Christmas celebrations Zanna documented every year in her too millennial way. I got a slice of that dream with a little effort.

I absorbed all this information about Zanna before we met, knowing it would come in handy one day when we became friends. I didn't need to follow her or go through her bins for information. It was all online, volunteered by her. I seized my opportunity at that party, where she wriggled around on the sofa with her bottle of prosecco, I kept my eye out for signs of her around town, and for snippets of information about her.

I did all my research, so when I next sidled up to her at a party and pulled out a packet of cigarettes — I'd practised smoking in front of the mirror before attending so as to do it without looking like a fool — she said: "Oh my gosh, menthol Vogues! I smoke those. And I have that leopard jacket too! Topshop, right?"

We had so much in common, she noted, because I made sure we did. I knew that she loved Ariana Grande, that her father was Portuguese, that she was obsessed with old photographs of Brigitte Bardot. I mean, not every effort to impress her worked. I bought a second-hand copy of *Howl and Other Poems* on Amazon, £1.99 for a battered version, because she wore a jumper with the text "Ginsberg is a God". But when I shoe-horned my memorised quote "I saw the best minds of my generation destroyed by madness" into conversation, Zanna stared at me wide-eyed, concerned.

"Did you?" she asked, knitting her brow (before Botox became a regular habit). "What happened?"

"Oh no, it's a poem," I muttered.

"You're so funny," she said, throwing her head back and laughing after a bemused pause. "Little Miss Literature."

"I'm a writer," I said, before drawing on my cigarette, no big deal.

"Are you now?" she said, eyeing me, head to toe. Was that the moment she considered working with me? Taking me on? Starting this whole mess? I never asked. And so I'll never know.

These were the questions tormenting me through that time. The reporting. The case. But every moment of it, strangely, felt like a blessing, too. I passed those hours in hiding in a hazy blur. My heart soared at Mason's arrest in the news. After all, it was a tenuous plan. A desperate plan. It might never have worked, the police might have turned their investigative gaze to Shane and me, if it weren't for Mr Mazur.

Life of Zanna
Documentary

Jessica Baines Interview

JB: After Ms White was taken away from the scene by an officer, we set about gathering evidence at the scene. The victim was not undressed at the scene but still, I suspected a potential sexual assault, so a pathologist was called to the scene to take swabs. It's ... well, it's very undignified. She was partially undressed, the clothes taken away by forensics, in case trace evidence was found on them. Seeing her body like that was hard. A woman not much younger than me, with so much drive, passion and promise. To have it so unfairly taken away from her. So unjustly. No one pictures their life ending this way. We all like to believe we have at least some control, a say in where we end. How we die. I resolved to do the best I could to solve this case for her.

A number of pieces of DNA were found on the victim. Her boyfriend, Shane's, to be expected. While blood and semen are often the most useful forensic markers, in this case, it was saliva that was illuminating. Sadly, saliva is nowhere near as reliable as those I mentioned before. It is not as rich a source of DNA, and the results can be variable and inconclusive more often. In this case, a few strands of DNA were found. Shane's, as previously mentioned, a strain that tested positively for Mason's and two more which had no match.

Time of death was estimated to be between 12 p.m. and 3 p.m. This laid out our enquiry parameters. We are able to cross-check alibi times. We were looking for someone who had been in the vicinity of the flat between these times who had a motive.

The phrase "caught red-handed" comes to mind, doesn't it?

He denied it, of course, but he was at the flat within the possible perameters of Zanna's time of death, as laid out by the coroner. Shane was with his father. Paige had worked at a café, as the owner testified, and then had bought things to bring back to the flat for a movie night. Still, I was hoping for extra corroboration to seal a case for the prosecution.

That's when Zanna's apartment building supervisor came forward and told us he had seen Mason entering the building. Had seen this man visiting before and had heard the pair arguing on numerous occasions. It was enough to make the arrest and put this dangerous man in prison.

PRODUCER: Did you ever suspect Paige?

SJB: Personally, no. I didn't. The nature of the body, the way it was found? No.

A crime like that, it would have involved brute force. I don't believe it's possible, or at least not remotely likely, that another woman would commit it. It was a classic stalking case. It's my honour to say I led the charge. It was one of the key reasons I was promoted.

Life of Zanna
Documentary

Andrzej Mazur Interview

AM: Yes, I saw Mr Hicks that day, when I went outside for a cigarette, he was coming into the building. I often saw him hanging around. I never liked the look of him. His long hair and tattoos. No. I never liked him, especially not for lovely Miss Zanna.

PRODUCER: So, you saw him coming into the building just before?

AM: Yes. He was entering the flat and he looked angry. Unhappy. He, erm, he had the expression ... [Passes hand over his forehead and pulls down.]

PRODUCER: A frown?

AM: Yes, a frown, exactly. I passed him in the hall. Then I went for my cigarette.

I had seen him before. I was suspecting an affair between him and Miss Zanna. He visited the times when Miss Paige and Mr Shane were away. I am the maintenance man. I notice all the things happening in the block of flats. Not much gets past me. [Laughs.]

When people are going to work, when they come home. Usually the days run like clockwork. I know the times. I notice everything.

He had been around maybe four times, or so. Never when the others were there. I cared about Miss Zanna, she was kind to me, not everyone is nice to the supervisor. So I worried about what she was doing. I listened, I heard sometimes Zanna shouting about Mr Shane. "He's bad, jealous. Angry."

[Sighs.]

Of course, it's not my job to get involved with personal things. I'm just the maintenance man. I fix things, the bloody rubbish intercom mostly. I take in parcels when residents are not home. I have favourites, like Miss Zanna and Miss Paige, but I try not to get involved. But, of course, I see a lot.

I don't judge Miss Zanna. Life is hard. We all try to get through. No one is perfect. Mason Hicks, I think he loved Zanna and wanted her to go be with him. And when she said no, he was angry and he killed her.

It was very sad. She was so lovely. A very lovely girl. She always asked after my children when I brought parcels. My children, Antoni and Julia, see?

[He takes his phone from his pocket and shows the screen-saver to the producer. There is a picture of two blonde children hugging on the screen.]

PRODUCER: Very sweet.

AM: Thank you. I love them very much.

[As AM puts his phone away, he has tears in his eyes. His voice breaks.]

When I think of Miss Zanna, I think of them. Someone hurting them.

[He sighs and blinks his tears away.]

As for that man, as we say in Poland, *baba z wozu, koniom lżej.*

[SUBTITLES READ: Good riddance to bad rubbish.]

The Present

It's a little dramatised, like any true crime I guess. I smile at Sissy on screen. She's such a sweet woman. Maggie, too, looks nervous but does well. When Shane comes on screen I run my thumb over his hand, to show him I'm there. That even though he didn't want to do it, and I gave him little choice, it's all going to be okay. He blinks at the screen, stiff. It's hard, as he talks about how he met Zanna, their relationship, but I bear it. It's history, I tell myself. The past. The past can't hurt you.

His last shot is of him speaking to the camera, so handsome.

"What is in the future for you and Paige?" the producer asks.

Shane smiles, shy like a little boy. "I don't know. All I know is I'm lucky. Your ex being murdered, it's a whole load of baggage. But Paige has been through the exact same thing, has the same baggage. We help each other carry it, you know?"

He looks so sweet. Like he means it. A rare look of innocence on his face when he talks about how lucky he is to have me. The sensation of new tears smarts in my eyes.

They kept the scene at the gala when Angela accused me. I had hoped they would, to stir some sympathy in the viewers. To show what I had to go through, the results of speculation. In the boutique cinema theatre, Angela's head swivels towards Sheryl now, faster than a cat who's seen a pigeon. Angela starts furiously whispering as she sways in the footage, pointing her finger in my face and her eyes narrowing. The cameras zoom in on me. My lip wobbles, meek and terrified.

Gianna takes her pot shots at me. But these are undignified slurs amid my sensitive interviews about the ramifications of trolling and online abuse. Jessica Baines singing my praises and proclaiming my innocence sounds like a beautiful melody.

A voiceover booms: "Mason Hicks was found guilty of murder by a jury. He is serving a life sentence."

I smile. It's still a relief, hearing that verdict, after all these years.

My breath hitches. It's myself on the screen for the final interview piece.

Life of Zanna Documentary

Paige White Interview

PRODUCER: It must have been hard, having so many people initially suspect you of harming Zanna.

PW: It was hard. Some people seemed convinced I had something to do with it. Me! Her best friend. There were the true crime bloggers, tearing everything about our friendship apart. Small things Zanna said about me in times of silly fights being brought up by her mother, and Gianna. People I know and strangers questioning me, my motives. Asking where I was at the time. There were some wild theories. There still are to this day. Sorry.

[Takes a tissue to blot her tears.]

It was awful. Just awful. Not only have you recently lost someone you love, someone you live with, someone who has been your best friend for years, practically your family, then some sick people have these dark, twisted, horrible things to say. I don't know what would compel someone to say something like that, to accuse someone of something so ... so evil. And it's even harder to countenance because, you know, there was no evidence, it was such a clear-cut case.

People thought, well, they had suspicions. I guess they always will. It's so much more exciting isn't it, shade and corruption. Women with knives in each other's backs, it's such a cliché. I hate it. People seem to think it's normal for female friends to turn on each other. It's a toxic, sexist belief. They love to see women fucking other women over for entertainment. That's especially why, in the real world, women need to stand together, and look after each other. That's partially why I kept the blog going. Because it represented mine and Zanna's amazing work together. We were feminist and sex positive for women, were all about girl power, making girls feel like they could do anything. Achieve their dreams in a male-dominated world.

To then be accused of having done something to hurt Zanna, something like that cuts into your soul. It hurts because it is *so* not what we were about. We celebrated women's successes, we would never do anything to tear another woman down.

And I would never have physically hurt Zanna. I'd never physically hurt anyone, I mean, look at me. I'm five foot three and I can't bicep curl six kilograms. But more than that, I'm not a violent person. I've never laid a hand on her, or anyone.

PRODUCER: And it still goes on to some extent — these accusations of you.

PW: [Nods.] Sadly, yes it does. People love to tell stories; the more salacious the better. People get attached to narratives. That's why I'm so happy we're doing this documentary. When it goes live, people will be able to see the whole truth. I will be able to put the past behind me. I said it before, and I'll say it again. I'll say it till I run out of breath. I never hurt Zanna.

PRODUCER: Both Angela and Gianna have claimed things weren't always so perfect between you and Zanna, shown us texts. What do you say to that?

PW: Look, nothing is ever perfect, is it? You can't apply a filter to life, can you?

PRODUCER: [Laughs.] You certainly can't.

PW: Sometimes Zanna and I argued. Sometimes over the blog — and yes, I can imagine there were times Zan was frustrated and wanted to fire me. There were times I wanted to quit. They were small, silly arguments mostly. Normal arguments all girlfriends have. Like siblings fighting. I tried to be the friend she deserved. That's what's important, what we should all do.

313

PRODUCER: And why have you not been entirely honest about that, in the past?

PW: For Zanna.

[Pause.]

And for the sake of justice being done. I didn't want to draw attention to the fact we argued. It was just so silly when Zanna had been killed by a dangerous man. That was the issue that needed drawing attention to. Not some petty squabbles.

The warring frenemies, it's such a classic trope, isn't it? You can see how desperate some people are for that story from the way they've held on to the idea that I hurt Zanna. I really didn't want that to overshadow Zanna's death. And I didn't want to play into this old sexist cliché.

PRODUCER: I understand that. One last question, Paige: do you have any regrets?

PW: If there's one thing I regret, I wish I'd told someone when Santiago cut her off. She was never the same after that moment. I think — perhaps — it's hard, something like that for someone like Zanna. Me, I mean, I've worked for everything I ever had, and I never grew up with money, never had that safety blanket. I've had to rely on ingenuity. Zanna, she was heartbroken by that. Really, she was. It changed her. Had that never happened, I don't think she would have ever entertained Mason, betrayed Shane and ultimately been killed. I feel as though I bear that responsibility. People say it's not my fault, but it's hard not to think that sometimes, you know?

PRODUCER: I'm so sorry. Here's a tissue. Have a moment.

[Paige dabs her eyes.]

PW: Okay. I'm okay to go.

PRODUCER: And so what was the impact of all that on your mental health, of people suspecting you of having something to do with Zanna's death?

PW: Oh just, just awful.

Trolling like this, you know, it devastates people. I've been a person of the internet, as it were, for many years, and even I really struggled to deal with this onslaught. These trolls, so many of whom seemed to think they were doing a good thing by trying to "solve" [Paige uses air quotes] Zanna's murder are so hypocritical. Trolling ruins lives, causes people to take their own lives. Trolling kills. And these people need to understand that. Not everyone is brave enough to speak out, so I do it for the other victims.

PRODUCER: So, how did you come back to the blog, after Zanna died?

PW: Well, the blog really saved me in a way. It was while I was feeling like there was no hope, no future, that I saw the demand for news on the blog. Prattle users, bless them, they were wanting to know what was happening. They cared so much about Zanna, and that touched me. So, I started by updating them with some Instagram posts. They had such a good response. Then I thought, well, people will want to see what Zanna and I were working on before she died. After that, I suppose, I built my own rapport with the followers and it seemed natural to keep communicating with them in the same way I was when I was writing before — but this time it would be the real face, sorry, my face, alongside my words.

Really, the blog was a lifeline because I was abandoned by Zanna's family and our old friends. No one called. I was left totally alone. Zanna was my only friend and she was gone. The only person who got in touch was Shane. He's my rock. The blog and Instagram, it's all I really have left of Zanna to remember her by. I carried on with the blog to stay close to her, but soon, under my control, it became a very thriving business, and I knew I could use that to keep Zanna's story alive. Zanna [laughs], well, she was never that good with money.

But now . . . it's become a huge burden, and I can't do it for much longer. Fans can expect to see some changes to the contents of the platform going forwards, but I will always keep Zanna alive in my heart.

PRODUCER: And I'm told you have some future plans for the blog?

PW: [Smiles coyly.] Yes, I do.

PRODUCER: Will you share them with us?

PW: Well, I don't want to say too much at the moment. But it's very exciting. *I'm* excited for it, anyway, and I think my followers will be. It's something new, and I'm a little bit frightened! But it's been a very long time coming now. So yes, watch this space. I know it's such an annoying cliché blogger thing to say "some very exciting things are coming", but — some very exciting things are coming.

I think when a friend dies like this, there is always an element of self-blame. I thought maybe if I'd got her some help after her father cut her off, suggested she see a counsellor, then maybe she wouldn't have made some of the bad decisions she made, and she'd still be with us. It's been a struggle all these years, grappling with that. I don't know how much longer I can dedicate myself to keeping Zanna's name alive. She'll always be with me, but maybe it's time to put her to rest, properly. That means no secrets for me. I think Zanna would be happy to know taking this action was benefitting my mental health.

PRODUCER: So, it will be impacting the blog and the socials?

PW: Yes, absolutely. And, on that . . .

I want to say that I'm so grateful to my followers, collaborators, those who have supported me since Zanna's death, who stuck by me as I took over the platform on Zanna's behalf. You're all making my dreams come true. And mostly, a big thanks to Zanna. Zanna, I couldn't have done it without you.

The Present

After a screening on New Year's Eve 2021

We travel home, in the back of the Addison Lee, in silence, our hands clasped together on the seat. As the lights came on, there had been applause from the journalists, smiles from Sheryl. Tom gave me a big hug and thumbs up and said: "You were great, really wonderful, really likeable, sympathetic."

Of course, Tom would say this, but there was more positive feedback to be had.

A journalist and reviewer tells me, "Wow, I didn't realise how much you had to go through, how much hate. You were so strong for carrying on with all that."

I give my sincerest thanks.

"You really gave us such an interesting, humanising perspective on being an influencer. It was so *real*, so honest and modest," another journalist says.

A familiar woman in a familiar quirky print silk shirt, with familiar red-painted lips, steps towards me, flanked by Tom. He introduces her to me.

"Paige, this is Emmeline Frithe, editor of the *Sunday Times Style* magazine."

I gush. "Oh, wow," I say, grasping her hand. "I've always been such a fan. I read the magazine when I was a little girl. It made me love fashion."

Her hands are so soft, probably massaged over the years with essential-oil infused creams. She smells like sparkling sweet green tea. Emmeline's peridot eyes sparkle and in her dazzling smile are two ever so slightly overlapping front teeth. It's a quirk that makes her face all the more alive. I immediately feel like perfect Invisalign teeth are so passé. Her home counties accent is smooth as an undisturbed Lake District lake and it echoes generations of wealth and status Zanna had never touched.

"I love to hear from people who love the magazine," she says, her deep yet breathy voice enchanting me. "I can't wait to speak with you about your column."

I fizz with delight, and clasp her hand tighter.

"I'll email you," she says, before she announces she must get home to her daughter, Pandora.

Shane holds me in his arms as we allow photographers to take pictures of us together. We go down a storm, if I may say so. Champagne and compliments are thrown around as liberally as condolences.

"I can only hope this helps others to be safe in this modern, digital age," I say to a crowd of nodding press people.

"Yes, so important," they murmur, "so important."

Far fewer journalists are talking to Angela and Gianna, who scowl over at me, the picture of envy. I smile. They wanted so much to prove what they think they knew, but they couldn't. I would always be multiple steps ahead of them, and now I'm so far out in front they couldn't catch me if they tried. I even reach out for a hug with Gianna as she walks past me, in front of the cameras and watching journalists, for the sheer joy of forcing her to endure it. She stiffens against my touch, but she must grin and bear it. I would like to be perceived as the bigger woman, after what she said about me. I hug Angela too, and her pride forces her into cordiality. So much for those accusations, drunk or otherwise. Look at us all now, the best of buddies, unified under a greater cause.

It's a real pleasure, to succeed where those who never wanted me around are forced to put up with it anyway, greeting me with these tortured false smiles under press camera lights. They have so much arrogance to think they see the reality behind Zanna's death. They never even saw the real Zanna. It takes a really honest person to see everything for what it truly is. These people will only ever see their narrow lives through their narrow narratives. I choose whichever narrative I want, and that's what has saved me over and over again.

Shane finally speaks, pulling me out of my reverie in shock.

"I think it's going to be okay, then?"

321

He still looks to me, like a child, to sort it all out for him, for us. I turn to him and nod.

"Yeah, it's okay," I say. I put a hand out to stroke his face. He flinches, catches himself, and then lets me touch him. I put a finger to his lips and lean over, pressing my own lips against the finger. Then it slips away and we are joined together at the mouth. Sharing air, sharing saliva, sharing our life, our guilt, our crimes, our culpability. Joined — by a force with more authority than the law, more sanctity than the church — in unholy matrimony.

We first slept together after the funeral. It sounds macabre, but it is what it is. We needed each other in those difficult, stressful, dangerous times. Those five weeks between the murder and the funeral were painful, holed up in the flat, too afraid to contact Shane, hoping he wouldn't contact me, hoping he had enough sense not to put in a message what he'd done, while also hoping to see him more than anything. My mind ran around in circles. *Would Shane ever speak to me again? Would Shane confess? Would Shane and I have any chance of being together now?* I followed news coverage of the case, all focusing on the shocking details of Zanna's death as well as pictures of her as scantily dressed as possible. I prayed I'd see Shane again. And then I did, in a room full of peonies.

Dotted in the spaces between the round tables and still filing in were bloggers, friends and acquaintances of Zanna's. I recognised PRs and photographers, various influencers with whom we'd taken press trips to France, or Portugal, or the Cotswolds, the kind of trips where bloggers and their photographers line up in front of the sunset to get "the shot". Chanel, Gucci and Stella McCartney shoulder bags bumped gently against hips as people shifted into little groups and around each other, murmuring. Noise reverberated around the tall-ceilinged room and guests spoke in hushed tones that entangled together like the hum of bees to create a vaguely menacing sound, far away and also close by. The sound of glasses clinking accidentally against one another amid air kisses is elevated above the buzz.

The glamorous guests nodded at me, smiled sad smiles, lips still together. People stepped around me, fell back as I walked past.

There was no "She lived a long and happy life" or "She's in a better place now".

I felt unmoored until I saw him in the crowd. I found my way to him, grabbed his hand, pulled him away. We bustled into a darkish corner of the funeral reception space and he pulled out a hip flask, half full. I unscrewed the cap and held it to my nose.

"It's whiskey," he said as the fuel-like fumes hit my nose, in the bottle and on his breath. He was drunk. It was the first time I had ever seen him like that. I wrapped my lips awkwardly around the nozzle on the small metal bottle. I fought back any involuntary reaction of my body to the alcohol, but my eyes watered. Shane smiled at me, a wonky drunk smile. I couldn't tell if the warmth in my stomach derived from the neat alcohol or disturbed butterflies. I looked after him, gave him water and those small sandwiches that get served at funerals, held him upright and took him home when he was too drunk to sober up. Back at the flat like old times, Shane kissed me. Our mouths rhythmically connected, his hand rested on my left breast and massaged it. I moved my hands down to his trousers, undid them and slid my hand inside. I couldn't have been wetter. He grasped tightly to me.

The next day he had his wobble. Bolting upright in bed, a cold sweat.

"We can't do this," he said, staggering over to his black suit trousers, trying to pull them on. I talked him down.

"Shane, Shane, come on, calm down. It's okay."

"It's wrong," he said, his hands shaking. He sank to the floor. "I can't do this."

I held him as she sobbed.

"I'm scared."

I draped my body over his, tried to comfort him, pulled him up, wiped his face.

"Shane," I said. "You don't have to be alone. I'm the only person who knows the truth, and I'll protect you. You love me, right?"

324

Tears pooled in his deep eyes, again. He wrapped his arms around his knees, buried his face in them and nodded.

"I love you too," I said, stroking his back. "And as long as we stick together, no one ever has to know what happened."

Shane was so lucky to have someone like me be the one who saved him. And now, the one who would always be there for him. Someone who would never let him down, and never let him go. Who doesn't dream of that?

He essentially never left the flat after that. It made so much sense to stay there, and stay together, for both of us. We had too much to lose to flee. The lifestyle, the money, our social media profiles kept us tied to our old lives. I thought about leaving the country forever, escaping to New York, to Bali, or somewhere. But what would I do? Start again? I had poured too much into Life of Zanna to leave now, I had put too much on the line to leave it.

We needed to heal. It was better to do that together. We understood what the other had been through — we protected one another with our complicity. Who's going to protect you better than someone whose fate is so implicitly tied with yours? Of course, it was hard. You can't see a therapist to deal with something like the circumstances of Zanna's death. Perhaps we leaned on each other too much, but there was no one else.

I was diagnosed, formally, with anxiety disorder for the first time, prescribed the first packet of diazepam for my PTSD, to help with the bad dreams and panic attacks. I know I take them too much, but any port in a storm. Shane drinks. We cope in the ways we have available to us.

We hid our relationship for a year, before finally going public on Instagram. Shane was keen to keep it to ourselves. I would have done it earlier. Eventually, though, Shane knew he had to capitulate. To compromise. Compromise really is key to making things work in a relationship. Shane has learned this, particularly. He knows he needs me.

"Shane," I say as the city lights swoop past us.

"Hmm?"

"I want to get married."

He swallows, gazes out the window with squinting eyes. He takes a moment. Breathes, and says, "Okay."

He'll come around to the idea. He always comes around to my ideas.

The Present

A boutique hotel in the Cotswolds

Awaking from a dreamless diazepam slumber, I thank the mattress beneath me. I'm in a thankful mood today. I remember to be gracious to the universe; another manifesting tool, an essential part of the process, Zanna had always told me. Ironic, since she was not exactly the queen of gratitude. Gurus don't always practise what they preach, but it doesn't mean their lessons can't be illuminating. After all, haven't Zanna's lessons brought me here? A farm-cum-luxury hotel. Chickens and C-list celebs cluck around the grounds, Shane and I among them now, recognisable in our own right. I'm not such a fraud anymore. Imposter syndrome? No more. We're in a suite to boot. All velvets, old woods and chintz.

At the foot of this lavish bed — the sheets, those cool, thick, slightly scratchy expensive ones — is a duck-egg blue sofa. That's where we started sex last night. Behind a huge glass pane is a rolling vista of the Cotswolds, shades of green in endless stripes. Rolling hills in hunter, olive, fern, moss, tea, army, asparagus, jungle. Each hue folds back to display a slither of the next, like petals in the bouquet Shane brought me. White roses, pure and bridal. I wrap myself in the ivory bed sheets. It's not easy to feel pure in these sheets after last night, after Shane and his antics. I sigh.

Focus on the here and now, my mindfulness app would remind me. The first day of the rest of our lives, that's what the motivational speakers say. I shift in bed, look up and see Shane, sitting on the sofa, staring out at the vista. I slept so well.

We didn't even set an alarm.

"What time is it?" I ask.

"1 p.m."

"You're joking!"

"No joke."

I'm not hungover, but I'm restless. I shut my eyes and lie here. I practise gratitude to the universe. I push away any negativity. Thank you, thank you, thank you.

"We slept so long," I muse. Shane makes an "mmm" noise.

"Imuhave a shower," he mumbles, leaving a warm spot on the bed that I roll into.

"I'll leave you a coffee on the counter," Shane calls, after a brief shower and gathering his gym kit together. No breaks from the gym, not even on this, our very special holiday.

"You are the dream," I say, reaching for my phone. Something stops me, though, before I navigate naturally to the Instagram app, the glinting orb of light on my hand. A brilliant, cut solitaire on a micro pave white gold band. Every element of it sparkles, it throws out candy pastel hues deep from within, where I imagine miniature ice castles. With each shift of my hand, the light changes it. I look and I look and I look. I tweak the Instagram caption I'm planning to include with the engagement announcement and a picture of this chip of diamond on my finger, held up with the country kitsch of this boutique farm-inspired getaway as a backdrop. How much would I roll my eyes at anyone posting this image if it weren't me? But it is me. Me and Shane. I got the ring, after all this time.

We were inseparable after all. But what choice did he really have besides being with me after what he did? With what I know? And I do know him, the good and the bad. Now, of course, it will be for better, for worse, for richer, for poorer, in sickness and in health, to love and to cherish, until parted by death.

What a two weeks it's been since the documentary aired, an exhausting rush of media attention, numerous calls for interviews. Even an offer to present a reportage-style documentary about the danger of stalking in the social media world. Zanna would really hate that, I think. But she's not here.

I've received a wave of sympathy and support from the fans after the documentary too, which is touching, really. They urged me to keep going with the blog. I smile, thinking about what I have in store for them. And a contract is signed for the *Sunday Times Style* magazine column, over the average UK yearly salary in a year for three hundred words a week. Can you believe it? I shook hands with Emmeline over dinner and Tom took me for cocktails to celebrate.

Emmeline briefed me: "We want the millennial woman's take on all things social media. Modern, funny, to the point. From an insider, an expert. Mental health, dating, style. More of what you do, with a *Sunday Times* gloss.

"We think you're a perfect fit. The epitome of what it means to be a modern, entrepreneurial, online woman. You're self-made, from a working-class background. You're savvy, and — most importantly — you're *real*. You're everything we're looking for."

I want more than anything to impress Emmeline. She's emerged from the picture on the Editor's Letter page and into my life. She embodies something I've only ever dreamed of. I know, because I've done my research. I've read all the think pieces she's ever written, absorbed her thoughts on life for the modern woman, business, publishing. I've searched as far back as her Instagram and Facebook pages go. Her elderly parents are wind-battered but happy with pink cheeks on shooting trips, holding dangling, bloodied pheasants in one hand and the straining lead of a demented, foaming-mouthed springer spaniel in the other. Their house does not only sit down a private road, it has acres and acres. Emmeline's family owns deer. They're not about mirror furniture and beige plush sofas like Angela's aspirational, fluffy home. They're about leather sofas and muddy boots. They're real class. It's something I've only ever seen on television, but Emmeline brings me closer to it. And I'm itching to get closer still.

I know it sounds so silly, but recently I've dreamed about what it'd be like to live Emmeline's life. To eat things like pheasant and pigeon. To wear Barbour. To have a National Trust pass and visit sites on the weekend from a house in Sandbanks, like Emmeline does on the weekend. Emmeline's wedding was held at Babington House and photographed for *Vogue*. I'm already adding snaps of it to my Pinterest board. She introduced me to her husband, Hugo, who happened to be stopping by the office when I dropped in for an introductory tour. He's tall, blond, with a strong jaw and floppy hair. His voice is gentle and soft, he's got a serene grace to him. He speaks in a low voice and handles Emmeline like she's precious and fragile, made of crystal. Nothing like how Shane handles me.

I've ordered a pair of Penelope Chilvers boots. Emmeline is arranging a staff getaway in Somerset. It's my chance to make a great impression. Something about the way Emmeline smiles at me tells me I'm exactly what they want, makes me feel so seen. I think she's my next best friend.

I bought a Smythson notebook to start journalling my ideas, its leather binding scent smells like real success. Tom and I have been excitedly planning the future, all the career opportunities ahead of me now. Tom is in talks for more TV appearances. There's been a suggestion of an interview on *Loose Women*, and maybe even a semi-regular panel spot at £3,000 a go. It made my head spin. Since the documentary went live, I've amassed 100,000 more followers. Renewed offers for collaborations are in, including written pieces for magazines and girl-power podcast appearances. He really is a very clever agent.

I said to him, in one of these meetings after the documentary went live, "You know, Tom, I can't work out who would have leaked the news of the documentary. It wasn't me."

He laughed. "Oh that was me, babes! That's just show business, hun. And didn't you get more jobs from it?"

He laughed again at my shocked impression. And then I said, "Yeah, I guess I did."

"We're really making the leap from influencer to media personality," Tom told me. "The only way is up from here. It's time to legitimise *you*, and move away from Zanna. That's the narrative, now."

Ah, the narrative. A useful device. After all, it's so easy to believe that Mason, with his criminal family and his history of stalking, is a deranged and violent man who killed Zanna in a fit of obsession. Zanna, leagues above him, a fact he couldn't stand.

It sent him mad. Poor Mason, unlucky for him. He got on the wrong side of the narrative, because he didn't have his own. I've spent years concocting mine. It doesn't matter how true they are, all that matters is they help you. When you believe it, other people will believe it too. Give people a good story, one they want to believe, and they will look for evidence to support it. It's called cognitive bias. It happens all the time.

And the DNA evidence, well, it backed it all up. Mason's was found all over her. So were mine and Shane's, but then, we lived there, didn't we? Of course our DNA would be there. All that manifesting it finally came through for me.

I felt a little sorry for Mason, I did. To see him cry in court, his mother there, a thin, wrinkled, baby-bird of an old woman, arthritic-knuckled hands clasping at a cross around her neck as she watched, tearless. I remembered how her partner, Mason's father, had been in and out of prison too. Here she was watching it again. But then, don't forget, Mason had been blackmailing Zanna himself, with his own sordid intentions. He is being punished for that crime, and that's something I soothe myself with. Mason was a bad person, with previous history. He would be likely to hurt someone again. He had a previous conviction for harassing his ex, after all. He even lied to me and Zanna about it. Called her a psycho. Some people are so brazen. I've only ever acted out of goodness and fairness. No, it's better for the public that he's locked up.

I sigh. It's a contented sigh, as I'm sliding my legs further into the marshmallow bed and wriggling under the covers. All these sacrifices, finally coming to fruition. I'm finally getting what I deserve.

And yet.

Every now and then my bliss is disturbed by a niggling, a recollection, like the fear that I've left the oven on. Then, that gurgling sound. Those intrusive thoughts come for me again.

If I did kill Zanna — if I did — then when did it start? When I decided I had to have her as my friend? When I sent those texts? When I didn't report Shane's behaviour to Zanna's family or friends, and I dismissed that smashed prom picture? Or was it when I faked that escorting profile and poured petrol on Shane's jealous spark?

I'd tried to make it look as real as possible. God, I'd been writing as Zanna long enough, faking her tone of voice. An advert for clandestine services wasn't a stretch. I never intended for her family to see it, or at least, I never thought about what would happen if they did.

But I shake it off, shake it away, and take a diazepam. Soon, I'll forget. Like a bad dream. I soothe myself. Deep breathing. I use my meditation app. It tells me, "You are not responsible for other people's actions."

It's simple: Zanna killed Zanna. Her own actions brought us all here. Her actions caused our rift, broke Shane's heart, and brought us, him and me, together. Zanna was responsible for her actions, and for the consequences of them.

We shouldn't live with guilt. As my mindfulness meditation app tells me, you can't let these kinds of critical inner thoughts win. It's all about reframing. It's exactly what Zanna told me when we first met, "Your thoughts create your reality." In reality, mine and the one everyone else accepts, I am a successful writer and a businesswoman. I own this. I'm the creator of my story. I'm killing it.

So, you write your own narrative, too. You've got a choice. What are you going to be? A victim, or a villain?

From creating the blog with Zanna to taking it on myself, running it over these years, I've learned everything there is to know about making that choice and following it through. And yet, the greatest success of all is the life I've created with Shane. Yes, he has his flaws. He can be mean, angry. But no relationship is perfect, is it? I've been in love — first my parents, then Talia, then Zanna, and I've been abused or abandoned each time, until now. I know what he did was wrong, but at least Shane cannot abandon me. Isn't that what love is? Shane and I are bound together now, for better or for worse. Tied together by our crime, safer together. We can face the world. Deal with anything that comes in our way. Even squash a threat like Talia if it persists. If needs be.

I sigh, finish writing and press post, and my news is out there in the world. Tears prickle my eyes with happiness.

An Instagram Post

I've always loved a new page. Clean, pure, full of anticipation. Every page is a new chance to start again. This time we'll do "our best", learn from the past, and tell ourselves we won't make any more mistakes. And if you fail, don't you worry, there's another page, another book, another chance in all those endless chances.

I'm so thrilled to tell you all that this morning, after whisking me away for some major relaxation after the stress of the documentary, Shane got down on one knee and asked me the most important, and yet easiest to answer, question of my life. Our romance came out of tragedy, and Shane has been my rock, and I his, through it all. Not to mention he somehow knew my dream ring. I can't stop looking at it and how it sparkles in the light.

We're so engulfed in the moment right now, we haven't planned anything for the big day yet. I've got some ideas, an English country wedding in Somerset, perhaps. Some place with a history, as Shane and I look into our very special future together. At this moment,

I sit among the hills, trees and nature of the gorgeous Cotswolds, and it's so peaceful. As we recover from the mayhem of the past five years, I find myself drawn ever more to the countryside. To the peace of it. I see Shane and I spending much more time here in the future. It's so fulfilling. It's like home. It's one of the many major changes coming in my life — but more on that in a moment.

Although my country retreat isn't yet over, I wanted so much to share our engagement with you, the very beginning of our happy ending. You'll all be invited to this big day, in one way or another, via our social channels. Fairytales do come true. Always remember that, my darling followers.

You have been asking questions about the documentary. We have had incredible support. I am so proud to have shone a light on an important issue, honoured the memory of my friend and hopefully proved to the vicious trolls that they have no idea about the truth, no matter what they think. But, given all of that, I say this — honouring all the joy and love of this job and communicating directly with all of you brings — we have nothing more to add when it comes to our dear, dear late friend. We are finally putting Zanna's death behind us and have no more comment to make publicly about it. Speculation hurts us, but nothing brings us down too far with the future now gleaming bright and beautiful ahead of us.

To celebrate the future and put the pain of the past behind us, we will be renaming this account and all affiliated social media "Pages of Paige". All posts prior to Zanna's death and/or relating specifically to Zanna and the charity work after her passing will be archived on a website where fans can still find her work.

We know this will be a controversial decision, but it's time to focus on the future. It's time for a fresh, new Paige.

#blessed #ad

Comments are off

Acknowledgements

Thank you to:

Haley Steed, who took a chance on someone with little to no experience with a half-finished manuscript and patiently helped her turn that into the completed novel before you. Hayley's belief in the book meant so much and without her dedication, I'm not sure Paige and Zanna would have ever made print. Thank you, also, to Valentina Paulmichl and to everyone else at Madeleine Milburn who played a part in supporting me and this novel.

Thank you to Clem Flanagan at Black & White for loving the book and taking a chance on it, and to all those at Black & White who have played their part in this process, including Thomas Ross and Rachel Morrell, Hannah Walker and Ali McBride.

Thank you, too, to Julia Kenny at Dunow, Carlson & Lerner for taking me on, loving this book too, and for the part she's played in the publication of this book.

341

Thank you to my parents, Jonathan and Kim Hodgkin, who read various iterations of the book and provided valuable insight. Thank you to them and my sister, Grace, for their forbearance during some of the more difficult moments in the process of writing this book.

Thank you to Vijay for listening patiently while I rambled on about this project, for joining me in solidarity to write in the caravan at the bottom of the garden, and for making sure there was wine on hand whenever I wanted it.

About the Author

Emily Jane Hodgkin is an author and editor from Derbyshire, who currently lives between New York and London. She has been a journalist for almost ten years, working at the *MailOnline*, the *Daily Express* and the *Mirror*. She is a horror and thriller fanatic, and *Life of Zanna* is her debut novel.

When she is not writing, she currently spends her time wandering around Greenwich Village, wishing she lived there, and practising embroidery, her latest new hobby.

Instagram @emilyjane.me
TikTok @emilyjanewritesthings
www.emilyjane.me